THE QUIET COUP

A POLITICAL THRILLER

ROB LUBITZ

THE QUIET COUP

PRAISE FOR ROB LUBITZ'S PREVIOUS NOVELS:

BEYOND TOP SECRET (2015)

"As the story progresses, Lubitz's rapid-paced novel maintains suspense by sprinkling information like colors dabbled on the canvas of a slowly forming portrait. Smart and sleek as the secrets slowly spill out."
Kirkus Reviews

"This stupendous thriller challenges both the heart rate and the moral compass. Trouble has a knack for finding the characters in Rob Lubitz's Beyond Top Secret, a complicated, entertaining thriller that explores the themes of love and ethics."
Forward Clarion Review: **Five Star Review**

"Beyond Top Secret by Rob Lubitz combines mystery, romance, espionage, and drama in a fast-paced action thriller. This is definitely one of the most enjoyable thriller/mystery books I have read in a while, and makes for great armchair reading." *Readers Favorite:* **Five Star Review**

"Combines elements of Tom Clancy's Jack Ryan thrillers, the identity hijinks of the Jason Bourne films and the courtroom high-wire of John Grisham novels. Readers who like twisty plots, secret conspiracies and cinematic action should find plenty of thrills…" *BlueInk Review*

BREAKING FREE (2011)

"This fascinating thriller wonders: What if you couldn't tie your shoes, walk down the street or save your own life without being told to do so?"
Kirkus Reviews

"As Butler goes further off path, he loses track of who he can trust: his government, his wife, his friend's wife, the police. So, the plot readily builds in tension from page to page and brings the reader along for the ride."
BlueInk Review

"Set in 1986, Lubitz's competent series kickoff introduces lawyer Ryan Butler, a former baseball prospect." *Publishers Weekly*

The tension in this skillful thriller begins when Ryan Butler, an unhappy corporate attorney in an unhappy marriage, learns that an old friend and baseball teammate is in a coma and this old friend's gorgeous wife needs his help." *Publishing Perspectives*

To my wife, Joanne:

The radiant, smart, vivacious, and beautiful woman I love.

In loving memory of:

My mother, Elizabeth Greenberg, and her two dearest friends,
Virginia Wilson and Mildred Hamil.

Special thanks to Harriett Russell, Fred Santesteban, Greg Bump, Tom Bly, Jim Drennan and Joanne Lubitz for their reviews of the manuscript and for their valuable insights and suggestions.

CHAPTER ONE

BILL DOUBTED THAT any man loved a woman more than he loved Cheryl. He doubted there was a more beautiful woman on earth. And although he had no memory of their lives together before their accident, he didn't care. All that mattered was the present.

"The view is so gorgeous here," said Cheryl, wrapping her arm around Bill's waist. Two thousand feet below lay Molokai's coastline, threads of silver sand and parallel lines of white breaking waves. Farther out the water shifted colors from translucent green to turquoise to azure to deep cobalt. In the distance the emerald islands of Maui and Lanai loomed up from the Pacific Ocean. Although not visible from the overlook, their beach house was below, farther to the west.

This was their special spot on the island, reachable only via a rugged dirt road tunneling through a canopy of thick jungle. The trip required steady nerves and four-wheel drive, as it crossed two streams and hugged the sides of vertigo-inducing cliffs. The place was unknown to tourists and rarely visited by the locals, but here they would share lunch, drink a bottle of wine, and make love on a blanket spread out near the overlook. Afterward, under an umbrella of orange-flowering poinciana trees, they would marvel at how a tragic turn in their lives had brought them to Hawaii—to paradise. They would repeat their conviction that they were the luckiest people in the world.

Since coming to the island, they'd lived idyllic lives, filling their days with swimming, snorkeling, sailing, hiking, kayaking, and making love like newlyweds. All remembrance of their previous sixteen years together in Colorado had evaporated like the morning mist.

They moved back from the overlook and began preparations for lunch. Bill set up the folding table and Cheryl lay a hibiscus-print tablecloth over it. She placed bright-red napkins, silverware, and two wineglasses on the table, and Bill uncorked a bottle of pinot noir. As he poured the wine, the glasses started trembling. They looked at each other wide-eyed.

"The ground is moving," screamed Cheryl.

They fell hard, struggling to stand up, their legs wobbling wildly. They were only a few feet apart, but it might as well have been a mile. Rocks rained down from the high cliffs above. A large one smashed into Bill's leg, causing his knee to buckle. Another struck him in the back, slamming him hard to the ground, scraping his face against the dirt. He forced himself up onto one knee, searching for Cheryl. She was behind him, her arm outstretched. He tried to grasp her hand but she stumbled backward, undulating up and down as the earth moved in waves. He called her name, but a deafening roar drowned out his voice. With all his energy, he threw himself over her, covering her body. He folded his arms over his head as the onslaught of rocks continued, bouncing off his arms, legs, and back. *We're being stoned to death*, he thought.

The shaking and rumbling slowly diminished and stopped. Bill pulled himself up. Every part of his body ached, especially his knee.

"Are you okay?" he asked.

She turned over and looked up at him. Blood streamed down her face from a wide gash above her hairline. "I feel woozy."

"You're bleeding pretty badly."

"I know, I can taste it. How are you?"

"I'm bruised, but I don't think anything's broken."

In front of them lay their smashed picnic table and cooler. Bill retrieved a water bottle and ripped off part of the tablecloth for a bandage. He pulled back her hair and cleaned her wound. "You're going to need stitches—it's a deep cut."

She lifted her big brown eyes. "How are we going to get out of here?"

Bill glanced back to their Jeep, buried under a pile of rocks. He wasn't sure he could move them, and even if he could, he knew the road out would be impassable. "I'm not sure."

Cheryl tried to stand up, shakily, and Bill rushed to steady her. Holding on to each other, they surveyed the scene. Rocks of all shapes and sizes riddled the area, and broken tree limbs littered the ground.

"We're lucky to be alive," said Bill.

Just then the piercing sound of sirens rose up from the beach below, stoking an unspoken fear in the backs of their minds. They looked at each other, sharing the same terror.

"A tsunami's coming," shouted Cheryl.

CHAPTER TWO

THE STAFF AT the *Beltway Insider* envied Connie Blythe's corner office. Not just for its size, but also for its floor-to-ceiling windows overlooking the Potomac River, Georgetown, and the Washington Monument. Connie kept her back to the view, not wanting to be distracted from her computer or the television permanently affixed to CNN.

Connie had joined the company two years earlier as its lead investigative reporter. The *Beltway Insider* had been among the first media outlets in the nation to go entirely digital. It was the brainchild of Aaron Retzler, a former assistant editor at the *Washington Post*. Available by subscription and published five times a week, it focused on political news, with an emphasis on Congress and the White House. Its website featured a whistle-blower page that encouraged readers to come forward with anonymous tips about political and governmental wrongdoings and scandals. Connie mined those leads for investigative potential.

At first Connie's hiring had raised eyebrows, because she'd previously worked for a disreputable tabloid, the *National Mirror*. It had been the low point of her professional life. After graduating from the Columbia University Graduate School of Journalism and spending fifteen years as an investigative reporter for a respected Pittsburgh newspaper, her world fell apart. She, like most of the staff, was let go when the paper faced bankruptcy. A shrinking job market for journalists finally forced her to accept the position with the tabloid. While she was there, however, her side investigation into a bizarre murder trial in North Carolina brought her to the attention of Aaron Retzler. She shared with him evidence suggesting hidden CIA involvement. Although her story couldn't be substantiated for publication, it won her a job offer.

A few months after joining the *Insider*, Connie got her big break: an anonymous tip from an enraged worker at the Congressional Printing Office who had taken umbrage when Senator Punting of West Virginia, a ranking member of the Senate Appropriations Committee, slipped three last-minute provisions into an appropriations bill. Few if any senators knew they existed. The language exempted the Appalachian Coal and Mining Company from certain environmental regulations and shielded the company from various financial penalties and lawsuits. It didn't take long for Connie to discover that the company had been a major contributor to the senator's campaign and had a long string of EPA violations.

The article's publication sparked general indignation, calls to reform the earmarking process, and a Senate Select Committee on Ethics investigation. The committee gently chided the senator for a lack of transparency but concluded that no laws had been broken. Senator Punting haughtily declared his complete exoneration.

The next shoe fell when Connie received a tip from a source in the banking business that the company had secretly funneled millions of dollars to Senator Punting's wife. The money, moving through accounts in her maiden name, had purchased cars, jewelry, clothes, first-class travel, and extravagant meals. Through considerable digging, Connie documented the money trail. Her revelations resulted in an investigation by the US Department of Justice, and, ultimately, the senator's resignation.

With the name recognition that accompanied the scoop, as well as a Pulitzer Prize nomination, Connie was on top of the world. She spoke at national conferences. Colleagues sought her out. Journalism students fawned over her. Her confidence blossomed; she shed weight, dressed more fashionably, highlighted her hair, cut down on the booze, and moved into an expensive town house in Georgetown. She even bedded a couple of her female admirers. Then the slump hit.

A year had passed since her blockbuster, and she had come up with little since. On the surface Retzler seemed sympathetic, telling her that something would eventually turn up if she stayed persistent. Then he would not so subtly remind her of his high expectations and the big salary he paid her. She felt increasingly desperate.

. . .

An announcement of breaking news on CNN drew Connie's immediate attention. The screen showed a satellite image of the Hawaiian Islands. Underneath, the banner read, "Earthquake hits Hawaiian island of Molokai, tsunami warning issued."

Connie turned her head away; it didn't involve politics, so it didn't interest her—or so she thought.

CHAPTER THREE

BILL AND CHERYL waited for hours on the blanket, not sure what to do. They knew they were fortunate to be high up on the island, away from the giant waves that would surely obliterate their house. However, they were in a remote area with little probability of rescue. They had no cell phone reception, and nobody would realize they were missing. Since coming to the island, they'd lived isolated lives, avoiding people as much as possible. Their only visitors had been Cheryl's aunt and uncle.

At the sound of helicopters, they rushed to the overlook, frantically waving their arms, but the choppers were too distant to see them. Their only chance was to hike out. It was only six miles to the main road, not too bad a walk under normal circumstances, but these weren't normal circumstances. Bill's knee had swollen, and Cheryl continued to bleed. Furthermore, she was acting spacey. Fortunately, they still had some food rescued from the picnic cooler: sandwiches, cheese, apples, grapes, two chocolate bars, and macadamia nuts. They also had another bottle of wine to help deaden some of the pain.

Bill decided they would spend the night where they were. He didn't want to be hiking in the dark. They ate quietly, on the blanket, not saying much. As the sky darkened, Cheryl drifted off to sleep while Bill's mind wandered.

. . .

Six months ago they'd set out to do some exploring and search for a new picnic place. They took the Kamehameha Highway from their house on the beach on the south shore of Molokai, past the small harbor town of Kaunakakai, and straight up the Kalae Highway, heading for Palaau State Park on the northern side.

Halfway across the island, Bill noticed a dirt road angling off to the right, nearly concealed by overgrown tropical vegetation. He pulled his Jeep onto the rugged road and followed it for two miles through dense, lush growth until they came to a sign: "No Trespassing—Private Property."

Next to the sign sat a dilapidated wooden table filled with bananas, guava, and breadfruit. Farther back, camouflaged by trees, sat a small run-down house of plywood and sheet metal.

They climbed out of the Jeep, took a few bananas, and left a twenty-dollar bill under a rock on the stand. Bill reasoned that whoever lived in the house could certainly use the money.

An old man suddenly appeared out of the trees on the other side of the road, startling them. "Aloha," he said. The man looked ancient: he was gaunt, with dark, wrinkled, prune-like skin, cloudy brown eyes, tufts of silver hair, and only a few teeth.

"*Aloha 'auinala*," responded Bill, meaning "Good afternoon."

The old man smiled at the response. "You're not tourists?"

"No, we live on the island. We've been here for two years," said Cheryl in a bright lilting voice.

The old man picked up a bunch of yellow bananas, glancing at the money under the rock. "*Ono*," he said, meaning "Delicious." "I used to sell them in town, but now it's too much work. Take as many as you want. Nobody comes this way anymore, not like the old days." He gave them another wide, mostly toothless grin. "Everybody calls me Eddie. I'd tell you my Hawaiian name, but you couldn't pronounce it, so Eddie's a lot easier."

"We were out exploring," said Cheryl, glancing at the No Trespassing sign. "We didn't know this was private property. We'll turn around."

"Oh, the sign. In the old days, I used to charge people to use the road. It goes on for another four miles. At the end there's an overlook—the best view on the island. Walk a little farther and there's a waterfall. It's a beautiful place…been in my family for years."

"Sounds lovely," said Cheryl, revealing a sweet wistful smile.

"The road is rough, steep in some places, starts flat, but then goes downhill. You have to cross two small streams, but you won't have any trouble in that Jeep," he said, pointing to the vehicle.

Bill wondered if it was an invitation.

Eddie smiled again. "Don't pay any attention to the sign. That's to keep tourists out. Since you live on the island, and seem to be nice haoles, you're welcome to go on."

Bill and Cheryl knew that the name for those who were not ethnically Hawaiian was *haole*, sometimes meant in a derogatory way, sometimes not. They thanked the old man and climbed back into the Jeep.

Driving forward past the No Trespassing sign, Bill glanced in his rearview mirror. Eddie was heading back to his house grasping the twenty-dollar bill. After that they made many trips to the special spot, always stopping at the stand and leaving twenty dollars, sometimes more.

. . .

Lying on the blanket, Bill observed the night sky. A billion stars shimmered across the glowing arc of the Milky Way. Next to him Cheryl slept quietly, her body slowly rising and falling with each breath. He knew that sleep would not come easy for him. He wondered what had happened to their house. He feared what tomorrow would bring. Mostly he regretted the day they had discovered their hideaway.

CHAPTER FOUR

THE HAUNTING COOS of Hawaiian zebra doves awoke Bill at dawn. His wristwatch read six fifteen, and he roused Cheryl. She had slept solidly through the night, but upon waking was not sure where she was or what had happened.

He had hardly slept at all, kept awake by the throbbing pain in his knee and the certainty that their lives would never be the same. He was sure that their house and everything they owned was gone. Most of all he worried about Cheryl. She needed immediate medical care.

They started out in a soft rain, but soon the morning clouds cleared and the sun rose high and hot. Yesterday's trade winds were gone, leaving the air stagnant and muggy. Withered flowers lay everywhere, their once-magical fragrance replaced by the odor of damp earth. The lush jungle was now a shattered wasteland—a chaotic tangle of boulders, rocks, fallen trees, and broken branches.

The road out was difficult to follow, and every painful step meant looking down to find footing amid cracking branches and tumbling rocks. Furthermore, the road gained nearly five hundred feet of elevation, making it a difficult ascent. Twice they felt aftershocks and terror gripped them. Fortunately, these were mild compared to what they had previously experienced and lasted only a few seconds.

As they approached the first stream, Bill recognized that something had changed. There was no running water, only scattered puddles. He figured the quake had altered the stream's course. The second stream confirmed his theory. Previously it had lazily trickled down from the cliffs above, but now it was the basin of a thundering waterfall, running deep and fast. A few hundred feet farther along, it narrowed into rapids and disappeared over a ledge.

Bill took Cheryl's hand, and they cautiously waded forward into the rushing water. Only a few steps in, Cheryl slipped and splashed in headfirst. Bill pulled her up, and they retreated to the stream's edge. Her vacant eyes and sheet-white complexion scared him. He faced an agonizing decision, whether to stay or go on. The stream appeared treacherous, but nobody was coming to rescue them. They had to cross it to reach help. He instructed Cheryl to climb on his back and hold on tight.

As they slowly approached the middle of the stream, the current deepened and Bill struggled to maintain balance. He cautiously inched forward, taking tiny steps, as the water began to lift them. Cheryl's arms tightened over his neck and her legs squeezed against his waist. He used his walking stick for leverage, and her added weight helped to anchor him, but it wasn't enough. In a flash his legs washed out and the current swept them up, spinning them helplessly in swirling rapids. Cheryl hung on to his neck, nearly choking him, her fingernails digging deep into his flesh. Each time Bill spun around he caught a glimpse of the rapidly approaching ledge and the water rushing over the side. *This is the end*, he thought.

As he faced back toward the cliffs, something hard and sharp smashed into his left side, near his kidney. The force of the impact sent them careening toward a twisted nest of trees and branches stuck together near the other side of the stream. With Cheryl desperately clinging on, Bill grabbed the jutting end of a tree limb. It wobbled wildly and then locked tight, bringing them to a jolting stop. He clawed his way up the limb, hand over hand, until they reached the heart of the nest. Bracing against tree trunks and branches, they crossed the remainder of the stream.

Safe on the other side, Bill lay on his back panting. Cheryl collapsed beside him. Both their bodies trembled. Bill raised his head and surveyed the stream as it rushed over the side, forming a new waterfall. A huge irregular boulder sat in the middle near the edge, dislodged from above during the quake. He marveled at their luck. If it hadn't been there, they would be dead. If he had hit his head against it, instead of his side, it would have killed him instantly.

Cheryl placed her head on his chest, and he examined her injury. Her bandage had come off, lost in the water. He pulled off his wet shirt, washed her wound, and tore off a strip of fabric. As he tied the makeshift bandage around her head, she stared at him with a dazed, childlike innocence. "I can't go on, I'm too weak."

"You have to. It's not that far to the old man's house. We'll find food there." He helped her to her feet, fearing time was running out.

. . .

When they reached Eddie's home, they had been hiking for nearly six hours and were sweaty, exhausted, hungry, and scared. The house lay in ruins, split by a river of rocks. Cheryl sat on the road as Bill circled the remains of the crushed structure looking for Eddie. There was no sign of him. Most of the trees that had previously crowded the house lay toppled. Bill picked through the debris, searching for ripe bananas. Heading back to Cheryl with an armful, he spotted a bloodied hand sticking up from the rocks. He dropped the bananas and frantically began digging, calling Eddie's name. He slowly realized the futility. The last rock dripped with blood, and beneath it the old man's head resembled a smashed watermelon.

He slowly walked back to Cheryl and handed her a banana. "He's dead."

"Who's dead?" she asked as she gulped it down.

"Eddie, the old man."

"What old man?"

The remainder of the hike was easier. The dirt road flattened and curved away from the high cliffs. Clouds formed above, drifting off the top of the island, drenching them in hard downpours and then misting them in a soft fog.

Cheryl kept quiet most of the journey, but occasionally asked Bill where they were going and what had happened. They had to rest often, and Bill kept a close eye on Cheryl's wound. Despite his pain and exhaustion, he intermittently carried her on his back or over his shoulder.

. . .

Two grueling hours later, they hobbled onto the Kalae Highway. After a mile Bill's spirits lifted. In the distance a dozen cars clustered around a bend in the road. His hope faded when he reached the abandoned vehicles. In front of them a huge crevice, at least eight feet across, split the highway. Going forward was impossible. He wondered what had happened to the people. He assumed that helicopters had rescued them.

They sat down near the crevice, and Bill studied Cheryl's face. Her eyes were wide and glazed. He couldn't imagine losing her; she meant everything to him.

Thirty months earlier, an eighteen-wheeler had blindsided them at an intersection in Colorado. Bill was in a coma for several days and Cheryl experienced significant brain trauma. Afterward neither could remember anything about their past lives. They saw a psychiatrist to help deal with their memory loss. The doctor found it exceedingly rare that they both would suffer from amnesia, but advised them to view it as a gift—an opportunity to build a new life and live fully in the present, unhindered by the past. They embraced that philosophy. That was why they'd moved to Molokai, to start anew, and to savor every second in paradise.

Bill pulled Cheryl to him and held her tight, and for the first time he could remember, he started crying. Suddenly living in the moment wasn't so great.

CHAPTER FIVE

ALTHOUGH SHE KNEW it was a bad habit, Connie Blythe continually checked her e-mails, hoping for a response from an anonymous source she was cultivating. Her quarry was Congressman Steven Luke from Missouri. Luke had been prominent in the news due to his surprise appointment by the speaker to chair the House Intelligence Committee. Prior to the appointment, most pundits had dismissed Luke as a warmongering fanatic. Years ago he had called for the preemptive nuking of Iran and North Korea, a statement that earned him the moniker of Nuke 'Em Luke. His sudden ascendance to such a critical position sent shock waves around Washington and world capitals. Nobody could comprehend why the speaker would make such a bold and unpredictable move, although speculation mounted that the vice president was behind it; he and Luke were friends.

After Luke's appointment, Connie had received a mountain of tips on the website: allegations of his meetings with oil lobbyists prior to introducing supportive legislation, suggestions that he was doing congressional favors for businesspersons in return for campaign contributions, and whispers of secret meetings with congressmen in leadership positions. However, those making the accusations insisted on anonymity, so without more detail, there was no fodder for further investigation. Besides, it sounded like business as usual in Washington.

What had caught Connie's attention was a message from a woman claiming that Congressman Luke had tried to rape her in his office. The woman wrote that she was willing to talk on the phone as long as her identity remained secret. Connie responded, providing her private e-mail address and her work and home phone numbers. She invited the woman to call her at any time, day or night. She had heard nothing back.

Connie realized that the message might be a prank or a fabrication. However, what gave it some credibility was an earlier tip from somebody named Jason, who'd said he worked in Congressman Luke's office. The message read, "Congressman Luke needs to stay away from the female interns and keep his trousers zipped."

Connie leaned back in her chair, pondering what to do next. From the corner of her eye, something on CNN caught her attention. The network was again cutting away to breaking news from Hawaii—the rescue of more earthquake victims on Molokai. The footage showed several people emerging from a helicopter and medical workers rushing to attend them. The camera focused on a woman with a bloodied gash across the top of her forehead. Connie froze, thinking there was something familiar about her. "Could it really be Alana Shannon?" she asked herself.

CHAPTER SIX

CONNIE STARED AT two computer screens in the dark and windowless media room tucked in the basement of the building. She was with the company's photography and media guru, Jack Gilmore, a short, baby-faced, middle-aged man wearing a ridiculous brown wig. One of the monitors displayed an array of screenshots of the woman's head taken from the CNN news clip.

"So you still think it's Alana Shannon?" asked Gilmore.

"I'm not so sure."

"She was quite the national sensation for a while, wasn't she? Former porn star kills real estate magnate husband in North Carolina, as I remember the headlines."

Connie shook her head. "That was my doing back when I worked for the tabloid. I never should have labeled her a porn star. She was photographed nude when she was young and appeared in men's magazines. Pretty innocent by today's standards."

"Did she really murder her hubby?" asked Gilmore.

"There's no doubt that she shot him, but she claimed self-defense. The prosecutor reached the same conclusion—he dropped the charges just as the trial was starting."

"Then she disappeared?"

"That was over two years ago, and there's been no trace of her since."

Gilmore pushed the mouse with his pudgy fingers, and a new collage of pictures appeared on the other monitor. "Here are the pictures of Alana Shannon from the newspapers and magazines. I tried to find ones showing similar angles."

Connie's eyes darted back and forth between the sets of images. "Aha, it's the nose that's different. The eyes and mouth look similar, but looking closer, it's not the same woman. I'm not sure why I thought it was her…maybe just wishful thinking. It's not just the nose, Alana Shannon had beautiful green eyes…This woman's eyes are brown. Sorry for wasting your time, Jack."

"Hold on. I've been beta testing some experimental facial recognition software and I ran it on the pictures. There's a sixty-five percent probability that the women on these two monitors are the same."

"That's not very high, is it?"

"No, but I saw the same thing that you did. The nose is different. So I separated the face into three sections: first the eyes and forehead, second the nose, and third the mouth and chin. Then I ran the software just on those sections."

"And?"

"The eyes match at ninety percent…not taking into account the color. The mouth and chin match at ninety-two percent, and the nose matches at thirteen percent. I think it's Alana Shannon after a nose job."

Connie moved forward in her chair. "She's had surgery?"

"That would be my guess. And I know there are procedures to change eye color."

Connie thought for a moment. "I know someone who might be able to identify her far better than me, her former defense attorney in North Carolina. He worked with her day in and day out."

"Why don't I e-mail him some of the screenshots from CNN? He might see something we can't."

…

Two hours later, Connie called Roger Calhoun in Raleigh. Calhoun had defended Alana Shannon during her murder trial, and most people credited him with persuading the district attorney to drop the charges.

"Did you get the pictures?" asked Connie.

"They're in front of me on my computer."

"So what do you think?"

"Looks a lot like her except for the nose and the eye color."

"But do you think it could be her?"

"I know it is."

"How?" asked Connie.

"You never met him in person, but the tall brown-haired man following her off the helicopter is Ryan Butler."

CHAPTER SEVEN

BILL AND CHERYL spent five miserable days and nights at the makeshift emergency center set up near the airport. For the first two nights they slept on blankets on the ground under hastily constructed tents. On the third night FEMA delivered cots, a welcome gift to the hundreds of exhausted and worried Hawaiians and tourists who had taken refuge there. With the airport runway damaged, helicopters ferried in food and medical supplies from the island of Oahu.

The medics examined Cheryl, treated and bandaged her head, and assured Bill that despite some significant blood loss she would be fine. They indicated that in addition to the bleeding, she had suffered a serious concussion.

Being among so many people at the shelter made them especially uncomfortable; they hated crowds. Their psychiatrist had told them they suffered from a mild form of agoraphobia, likely triggered by the trauma of their car accident. However, except for Bill's recurring nightmares, they showed no symptoms of posttraumatic stress and were extremely content living in their own private world.

Cheryl's aunt Janet and uncle Doug had been their only visitors. Although she didn't remember her, Cheryl had taken an instant liking to Janet, a tall, dark-haired, long-limbed, gregarious woman. Cheryl's husband, Doug, was short, gruff, and very inquisitive. His job as a bank examiner brought him to Hawaii every six months, and Janet tagged along. They had visited three times, and Janet phoned Cheryl every few weeks. Cheryl looked forward to the calls and visits—they were her only connection with her past.

From what Bill could learn from the authorities, the quake had been limited to Molokai, although the islands of Maui, Lanai, and Oahu had experienced some tremors. The quake, centered a few miles off Molokai, had sent a fifteen-foot tsunami crashing against the cliffs on the island's mostly unpopulated north side. By the time the waves circled around to the south, where most of the population lived, they were only five feet high, causing minor flooding along the shoreline. The main problem the island faced was repairing the roads and the airport runway. Bill and Cheryl couldn't get any information about the condition of their house, but the authorities were hopeful that it still stood.

On the fourth day the airport runway opened, and a steady convoy of flights arrived carrying much-needed supplies and equipment. On the fifth day Bill and Cheryl received the news they had been hoping for: they could return home. Cheryl had fully recovered and had regained most of her bubbly personality.

A Molokai police officer, Sergeant Keahi, drove them along the newly repaired highway to their house. On the way they could see the damage caused by the quake and the tsunami. Many of the palm trees were down, and sand and mud covered parts of the road. A few of the houses had collapsed, but FEMA had assured them that theirs was structurally sound.

Sergeant Keahi didn't seem like the stereotypical happy islander. He had the brown complexion, black hair, and native facial features, but his face was sunken and his lips drawn tight. He appeared very distressed. "So you're the people who found Uncle Eddie?" he asked.

"Yes," said Bill, surprised by the question. "Are you related?"

Sergeant Keahi revealed a trace of a smile. "Hey, we're all related here. We're one big happy Molokai family." He seemed more Hawaiian. "I knew Uncle Eddie. Everyone did. He used to sell bananas on the street in town. He would set up his stand outside the main grocery store." He chuckled at the memory. "In the last few years, after his wife died, he lived alone in that shack. My auntie and others took him food and supplies every week. He just wanted to be alone. I'm surprised he let you use his road to the overlook. He normally didn't take to haoles."

"He was friendly to us...told us we could use the road anytime."

"He must have really liked you. He was possessive of that road. Used to charge people five dollars to use it—even family. So people stopped going."

"We gave him twenty," said Cheryl.

Keahi laughed. "No wonder he liked you."

. . .

Bill took Cheryl's hand as they approached their house. It looked fine from a distance, but most of the surrounding gardens were gone, replaced by patches of sand and gravel. The coconut palms that had lined the front were either missing, broken, or bent way over. Fortunately, the house was built on stilts, twelve feet above the ground, so the water hadn't reached the first floor, although it had flooded their car, parked underneath.

Sergeant Keahi pulled into the remains of the driveway. "Good luck," he said, letting them out. "I'll check back on you later today to see what you decide."

Based on the instructions from FEMA, they were to examine the house and decide whether to stay or return to the shelter. If they stayed, FEMA would deliver water and rations. FEMA had indicated it would be a long time before electricity and water were restored.

Although the house appeared undamaged from the outside, it was a different picture inside. It appeared ransacked. The quake had knocked shelves over, thrown paintings and mirrors to the floor, and shattered several windows. A stench of rotting food emanated from the refrigerator. They walked in silence out to the veranda that backed the house. Except for mud and sand piles on the lawn and the beach beyond, everything looked the same.

Bill and Cheryl sat down on the red-and-yellow patterned sofa. They knew they faced a long and difficult struggle.

"It will be okay," Bill said, putting his arm around Cheryl. He expected her to smile in her usual happy, optimistic way, but instead she sobbed.

The view of the islands of Maui and Lanai in the distance were still just as beautiful as ever, seemingly unchanged, but something felt different. Her crying shocked him. In the two years since they had come to the island, he had never seen her cry. Never. They had always been so happy, as if they were immune from anything bad; as if they lived in a state of grace.

Watching her cry, Bill had the strangest feeling. This September would mark their eighteenth wedding anniversary, and yet all he could remember of her was from the past two years. "Who had she been before that? Who had he been before that?"

He had a tremendous love for and physical attraction to her, but despite their long history together in Colorado, he felt he was seeing her for the first time. He had a vague sense that something had been irrevocably broken, like a precious vase that has crashed to the floor. You can piece it back together, but it will never be the same.

CHAPTER EIGHT

CONNIE'S BOSS, Aaron Retzler, gave her a skeptical frown. "You want me to fly you to Hawaii in the middle of a disaster recovery?"

"Yes."

Retzler sighed, took off his tortoiseshell glasses, and dangled them in front of his face. His head was completely shaved, and his usual black turtleneck and blue jeans draped his thin frame. "So you are absolutely sure it's Alana Shannon and Ryan Butler?"

"Absolutely."

"How do you know they will still be there?"

"I don't, but it's a window of opportunity that's rapidly closing."

"Maybe they were just tourists and are headed home…somewhere unknown."

"No. I checked with the relief workers—they have a house on the island. They listed their names as Cheryl and William Parker. I searched the real estate records online; they bought the house about two years ago, not long after Alana Shannon disappeared."

"Then there's no hurry. You can call them when they get phone service restored."

"Some of the homes on the island have been destroyed or severely damaged. I don't know about their house, but it was on the beach, so there's a good chance the tsunami took it out. They may have to relocate. There's a big risk I could lose them if I don't act quickly."

Retzler leaned back in his chair, crossing his arms. "What do you hope to achieve, Connie? Do you think they will really talk to you? After all, there's a reason they disappeared."

"You mean the CIA?"

"Yes."

"Well, it's a chance for us to find out for sure, isn't it?"

"I don't know, Connie. How about your other investigations? What's going on with that woman who said Congressman Luke tried to rape her?"

"It's been two weeks, and I messaged her twice suggesting we meet or talk on the phone, promising her complete anonymity. I haven't heard back."

"You need to be aggressive on this—reluctant sources need to be encouraged and coaxed."

"I know that…I just don't want to scare her off, so I'm giving her a little more time."

"Anything else ready to break?"

Connie frowned. "Well, I'm still working on a couple of leads, but nothing significant, nothing like Congressman Luke."

Retzler brought his hand to his face, squeezing his chin. "Your draft article on Alana Shannon and the CIA first brought us together."

Connie rolled her eyes. "Yeah, the one you wouldn't publish."

"Don't get snippy with me. We've been through this before. The article was weak, and the CIA categorically denied everything. Even if you get something in Hawaii, they'll move to prevent publication."

"Are you going to let the CIA dictate our stories? Remember, when you hired me you promised I could resume work on the Shannon story if anything new surfaced. Well, it has." She placed her hands on her hips.

Retzler shook his head. "All right—you win. I doubt they'll talk to you, but you're right…I made you a promise. I'll issue press credentials to get you on the island—indicating that you're covering the earthquake for our company. It's going to be chaotic when you get there—it may be hard to find them."

"Don't worry. If they're there, I'll track them down."

Retzler grinned as she walked out of the room. Despite her small stature, she was quite a dynamo.

CHAPTER NINE

"**HOW ARE YOU** holding up?" Bruce Marko asked James Lamont, the deputy director of the CIA. They were together in a secure conference room in the executive offices of the White House, awaiting the arrival of two others.

The question surprised Lamont. Bruce Marko was in charge of covert operations and never displayed the slightest concern for anybody's feelings. Although he had Hollywood-good looks, his facial expression never varied from blankness. He seemed more like a robot than a human being.

"I'm hanging in there," answered Lamont, eyeing Marko's familiar blue-and-yellow striped tie. He wondered if it was the only one Marko owned, or did he have a drawer of duplicates at home?

"Congressman Luke doesn't let up, does he? Blaming us for 9/11…claiming we're too soft and timid. Do you think Luke's getting to the president? Is he going to fire the director and Olds?"

Now Lamont knew the real reason for Marko's feigned concern. He wanted to gauge his own job security. Before he could answer, Scotty Olds and Wilhelm Kronig walked in. Olds, the president's security adviser, was of medium height, dark haired, and impeccably dressed, always looking as if he had walked off the pages of *GQ*. Kronig, a former CIA deputy director himself and now a special consultant, was elderly, bald, of medium height, and slightly overweight, with a kind face that radiated wisdom. The old Black Box team was together again, minus Al Wolaski. Eight months earlier, hunters had stumbled upon his bullet-ridden body in a remote area of Montana.

The team was responsible for the CIA's ultrasecret Black Box program—high-risk, high-payoff operations run off the books with only the verbal approval of the president. None were currently in play, but they were still cleaning up from the last one, a failed attempt to find and kill Osama bin Laden.

The leader of the team, Scotty Olds, was a close friend of the president. He smiled with bemusement at Marko's tie. "You called the meeting, so go ahead, Bruce."

"I need to brief you on the drug manufacture. Something doesn't add up."

"What do you mean?" asked Lamont, sitting erect in his chair, peering over thick glasses. His dark mustache nearly concealed his lips.

"Recently I was talking to our man at Guantánamo, checking on how the special interrogations were going and whether the drug was still working its wonders. He mentioned an issue he had with the central CIA lab—claims he was being shortchanged on the shipment. You know the protocol—the drug's weighed at the lab and rechecked at the destination. Seems the weight had been consistently off by a small percentage, less than one-half of one percent. Naturally we would expect tiny variations, sometimes above and sometimes below, but all the shipments were underweight by the same percentage."

"So maybe there's a problem with the scales?" asked Lamont.

"That's what our man at Gitmo thought. He double-checked his scales—no problem there, so he contacted the central lab, thinking they might need to recalibrate at their end. The lab head said he would look into it. That was six weeks ago, and since then all the shipments have been right on target."

"If the problem's been rectified, why are we meeting?" asked Olds, fondling his gold cuff links.

"Because I checked our other two interrogation sites in Poland and Uzbekistan. They also said that their shipments have been consistently underweight, but unlike Gitmo, there's been no change…They've continued to be shorted." Marko waited for this to sink in.

"Go on," said Lamont.

"If it was only an issue of faulty scales, all the weights should have returned back to normal six weeks ago, just as they did at Guantánamo…but they didn't."

"Are you implying that some of the drug is missing? That somebody's been skimming it?" asked Lamont, wringing his hands.

"I don't know, but I thought it deserved investigation."

"Who would even know what the drug does?" shouted Lamont. "Nobody at the central lab knows that. Their job is to produce it based on the formula. For somebody to steal it, they would have to know its purpose." Lamont took a handkerchief out of his pocket and wiped his brow. He was prone to sweating when agitated.

"I did some calculations," said Marko. "Over the past twenty-seven months, the lab has produced and shipped 923 grams of the drug. A shortage rate of point zero zero five would net about five grams."

Lamont exhaled a deep breath. "We all know the tremendous power of the drug. It only takes a small dose…Five grams could go a long way."

"I've done some further investigation," added Marko. "The weight of the drug is verified by the lab's chief chemist, Dr. John Cameron. He's been at the agency for twenty-six years. I checked his records…There's nothing negative there. He's been an exemplary employee."

Kronig shook his head sadly. "You won't find anything in the official record, but Cameron was under internal investigation as a suspected homosexual when I took over as deputy in 1982. The previous director was hysterical about gays—thought they were security risks and vulnerable to blackmail. A purge was under way. I put a stop to it. I could understand security concerns about field agents, but certainly not a chemist."

"So nothing came of it?" asked Olds.

"No, but there were others under investigation—including Wolaski."

"What? I never would have suspected him," said Lamont.

"He denied it, and since there was no proof, the inquiry was dropped. However, after Wolaski left the agency he applied for a job with the House Intelligence Committee. The investigator doing his background check asked me if Wolaski was a homosexual. He said there were rumors that he was intimately involved with another CIA employee named John Cameron."

"Shit," said Lamont, pounding his fist on the table. "You mean that Wolaski and Cameron could have been lovers?"

Marko interrupted. "I heard the rumors too, so I checked their files. They both lived in the same apartment building…different units, but on the same floor."

Lamont sat forward in his chair. "Fuck—so Wolaski could have told Cameron everything about the drug…what it's being used for."

"It's possible," said Marko. "And who knows what else he might have told him about the Black Box operation? We all know the son of a bitch couldn't be trusted. Maybe we waited too long before taking him out."

The room turned quiet. Finally Lamont broke the silence. "For the sake of argument, let's assume that Wolaski told Cameron about the drug and the Black Box operation. The question is why Cameron would risk everything to skim it. He wouldn't do that unless he had a specific purpose."

"That's a scary thought," said Olds.

"How do we find out?" asked Lamont. "We can't use internal investigators—the existence of the drug is too secret. An investigation would shine a light on what we're doing, and we can't risk that."

"We could confront him," said Olds.

"I don't think that's a good idea," interjected Kronig. "He'd probably clam up, which would leave us at a dead end. I suggest we use private sources—hire somebody from outside the agency to follow him. If he's stealing the drug, we need to catch him in the act or at least find out who's at the receiving end."

"Do you have someone in mind?" asked Lamont.

"Patrick O'Brien—an asset I had in Moscow. I managed to pull him out in 1992. Later I secured him a job as an investigator with the DC police department. He retired a few years ago but still does special assignments. He's an expert in surveillance."

"You had a Russian agent named Patrick O'Brien?" asked Olds, laughing.

Kronig smiled. "Well, it's not his real name, for sure. We gave him a fake background and he now speaks fluent English with a slight Brooklyn accent. He's amazing to listen to...Nobody would suspect. He can change his dialect at the drop of a hat. He's a chameleon...can impersonate anybody using voice, gesture, and posture. He has the whole toolbox."

"Bring him in," said Olds, tugging at end of a starched white shirtsleeve.

CHAPTER TEN

BILL WAS AT the back of the house, by the beach, removing debris and raking sand. Cheryl was inside sweeping up shattered plates and glass. Bill came into the house when he heard the car pull into the driveway, and they both looked out through the broken front window. A very short, stylish blonde woman dressed in a dark business suit and white high-heeled shoes emerged from a black Chevy. They certainly hadn't been expecting visitors. Bill and Cheryl walked out to greet the woman as she quickly approached the house. She stretched out her hand, holding a business card.

"Hello, I'm Connie Blythe with the *Beltway Insider*. I'd like to talk to you."

Bill examined the card and noticed that the business address was in Rosslyn, Virginia. For some reason he knew Rosslyn was a suburb of Washington, DC. He handed the card to Cheryl. She read it and handed it back to him.

The woman stared at them with a look of expectation.

"We don't want to talk to the press," said Bill. "We told our story to the Red Cross and to FEMA, and that's it. We don't want our names or faces in the news."

"Do you recognize my name?"

They both indicated no. "Are you a well-known correspondent or something?" asked Cheryl.

"No, but I thought you would know who I am. Can I come in?"

"The house is a mess," said Cheryl. "We're just beginning to clean up. We can sit on the veranda if you would like."

Connie followed them around the side of the house to the back and sat facing them.

"You really don't remember my name," Connie said, making it sound more like an accusation than a question.

"No," they said in unison, mystified by the repeated question.

"So now you go by Cheryl and William Parker…When did that happen?"

"I don't understand," said Bill.

"Let's cut the crap," said Connie. "I know who you are. There's no point in pretending."

Bill and Cheryl exchanged bewildered glances.

"Pretending what?" asked Cheryl, with rising annoyance in her voice. "You must have us confused with somebody else."

"I don't think so. I have been searching for you ever since you disappeared." Connie shook her head. "Look, I understand that you might not want to talk to me, but I promise I'll keep your location secret. If you want, everything will be off the record. I just want to know what happened to you. Was it the CIA?"

They looked back dumbfounded.

"We have no idea what you are talking about," said Cheryl. "We're from Colorado. We were injured in a car wreck two and a half years ago. After that we moved to the island."

"So you are telling me with a straight face that you are not Alana Shannon. That you're not the woman who killed her husband in North Carolina?"

"What?" exclaimed Cheryl.

"That's enough," shouted Bill. "You're crazy, lady. I want you off our property, now!"

"So you want to play it that way?"

The anger welled in Bill. He moved toward Connie with an aggressive posture, looming above her and shepherding her to the front of the house, back toward her car. "Go, lady," he barked.

"Please," she said. "I promise you complete confidentiality. I've come a very long way to find you. You know you can trust me, Ryan."

Bill froze for a second. "I'm not named Ryan," he shouted. "I'm William Parker. Now go!"

Connie trudged to the car as they followed her. She opened the door and looked at Bill. "I expected more from you, Ryan Butler, after everything we went through together." She positioned herself in the driver's seat and slammed the door.

They watched as she pulled away a little too fast, spinning her wheels in the driveway.

"What was that all about?" asked Cheryl, with tears streaming down her cheeks. "First the quake, the tsunami, and now some crazy woman."

"It will be all right, darling. Let's forget all about this. It must be a case of mistaken identity." He put his arms around her, looking out to the car tracks in the sand. He had an uneasy feeling—it wasn't the first time he had heard the name Ryan Butler.

CHAPTER ELEVEN

CONNIE FUMED ON the flight back from Hawaii. She couldn't comprehend why they wouldn't acknowledge her. She could appreciate that they might not want to talk, but she couldn't understand why they would act dumb. At first they were so convincing that Connie had doubted that it was really they—but when she mentioned Ryan's name she had seen a flash of recognition in the man, a sudden pulling back of his head and a widening of his eyes. It lasted only a fraction of a second, but long enough to convince her that he was Ryan. She couldn't detect any recognition in Alana.

Returning to her office in Washington, Connie wanted to pursue the story, track down William and Cheryl Parker's background, and follow the money. She could check with the mortgage company that had handled their real estate transaction on Molokai. She could trace credit cards and other financial records. However, after much argument, Aaron Retzler convinced her the story was dead. He said that if they wouldn't talk, or even acknowledge their past lives, continuing was pointless.

Softening Connie's disappointment was a new message from Jason in Congressman Luke's office. This time he also gave his last name, Cassidy, and suggested setting a time to get together to discuss "certain strange meetings the congressman has been having with other representatives, including the speaker."

Connie assumed he was talking about Congressman Luke's tea sessions, which had recently come out in the news. Connie had seen the clip on CNN in which a reporter had cornered the congressman as he was leaving the Sheraton Hotel in DC after delivering a speech to the Council on Foreign Relations. The congressman towered over everybody.

Shoving a microphone into the congressman's chin, the reporter yelled, "Congressman Luke, is it true that you have been holding secret meetings in your office with the speaker of the House and other congressmen?"

Luke appeared surprised by the question, but he quickly recovered, revealing a broad smile. "I believe you may be referring to the times I have invited one of my esteemed colleagues back to my office for tea…an opportunity for an informal exchange of ideas and perspectives. These meetings do not appear on my official calendar because they are impromptu get-togethers that take place when our schedules unexpectedly open up." He laughed. "I assure you these meetings are not secret, and there is nothing unethical or unsavory about them." His face soured. "It is a sad commentary that the media would read something sinister into the friendly sharing of a nonalcoholic beverage in the privacy of someone's office."

The congressman shook his head sadly. "You know, I just came from delivering an important policy address about how the CIA is failing this country with faulty intelligence and overly cautious analysis. You would think I would get a question on that issue, instead of my personal schedule. The American people are more concerned about the threats posed by Iran, Iraq, and North Korea than they are about my tea-drinking habits." He started walking off again.

The same persistent reporter shouted a follow-up question, again shoving the microphone into the congressman's face, almost poking him. "Congressman Luke. Is it true that you have had at least three meetings with the speaker of the House in your office in the past few weeks?"

"Yes, it is true, and so what? Have you listened to anything I have said?"

"Why would the speaker come to your office instead of the other way around?"

The congressman concealed his anger and smiled broadly. "I guess he just likes my tea."

CHAPTER TWELVE

CONNIE PARKED AT Great Falls Park, sixteen miles north of Washington, and followed a path through the woods to the picnic area where she had agreed to meet Jason. She spotted a cluster of tables with the cascading waterfalls of the Potomac River in the background. They were empty, except for one occupied by a man in blue and a young woman in a heavy white sweater. Jason hadn't mentioned that anybody would be with him.

Connie approached. "Jason?"

He shook her hand. "As you can see, I brought someone else…She's an intern. She wishes to keep her identity private."

Connie examined the woman, who was thin with dark-brown hair and just a light touch of pale lipstick. She wore a long dress under the sweater. She smiled nervously and gave Connie a limp handshake.

Connie spoke first. "You hinted in your message that there was more to the tea sessions than reported."

"I don't believe the congressman has been truthful. He said they are spontaneous meetings, but they are carefully planned and choreographed."

"How so?"

"Before we go on, I want you to know that I have worked for Congressman Luke for over ten years in constituent relations. I was a great admirer and, until recently, thought he had the best interests of the nation in his heart. I believed he was an honest Christian man, but now I'm not so sure. I support his opposition to abortion and gay rights, but I believe his foreign policy views are extreme."

Connie nodded, giving no hint that she was a lesbian.

Jason continued, "I know there is something strange and unethical going on. What I am going to tell you is off the record."

"If you want," said Connie, disappointed.

"There is great secrecy regarding these tea sessions—not only about who he is meeting with but how they are conducted. The staff receives advance notice that a meeting is going to take place. They are instructed to try to schedule business outside the office. Those remaining must stay in their offices until they receive the all clear. There is to be no milling around, and the break room is off-limits—where the tea is prepared. Only the chief of staff has access to the break room during that time. We are told that if we see congressmen entering or leaving, not to mention it to anybody else."

While Jason talked, Connie examined the young woman. She appeared frightened, with a mouse-like demeanor. She focused on her hands folded in front of her on the table, avoiding all eye contact.

Jason continued. "The meetings started five months ago. At first just one or two a week, now maybe three or four. I know the speaker has come several times. There have been lots of rumors circulating about what's going on. I think somebody in another congressional office—not ours—tipped the press."

"That would explain the questions from CNN."

"After CNN ran the story, there were no meetings for a week, but they've started again."

"So what do you think is going on in these meetings?"

"First let me give you some observations. There is an informal network of staffers on the Hill. Most come and go, but you get to know the ones who stay on. It was clear to me from the beginning that the other staffers and most of the other representatives didn't think much of Congressman Luke...They thought his foreign policy views were on the fringe. The House minority leader once called him a crazy bird."

"I remember that."

"Back then nobody imagined him being appointed chair of the foreign intelligence committee. When the speaker made the announcement, everybody was shocked, including me. How can you explain his sudden rise to power?"

"I don't know—you tell me what you think."

"The other congressional staff keep asking me the same question—what's going on in those tea sessions? They say that afterward, their bosses shift their positions and their votes. When they question the sudden change of heart, they hear the same response, almost in the exact same words. They say that Congressman Luke is very convincing and he knows things that nobody else knows. I've heard that over and over again—he knows things that nobody else knows."

Jason lowered his voice to a whisper. "He goes from being on the back burner in Congress for the past twelve years and then, overnight, ascends to one of the most powerful positions in Washington…all this right after the tea sessions started."

"Maybe it's a coincidence," said Connie.

"Maybe, but there's something else. He hasn't only been meeting with other congressmen…He's been meeting privately with female interns."

The woman lifted her eyes from her hands and spoke in a meek voice. "I'm the person who sent you the message that Congressman Luke tried to rape me. I'm Aubrielle Blake, but please don't use my name."

CHAPTER THIRTEEN

SITTING AT THE picnic table, under an overcast sky, the intern began her story.

"It was after seven in the evening, and I was packing to leave when the telephone rang in my cubicle. Most of the staff had already left. I was shocked when Congressman Luke was on the line asking me to come to his office. I was very nervous. I had only been to a few meetings where he was present. I was shaking."

"I can understand that," said Connie.

"When I entered the room he told me to sit on the sofa. He said he invited me because he wanted to get to know the interns better. He said he was interested in the perspectives of young people. He asked me to share some tea and have a chat. I was aware of his tea sessions, so the request didn't seem out of the ordinary. What he didn't know was that I'm a Mormon and I'm not supposed to drink tea, but I said nothing and I let him pour me a cup. He asked me how I liked my tea. I told him I had never had tea before, and he laughed. He said that in that case I should take it with cream and sugar. I took a sip…It tasted like hot sweetened milk. We spoke for a few moments, and the phone rang. He told me it was a private call. I started to leave, but he instructed me to stay. He said he would take it in his interior office, and he left the room.

"I took another sip of the tea. It tasted good, but I started feeling light-headed. I didn't think it was the tea, just my nervousness being with the congressman. I also felt guilty about drinking it. I questioned what my parents would think, so I poured the tea into a big potted plant by the sofa. I didn't think it mattered if I drank the tea or not. I was feeling a little shaky."

Connie gave her a sympathetic smile.

"When the congressman returned, he asked me if I had finished the tea. I said yes and he asked me to show him the cup. I remember thinking it was a strange request, but I tilted the empty cup for him to see. I remember him saying, 'Good girl,' which I also thought was odd. Then his whole demeanor changed. He asked me if I was a devout Christian. I said yes. He asked me if I believed that God forgave our sins. Again I answered yes.

"He sat next to me on the couch and took my hand in his. He said something about what a difficult struggle it was to save the nation from the liberals and atheists. He told me it was hard for him to be away from his wife for such a long time…She stayed back in Missouri with the children. He kept saying that he was very lonely and it was difficult for a man to be without female companionship. He told me I was beautiful and that I could give him a great gift that would help him to carry on in his struggle. He said that I had to do everything he asked without question. He stood up in front of me and told me to part my legs—I was wearing a skirt. I didn't know what to think, but I parted them.

"Then he told me to unbutton my blouse. I asked why and he acted startled. I remember his exact words: 'Because I want to touch your tits.' His face had changed…He looked crazed. He started unbuckling his pants and pulling down his zipper. I jumped off the sofa and ran out of the office in shock. I remember passing Jason in the hall. He asked what was wrong, but I ignored him. Jason followed me to my cubicle, but I told him I wanted to be alone. I sat at my desk and cried. I didn't know what to do."

Connie reached into her purse and handed her some tissues. "Take your time," she said. "I know this is hard."

"I thought maybe I should tell my parents, but I wasn't sure they would believe me. I thought of going to the police, but I knew it would be my word against his, and nobody would take mine over a congressman's. Finally I went to Jason and told him what had happened. That's when he suggested I go on your website."

"Did you tell anybody else?"

"No."

Connie sighed. "Of course I believe you, but I don't have enough to go on. There is no way to corroborate your story, and from what you told me, he didn't touch you, did he?"

"No, but he was going to."

"When he started taking his pants off, did he expose himself?"

"I didn't see anything; I just got up and ran away."

Jason stepped in. "This isn't an isolated instance."

"What do you mean?" asked Connie.

"I know for sure that he met alone with at least two other female interns, all late in the evening after most people had gone home, and always when his chief of staff was away."

Connie perked up. "Go on."

"I was miffed that he would meet with the interns when he had never bothered to meet alone with me. Then I realized it was the young females he was interested in. Finally I went to our chief of staff, Laura Jansen, and asked her if she knew that the congressman was meeting alone with female interns. She didn't seem surprised, but she did seem angry. She told me not to worry about it…She would talk to the congressman. She said he was naive about certain matters and didn't always realize how others might misinterpret his behavior. Then she asked me not to mention it to anybody else. At that moment I knew something was wrong. So when I saw Aubrielle come out of the office, I realized something needed to be done."

"Will these other interns be willing to talk to me if I promise them confidentiality?"

Jason shook his head. "These are all good girls, raised in strict religious and conservative homes. They would never knowingly let anybody molest them."

"So they won't talk."

"I didn't say they wouldn't talk to you, but you'd be wasting your time. I'm sure they don't know what happened to them."

"What do you mean?"

"I think the tea must be spiked with some kind of drug—the same drug he is using with the congressmen during his tea sessions. Somehow it gives him power over people. The only reason Aubrielle escaped is that she didn't drink the tea. There's more to the story, but I'd prefer to tell you the rest in private."

CHAPTER FOURTEEN

PATRICK O'BRIEN, once known as Pyotr Kloskov, was a professional at tracking people. In 1976 he began working for the KGB in the province of Kursk, 280 miles south of Moscow. Smart and resourceful, he quickly rose through the ranks, but hit a dead end in 1983 when the authorities arrested his younger sister, Lenka, accusing her of anti-Soviet sympathies. The charges were vague; she had American rock and roll records in her possession. So did most other Soviet university students at the time. Lenka's real crime was being young, beautiful, and unwilling to submit to the sexual advances of a prominent Communist Party boss. In a closed-court proceeding, a Soviet judge sentenced her to five years of hard labor.

Having a traitorous sibling was enough to block Kloskov's advancement, but insufficient to get him drummed out of the KGB. They transferred him to a dead-end position in Moscow trailing foreign diplomats and members of the politburo suspected of harboring dissenting views.

For nine years he honed his craft, learning how to follow people without detection, how to break into people's houses or hotel rooms and leave no trace, and how to clandestinely photograph the unsuspecting. He became adept at bugging apartments, planting evidence, framing foreigners, and tricking the innocent into confessing.

He also discovered that he had a great talent for language, both verbal and nonverbal. He spoke fluent English, German, and French without anyone's suspecting that he wasn't a native speaker. He studied the subtle, unconscious mannerisms of people from other cultures— their gestures, facial expressions, and postures. He took great pride in mimicking them—especially the Americans. Like his sister, he had a keen interest in American culture, and he harbored a deeply hidden hatred for the Russian authorities for whom he worked.

Through chance and some degree of recklessness, Wilhelm Kronig recruited Kloskov to work as a source for the CIA. In addition to his formal duties, he moonlighted by spying on high-ranking political and military figures in the Soviet hierarchy. In 1992, as the Soviet Union collapsed, Kronig smuggled him to the United States. With Kronig pulling the strings, he officially became Patrick O'Brien, a second-generation Irish American born in Brooklyn who had found work for the Washington, DC, Metropolitan Police Department and eventually become a detective. In addition to his regular duties, he performed side jobs for the CIA.

. . .

With the advances in technology, trailing people was much easier than in the old days. O'Brien placed a transponder on Dr. John Cameron's Lexus that broadcast its real-time GPS location. He also affixed an almost microscopic motion detector to the door of Cameron's apartment that alerted him whenever the door opened or closed. Using these two devices, he could track most of Cameron's movements from his laptop.

It took him a couple of weeks to map out Cameron's routine. Most workdays he drove his Lexus from his apartment in Arlington, Virginia, to the CIA offices in Langley, arriving by eight in the morning and leaving by seven at night. On Friday nights he headed for the same gay bar in Georgetown and usually departed with a pickup before midnight, returning to his apartment.

Most Saturdays he put in a half day at Langley, and on Sunday mornings he attended Catholic Mass. That was his usual pattern, except for Thursdays. On those evenings he worked late, usually leaving around nine, and drove into central Washington, parking near an exclusive apartment complex on Pennsylvania Avenue adjacent to the United States Navy Memorial.

. . .

O'Brien discreetly followed Cameron into the apartment building's lobby. A guard station blocked access to the elevators, suggesting that some very important people lived there. O'Brien watched as Cameron spoke briefly to the guard, who opened the gate to the elevators. Cameron climbed in with two other people. He also noted that Cameron carried a small brown case. Eleven minutes later Cameron exited the elevators still carrying the case, returned to his car, and drove home.

O'Brien had videotaped the entire scene with the miniaturized camera in his lapel. Back home he examined the footage. Zeroing in on the brown case, he realized that the one Cameron had exited with was slightly darker than the one he'd brought with him. He ran spectrographic analysis to confirm that the colors were different. He then focused on the elevator floor indicators; there were four in all. He had already noted that the one Cameron had taken stopped on the sixth and ninth floors before returning to the lobby. By monitoring the sequence of the elevator lights for the eleven minutes that Cameron was gone, he determined that the one he had come down on had traveled from the lobby to the eleventh floor to the sixth floor and back to the lobby. Cameron walked out with one other person, an elderly woman. O'Brien deduced that whomever Cameron had visited, and exchanged cases with, lived on the sixth floor.

O'Brien repeated his surveillance over the next two weeks and confirmed the pattern of late Thursday visits to the upscale apartment building. He obtained a listing of the twelve people who rented apartments on the sixth floor. Six of the residents were lawyers for big-dollar lobbying firms on K Street, two held high-ranking Justice Department positions, two were senior State Department officials, one was the senate's deputy budget director, and one was the chief of staff to Congressman Steven Luke.

CHAPTER FIFTEEN

FOR THE FIRST four weeks after returning to their house, Bill and Cheryl powered the refrigerator and the fans with a generator supplied by FEMA. They cooked on their propane grill or on their Coleman stove. FEMA provided water in large gallon jugs, and they carried seawater from the beach to flush the toilets.

On the fifth week the utility company restored power, and they opened a bottle of champagne to celebrate. The next week they had running water. The house was clean and the windows repaired. The back, front, and side yards even showed new growth. The authorities told them that phone, television, and Internet service would be back soon.

However, Connie Blythe's sudden and strange appearance continued to haunt Bill, especially her mistaking him for someone named Ryan Butler. It seemed an amazing coincidence that almost two years earlier, Cheryl's uncle Doug had mentioned how much Bill reminded him of a high school classmate from Allentown, Pennsylvania. He said this kid, named Ryan Butler, had been a great baseball pitcher and everybody had expected him to be in the major leagues someday, but nobody knew what had happened to him. Bill wondered who this Ryan Butler was. Despite his curiosity, he was hesitant to investigate further…as if a voice in the back of his head was warning him not to go there.

Bill vowed not to pursue the matter, but a few days after the restoration of Internet service, he awoke in the middle of the night with the name Ryan Butler swirling in his head. Against his better judgment, he went on the computer and Googled it. The screen filled with Ryan

Butlers from all over the world, so he narrowed his search to *Ryan Butler Allentown Pennsylvania baseball pitcher.* One article appeared:

"Former Allentown Pitching Ace Drafted by Chicago White Sox."

The article provided little information and no pictures, just a statement that after graduating from Allentown High School, Butler had gone to Temple University on a baseball scholarship.

Bill tried another search, *Ryan Butler Chicago White Sox.* A website of minor league baseball statistics appeared. He clicked on the page and found a short profile for Ryan Butler, listing his birth date, height, weight, and pitching stats for two minor league teams. Butler's cumulative two-year statistics were impressive: 16 wins, 6 losses, and 202 strikeouts. However, Bill riveted his attention on the accompanying photograph of a young man under a baseball cap. Despite his youth, the resemblance was strong. Furthermore, the website listed Ryan Butler as six foot two, with brown hair and blue eyes, the same as Bill. However, Butler was three years older.

Bill spent another hour searching the Internet and found plenty of Ryan Butlers, but none appeared to be the one he was seeking. He wondered what had become of the man, especially after such a promising start as a professional baseball player.

Bill went back to bed relieved. Ryan Butler was just somebody who looked a lot like him, that was all. However, the uncanny resemblance continued to intrigue him, and the next morning he called Allentown High School to obtain a copy of the yearbook. It was a huge mistake.

CHAPTER SIXTEEN

"SO WHAT'S THIS news you have to tell me?" Jason asked Hannah as they ate lunch together in the cafeteria in the basement of the Longworth House Office Building, surrounded by a frenzied swarm of congressional staffers, all gulping food and exchanging gossip.

Jason had known Hannah for eight years. She was tall, blonde, in her early thirties, preppy, with strong liberal leanings. She had come to Washington as an intern right out of Swarthmore College and now served as deputy chief of staff for an influential Democratic congressman. Although they were opposites politically, they had become instant friends.

In the beginning nobody had thought anything of their sharing lunch, and they enjoyed trading inside information and arguing politics and morality. Now having lunch with a staffer from the other party was suspect, so their meals together had become rarer. Lately he'd hesitated to see her for another reason…She kept drilling him about what was happening at Congressman Luke's tea sessions. He told her the truth, that he didn't know, but he knew she didn't believe him.

Soon after they sat down, Monica Rigleman walked by carrying a tray of food. "Nice to see elephants and donkeys conspiring," she said, and, without waiting for an invitation, plunked herself down at their table. "So what secrets are you two sharing?"

Neither Jason nor Hannah liked Monica, nobody did. Just out of college, she was the dark-haired, attractive daughter of a prominent senator and was serving as a congressional aide. Despite her junior position, she was outspoken, brash, and opinionated. Everybody knew she hadn't gotten her job based on her brains or charm.

Jason frowned and Hannah almost imperceptibly shook her head when she joined them. Hannah continued the conversation, directing a question to Jason while ignoring Monica. "Do you remember Annie Weaver?"

"Sure, she was one of our interns. She left four months ago. Why?"

Monica immediately interjected herself into the conversation. "How could anyone forget her?" she said, rolling her eyes. "That girl stepped right out of the nineteenth century; what a loser."

"She was extremely religious," said Jason. "She came from a very sheltered background."

Monica smirked. "She was so laughable. Everyone made fun of the way she dressed, all those long skirts and high necklines. If anybody said anything off-color, she'd blush like a tomato."

"She was a sweet kid, just out of her element here," said Jason, turning back to Hannah, trying to ignore Monica. "Why do you ask?"

"I passed her on the National Mall the other day. I said hello, but she walked right past me. I'm not sure she heard me. She was staring at the ground and seemed withdrawn, all shriveled up. She looked so desolate and dejected that I followed her and tapped her on her shoulder. She jumped liked a scared frog."

"I always thought she was a pretty girl," said Monica, interrupting again. "She even could have been hot if she wore some makeup and dressed sexier. You know, maybe show a little cleavage."

Hannah stared disapprovingly at Monica and turned her attention back to Jason. "I asked her if anything was wrong. She said no, but then she burst into tears and hugged me like a lost friend."

"That doesn't sound like her," said Jason. "She was always so reserved."

"We sat together on a park bench and she dropped a bombshell. She told me she was pregnant. I was shocked. I would never have expected that from her. I asked her how long and she said the doctors indicated about four months."

"I can't believe she got pregnant," said Jason. "Not her."

"Me neither," said Monica. "I didn't think she knew what sex was."

Hannah gave Monica another disapproving glance. "I asked her who the father was and she started sobbing. She said she didn't know."

"What? Our prim and proper Annie Weaver was a slut all along," said Monica, grinning.

"This is serious, Monica," scolded Hannah. "The girl has mental problems. She told me she didn't know who the father was because she's never had sex."

Monica spit out the food she was chewing, laughing. "Oh, I understand, it's another Immaculate Conception…She's the new Virgin Mary."

"Lay off her, Monica," admonished Jason. "She is obviously in serious trouble. There is nothing funny here."

Monica shrugged her shoulders and took another bite of her sandwich.

"She asked me something very disturbing," continued Hannah. "She asked if a woman could get pregnant without having sex. She seemed sincere. I felt so bad for her. She's obviously delusional. Of course I told her no, and I suggested that she seek psychological counseling. She looked at me in horror. She said her family were Pentecostal and only believed in faith healing. She also said that she hasn't told her parents yet. She's scared they'll disown her."

"So why are you telling me this?" asked Jason.

"Because she asked about you. She thought that you might be able to give her guidance. She said you were one of the few really moral men she ever met."

"She said that about me?"

"Yes. You know, everyone likes you and respects you, Jason. You have that effect on people. You might be able to convince her to get help. She's obviously repressed, whatever happened. I'm sure she's dealing with tremendous shame and guilt."

"Where is she working?"

"Some administrative position with navy procurement. She gave me her card." Hannah handed it to Jason.

Monica stared at both of them. "I know you don't want me to say this, but what she really needs is to get rid of that thing."

Jason and Hannah just glared at her.

...

Later, back in his office, Jason did the calculations. Annie Weaver was four months pregnant, and it had been four months since he had seen her coming out of the congressman's office, her face and lips red and her clothes rumpled. He knew he had two phone calls to make, one to Annie Weaver and another to Connie Blythe.

CHAPTER SEVENTEEN

CHERYL WAS GROCERY shopping when the yearbook arrived. Sitting in his study, Bill examined the cover. It read, "Allentown High School." He scanned the index and saw that Ryan Butler appeared on two pages. One displayed an array of photos of graduating seniors, twenty to a page. He stared at the picture of Butler. It looked like a younger version of himself. Underneath, the caption read, "Future major league baseball player."

On the other page, Butler appeared in two pictures: a group photo of the baseball team with Butler in the middle and a larger picture of just him, in his baseball uniform, holding a large trophy and grinning. Underneath it was the caption "Pennsylvania Division II High School Pitcher of the Year." The man could be his twin, except Butler was three years older and had grown up in another state.

Bill strained to remember his high school years, but, like everything else before the accident, they were a blank. He reconstructed what he knew about his past: he had been born and raised in Lawrence, Kansas, gone to college at the University of Colorado, met Cheryl, married her, bought a house in Boulder, and worked for the university before the accident. How he knew all this, he wasn't sure—he didn't remember anyone telling him, and he had no documentation except for a copy of his birth certificate.

Cheryl's return interrupted his ruminations. He called her into the study. The yearbook sat on his desk, open to the picture of Ryan Butler holding the baseball trophy. Bill's hand covered the caption.

She walked in and gave him a quizzical look. "What's up?"

"Look at this picture and tell me who it is."

Cheryl stared for only a moment. "That's you when you were younger," she squealed. "How did you get that picture?"

He turned to the other picture of Butler; again his hand concealed the name. "And who is this?"

"It's you again. I didn't know you played baseball. So how'd you get a copy of your high school yearbook?"

He closed the book to show the cover.

"'Allentown High School, Pennsylvania'?" she said, her head tilted. "I thought you went to high school in Kansas."

"I did. Amazingly, that isn't me." He removed his hand, showing her the name under the picture.

"Ryan Butler," she whispered. "He looks like he could be your—what's the term—doppelgänger?" She paused. "Why do you have a yearbook from Pennsylvania?"

"Does the name Ryan Butler sound familiar?"

She thought a moment, and a worried frown crossed her face. "That crazy woman who showed up at our house called you by that name, didn't she?"

"Yes."

"Well, maybe that explains it. I can see why she thought you might be him. But how did you find his high school yearbook—how did you know where to look?"

"Remember when your aunt Janet and uncle Doug first visited us?"

"Of course."

While you were talking to your aunt, Doug and I walked out to the beach. He told me I looked like somebody he went to school with in Allentown, Pennsylvania, named Ryan Butler. He said I was the spitting image of him. He told me he had been a great baseball player. So I called the high school and ordered a copy of the yearbook. Strange, though, I didn't see any mention of your uncle Doug in the book."

"Why didn't you ever tell me this?"

"I didn't think anything of it until that crazy woman showed up. It piqued my curiosity, so I ordered the yearbook. I also did some research on the Internet. Turns out that this Ryan Butler was a very good minor league baseball player. I found a picture of him on the Internet, and again, he looks a lot like me. He was also listed as six foot two—exactly my height, but born three years earlier."

"Well, it's all a case of mistaken identity," she said, sighing. "I feel much better. That lunatic woman must have thought that you were this Ryan Butler fellow. That explains it."

Bill stayed quiet for a few seconds, thinking. "You know what would be interesting—to get a copy of my own high school yearbook from Kansas and compare the photographs."

"Do you remember the name of your high school?"

"No, but there can't be that many high schools in Lawrence, I could call around."

Cheryl bit her lip. "Why would you want to do that? Remember, we're supposed to live in the present. Why look back?"

"Why not?" answered Bill, realizing that neither of them had ever seen a picture of him- or herself from before the accident.

CHAPTER EIGHTEEN

BRUCE MARKO AND Wilhelm Kronig waited in James Lamont's office at CIA headquarters at Langley. They had just heard that the president had fired Scotty Olds and the CIA director. They knew that the vice president had engineered the dismissal at the urging of Congressman Luke, and they had rushed to Lamont's office for more news.

Lamont walked in glumly, barely acknowledging their presence.

"Did they fire you too?" asked Marko in his usual flat monotone.

"Not exactly. I've been demoted."

"How can they demote the deputy director?" asked Kronig.

"They want me to stay on to handle administrative duties during the transition, but they're shutting me out of the intelligence side."

"That's ridiculous," stated Kronig. "They don't have a clue as to how things work here."

"Who's the new director?" asked Marko.

"Former congressman Craig Goodwin from California…Recently he's been working for the American Military Leadership Council—a group that advocates for increased military spending. I just met him. He told me he's a friend of the vice president."

"I remember him," said Kronig. "He sat on the House Appropriations Committee a few years back. He's a former Army Ranger, tough as nails and a super hawk. But he has a terrible temper and can't take criticism. That's how he lost his congressional seat. He attacked his opponent during a debate—punched him in the nose. Unfortunately, he knows nothing about the intelligence world."

"That's what they want," said Lamont. "A fresh face. Somebody to clean house."

Kronig shook his head dejectedly. "He'll need somebody with him who understands how the agency operates."

"They've already promoted someone from within…to serve as his *special adviser.*"

Kronig read the pain on Lamont's face. "Who?"

"Arnie Crowder. He was at the meeting too."

"Crowder? Are you kidding?" yelled Kronig. "He's the biggest asshole in the agency. A loudmouth know-it-all. All bluster and no substance."

"Everybody hates him," added Marko. "He's a fraud and a liar. So what about me? Has my position changed?"

"It's still unclear. It looks like you'll have two bosses. You'll come to me for everything except intelligence matters, for those you'll go to Crowder."

"You can't split it up like that, there's too much overlap," said Kronig.

"I know," said Lamont. "And by the way, Wilhelm, they're terminating your contract at the end of the week."

"I figured I was gone, but why are you staying on? It's an impossible situation, and they're going to squeeze you out in a few months anyway."

"I don't feel I should abandon ship. If I stay, maybe I can mitigate some of the damage. Several of our top analysts are already threatening to quit. If they leave, Goodwin will replace them with flunkies who will do whatever he wants. They'll wreck our intelligence capabilities."

"They just want the CIA to back up their preconceived beliefs," said Kronig.

Lamont slowly sat down in his chair, as if it hurt to move his body. "Director Goodwin and Crowder want everything on the fast track. The order is to drop everything and find evidence that's supports Iraq's chemical weapons program and its complicity in 9/11."

"But there's nothing there," yelled Kronig, throwing his arms in the air.

"They don't believe that...They believe the problem is us—that we're too timid and too cautious to find it. They're insisting that our analysts find evidence or hit the highway."

"That undermines the whole objectivity of intelligence analysis," complained Kronig.

"You're wasting your time preaching to us—we're the choir," said Marko. "Did you brief the new director and Crowder on our covert matters?"

"Yes."

"And the drug?"

Lamont hesitated. "No, nor did I mention our situation in Hawaii. Can you imagine what these idiots would do if they knew about the drug?"

"You may be on shaky ground," said Kronig.

"Maybe, but we've already withheld the secret from the past director and the president—because of the Black Box protocol. So what's different now? I'm not going to turn that information over to a person in some newly created dubious position of special adviser."

Marko interrupted. "You realize that you're putting me in a difficult situation. If I'm going to continue to be responsible for overseeing the drug's manufacture, and I'm reporting to Crowder, how can I keep that secret?"

"I suggest that you keep quiet about the drug. If asked, you will have to tell them. But now they're focused on other matters, mainly Iraq."

"And what about Patrick O'Brien's investigation and the apartment surveillance?" asked Kronig.

"That stays here—just between us," answered Lamont firmly.

CHAPTER NINETEEN

"**WHAT'S THE MATTER?**" Cheryl asked, reading Bill's pensive expression.

"I told you I wanted to order my high school yearbook from Lawrence, Kansas. Well, I called around to the two public high schools and neither had any record of my graduating or ever attending school there. I also checked a couple of private schools and even the Catholic high school—same story."

"That's strange."

"So why do I think I went to high school in Lawrence?"

"Somebody told you. We obviously have no memories of our own."

"For that matter, who told me that I went to the University of Colorado? Who told me that I met you there? Who told me we had a house in Boulder? We have no documentation of any of this—all I have is my birth certificate."

The color faded from her face. "I thought we agreed we weren't going to worry about our past, we should live in the now."

"I know. But what do you remember from after the accident?"

"I remember talking to the psychiatrist—the doctor who explained our brain injuries and amnesia."

"Do you remember actually selling our house in Colorado?"

She thought a moment. "Except for meeting with the psychiatrist, my first memories are when we arrived on the island." A worried frown cracked her face.

"Me too. Doesn't that seem strange? I mean, we decided to come here, we sold our house in Colorado, but neither of us remembers doing that."

"We were still recovering from our injuries…Oh my God—maybe the amnesia is expanding."

"Who does our tax returns?"

Cheryl's eyebrows knotted. "Our lawyer does."

"Who is our lawyer? Do you ever remember meeting our lawyer?"

"No. I know that we turned over our affairs to the law firm after the accident. We weren't mentally fit to handle our finances while we were recovering. I guess the firm has continued to handle them."

"Yet we don't know who the law firm is or how to contact them?"

"Not really." Her face paled even more.

"Shouldn't we know?"

"Unless we once knew and have forgotten. Maybe our memories are still bad. Maybe we're continuing to forget things but are unaware of it—there's no way we could tell."

"That's scary," said Bill. "Why don't you call your aunt Janet…She can probably tell us who our lawyer is, or find out for us."

"Good idea," said Cheryl, regaining some color.

. . .

Cheryl left a message on her aunt's voice mail, asking Janet to call her back. She walked over and put her hand on Bill's chest. "This is upsetting. I'm thinking we should leave everything alone. I have a bad feeling…like something inside is telling me not to look back."

Bill hugged her. "I have that same feeling, that we shouldn't be searching our past. It's a strange sensation…almost ominous."

"Then let's forget all about it. Let's take the sailboat out. I'll grab my swimsuit and we'll go. We can snorkel at the reef. Let's never talk about this again."

"Agreed."

Just as they were leaving, the telephone rang. They exchanged glances, unsure whether to pick it up. They waited for the answering machine to begin.

"Hello, Cheryl. This is your aunt Janet—you just called me. What's wrong, dear—you sounded upset."

Cheryl picked up the phone. "Hi, Aunt Janet. I'm sorry. We're not really upset; we just wanted to get some information, but it's not important now."

"Well, you certainly sounded upset. What information?"

"We realized that we can't remember the name of our lawyer. We thought that maybe you would know. That's all."

"Is there a reason you need a lawyer? Nothing bad has happened, I hope."

"No, we were curious. Neither of us remembered the name and it upset us. We're concerned that we're still forgetting things."

"Well, you probably are still suffering from the lingering effects of your brain injuries."

"Something else strange happened. Bill was trying to order a copy of his high school yearbook in Kansas, but they told him they had no record of his attendance."

"Why did he want a copy of his yearbook?"

"It's a bizarre story. Bill said that your husband told him he looked a lot like a guy he went to high school with back in Allentown, Pennsylvania—a baseball player named Ryan Butler. Then some woman came to the house a few weeks ago and mistook him for some person with the same name, Ryan Butler. Bill was curious, so he ordered a copy of Butler's yearbook from Pennsylvania. There is a remarkable resemblance, although Butler is three years older."

"I remember Doug mentioning to me that Bill looked like this kid he knew in high school, but, then again, a lot of people look similar. So tell me about this woman who came to your house."

"I don't remember her name. She gave us her business card, but we threw it away—she was a reporter. At first we thought she wanted to interview us about the earthquake, but all she wanted to talk about was some murder trial in North Carolina. We kept telling her that we weren't the people she thought we were. She kept calling us Ryan and Alana. She acted crazy."

"Have you heard from her again?"

"No, that was it. But after looking at those high school pictures of Ryan Butler, I can see how she could have mistaken Bill for him—there's an eerie similarity."

Janet's voice was soothing and reassuring. "I'm sure it's all a case of mistaken identity. I wouldn't worry about it, and I'd stop looking backwards. You told us that you only lived in the present. Doug and I were so impressed by that philosophy that we've been working on it ourselves—to live in the moment and try not to think about the past or worry too much about the future. We're getting better at it, and it's helping our marriage."

"You're right. I don't know what came over us."

"To make you feel better, I'll tell you what I'll do. I'll check with our cousins who are still in Colorado. I'm sure that they know who your lawyer is…probably the same firm that handled the sale of your house and your financial accounts. I should be able to get back to you in a few days. How does that sound?"

"Thanks so much, Aunt Janet. I feel so much better after talking to you."

CHAPTER TWENTY

JASON AND CONNIE were tired by the time they reached the church outside Lexington, Virginia. It had taken three hours to drive from Washington through the long valley that separates the Blue Ridge range and the Appalachian Mountains. Connie had driven the road before, in the fall, when everything was ablaze in red, yellow, and orange. Now the trees were dark skeletons protruding from bleak snowy mountains.

They drove through the picturesque twin-college town of Lexington, past the Virginia Military Institute and the Washington and Lee University. Another ten minutes down a rural road brought them to the Pentecostal church, a small brick structure with a white steeple in the middle of nowhere. Inside they met Annie Weaver's parents. Annie wasn't present.

Mr. Weaver was of medium height with a long face, short hair parted in the middle, and dark glasses. He wore a brown sports jacket and a brown tie. Only his calloused hands hinted that he worked outdoors. Mrs. Weaver was plump, with a soft rounded face. Her long brown hair reached to her waist, and her skirt landed at her ankles. She eyed them with apprehension.

"I agreed to meet because you said you might be able to shed light on our daughter's pregnancy," said Mr. Weaver, staring intently at Jason. "Annie encouraged me to talk to you...She said I could trust you." He redirected his gaze to Connie. "I have no idea what you are doing here. You say you're a reporter?"

"That's right, sir, but I promise you the strictest confidentiality. Nothing you or your daughter say will be revealed without your permission."

Mr. Weaver frowned. "You still haven't told me your purpose here."

"That will become clear as we discuss your daughter's situation," answered Connie.

"Where is Annie?" asked Jason.

"She's waiting in another room," said Mr. Weaver. "We wanted to talk with you before bringing her in, if at all. It all depends on what you have to say." Mr. Weaver took off his glasses and looked hard at Jason. "Are you the father?"

Jason recoiled. "No. Not at all."

"Oh, I thought maybe that's why you came."

"We hoped that you were here to confess and take responsibility," said Mrs. Weaver.

"If you're not the father, do you know who is?" demanded Mr. Weaver.

"I have a suspicion," said Jason.

Mr. Weaver brought his hand to his heart. "This is a heartbreaking situation for all of us. We love our daughter very much, but in our faith, sex outside of marriage is a sin deserving of condemnation."

Mrs. Weaver started tearing up. She dabbed a tissue to her eyes.

Mr. Weaver waited for her to regain her composure. "However, as Christians we have compassion. We can never forgive the sin, but we can forgive the sinner. But that requires the sinner to acknowledge the wrongdoing and seek forgiveness. Our daughter continues to be unrepentant, insisting that she has never had sex despite the clear evidence to the contrary."

Mrs. Weaver sobbed.

Jason smiled sympathetically at Mr. Weaver. "I share your Christian faith and I understand your heartbreak. However, seeking forgiveness requires knowledge of the sin. I don't believe your daughter has any memory of what happened to her...I believe she is telling you the truth as she knows it."

"How can that be?"

"We believe there is a high probability that your daughter was raped under the influence of an extremely powerful drug that has erased any memory of the occurrence. Furthermore, we don't believe that your daughter was the only one raped in this manner. We believe there are multiple victims. That's why Ms. Blythe is here. We are beginning an investigation."

Fury burst across Mr. Weaver's face. "Who raped her? Do you know who did it?" He clenched his fists.

"You're not going to like the answer…Congressman Luke."

Mr. Weaver stood abruptly from his chair, his face turning scarlet. "That's absurd. Congressman Luke is a fine religious man; he would never do such a thing. You should leave—now." He gestured to the door.

Connie spoke. "I know this comes as a shock. Would you at least let us provide the evidence before throwing us out? We've come a long way and we're talking about your daughter's life. For her sake, please hear us out."

Mrs. Weaver placed her hand softly on her husband's shoulder. "We should at least listen to what they have to say."

Mr. Weaver slowly sat back down. "All right, go on, then."

Jason took over. "Congressman Luke has been meeting alone with some of the female interns, usually for an hour. The meetings are impromptu, and always take place when his chief of staff is away. I am aware of several such meetings, there may have been more.

"When I ask the interns about the meetings they become confused. They tell me that the congressman was interested in their views on issues related to young people, but strangely, they can never recall any of the discussion. Congressman Luke met with your daughter like that four months ago, which coincides with the time of her pregnancy. I happened to see her when she came out of his office. Her face was red and her clothes disheveled. She looked very upset. I asked her what was wrong, but she ignored me and ran back to her cubicle. I walked by later and she was slumped over with her face in her hands. I thought I heard her crying.

"When the chief of staff returned I confronted her. I told her that I didn't think it was a good idea for the congressman to be meeting alone with the female interns. She appeared mad and told me she would speak to the congressman about it. She said that the congressman means well but doesn't appreciate how things might look to others."

"That's all you have?" asked Mr. Weaver.

"No, there's more. About a month later, another female intern came into my office. She looked distraught and asked to speak to me privately. She told me that the congressman invited her into his office for a discussion. He offered her some tea…Perhaps you've heard about his tea sessions?"

"Yeah, I think so."

"The intern is a Mormon and not supposed to drink tea, but she didn't want to insult the congressman. She took a few sips, but when the congressman excused himself to take a call, she poured the rest of the tea into a potted plant. When he returned, he seemed pleased that she had finished it. He made several crude sexual remarks and told her to spread her legs and remove her blouse. He started to take off his trousers. The intern ran out of the room."

Mr. Weaver tightened his lips in revulsion.

"Later that evening I decided to confront the congressman. I was just outside his office when I heard him arguing with his chief of staff. She was shouting at him. I couldn't make out all the conversation, but she was berating him. I heard her say that the drug wasn't meant to satisfy his dick, and his sexual perversions could jeopardize everything. That's when I contacted Ms. Blythe."

Mr. Weaver turned to his wife. "Go get Annie."

CHAPTER TWENTY-ONE

ANNIE ENTERED THE room cautiously, smiling shyly when she saw Jason but looking uneasy when Connie introduced herself. Her long dishwater-blonde hair flowed down her back. Like her mother, she wore no makeup and a simple dress that hung to her feet.

Connie examined her closely. Despite her initial plain-Jane appearance, she was quite attractive, with pale-blue robin's-egg eyes and a button nose.

Mr. Weaver smiled at his daughter. "I need to ask you a few questions, Annie. Did you ever meet alone with Congressman Luke?"

She seemed stunned by the question. "Yes, once."

"And why did you meet with him?"

"He wanted to hear my views about politics from the perspective of youth. It wasn't a surprise or anything unusual…He had met with a lot of the other girls." She turned her head back and forth between Jason and her father. "What does this have to do with my pregnancy?"

"Tell me what happened in the meeting." asked Mr. Weaver.

"He sat across from me on a couch. I was very nervous and struck by how tall he is. He was very courteous and reassuring. He asked about my background and interests. He offered me some tea. At first I declined—I'm not a tea drinker—but he said he would be insulted if I didn't share a cup with him. So I drank the tea. That was it."

"What do you mean 'That was it'? What happened next?" asked Mr. Weaver.

"We discussed things; politics and world events, I guess."

"You guess?"

"I don't remember," she said with increased agitation. "Why are you asking me about my meeting with the congressman? I'm pregnant and I don't know how." She glared at Jason. "I thought you were here to help me."

"I am," said Jason. "But you need to answer your father's questions."

Mr. Weaver smiled sympathetically at his daughter. "Please tell me one specific topic that you and the congressman discussed, after the tea."

She hesitated, deep in thought. "I don't recall. I guess I was very nervous. I really don't remember any specifics."

"Annie, dear, do you normally forget things when you get nervous?" asked Mrs. Weaver.

"No, not normally."

Jason interjected. "Do you remember seeing me when you came out of the congressman's office?"

"I don't know, maybe. I don't remember much of anything that evening."

"I asked you what was wrong; you seemed upset."

"I did?"

"Yes. Later you sat at your desk with your head in your hands. I heard you crying. Do you remember that?"

She stayed quiet for a long time. "No, but I do remember a feeling. It's starting to come back."

"What feeling?" asked Mr. Weaver.

She looked up, her chin trembling. "I remember feeling dirty. Like I needed to take a shower. No, it wasn't only that I felt dirty...I felt disgusted."

Mr. Weaver reached over and patted her hand. "That will be all, Annie, please go back to the other room and wait."

Her face reddened and she ran out of the room, starting to cry.

Mr. Weaver stood up, pacing. "You've convinced me."

Mrs. Weaver nodded in agreement.

"I'm going to Washington and confront the bastard," he shouted.

"I would advise against that," said Connie. "There's no proof, and he'll deny everything. He'll have the security guards remove you from the building. If you touch him, he'll charge you with assault. He's very powerful, and all we have is the accusations of two young women."

"And Annie doesn't remember any of it. There's no physical evidence," said Mrs. Weaver, trying to calm her husband.

Connie spoke. "Well, actually there is physical evidence—there's the baby. If you and Annie are willing, it's possible to determine paternity now. There is state-of-the-art technology called the noninvasive prenatal paternity test. It works by analyzing the DNA of the fetus that is naturally found in the mother's bloodstream."

CHAPTER TWENTY-TWO

IN A FIT of rage, Bill repeatedly fired his gun into the chest of a large menacing blond man, splattering blood all over the deck of the boat.

Cheryl shook him. "Bill, Bill, wake up. You're having another nightmare. You've been moaning. Wake up."

It took a few moments for Bill to recover his bearings.

"Is it that same dream about killing a man on a boat in the Caribbean?"

"Yes. I'm getting up...I don't want to fall back into it."

This was often his pattern. He would awake from the same nightmare sometime between two and four in the morning. He would get a beer and turn on the computer in his study—anything to distract him from the dream.

Despite his agreement with Cheryl not to look into their pasts, he Googled *Ryan Butler Lawrence Kansas*. There were no hits. He tried typing *Ryan Butler Boulder Colorado*. Again, nothing. He took a sip of beer while staring at the screen. Then it hit him: he suddenly recalled that the crazy woman had mistaken Cheryl for somebody named Alana Shannon. He typed in the name and the computer screen immediately filled with references and articles. There were hundreds of them. He felt goose bumps as he read the headlines:

"Alana Shannon charged with murdering husband."

"Alana Shannon pleads not guilty to murder."

"District attorney drops murder charges against Alana Shannon."

"Alana Shannon had secret past."

"Alana Shannon goes into hiding; lawyer issues statement."

It went on and on. The sources for most of the headings were newspapers in Raleigh and Durham, North Carolina, but there were also some from the national press and television tabloids.

As Bill scrolled further down the pages, the headlines changed, taking on a lascivious tone:

"Raleigh socialite Alana Shannon was a former porn star."

"Alana Shannon's scandalous past."

"Alana Shannon had criminal record."

"Alana Shannon, the Porn Star Murderess, now and then."

Bill clicked on the last one; the source was a tabloid, the *National Mirror*. Two pictures appeared on the screen side by side: a dignified blonde woman in a gray suit looking to be in her late thirties, and a young redhead in a skimpy bikini.

Bill sweated. Both women bore a close resemblance to Cheryl, but it couldn't be she—the eyes and mouth looked identical, but the nose was different and the eyes emerald. The women on the screen were prettier than Cheryl, but still the similarity was striking. She looked as if she could be Cheryl's sister.

Bill devoured the articles. The authorities had arrested Alana Shannon for killing her millionaire husband in their mansion in Raleigh. She claimed she'd shot him in self-defense after he threatened her with a gun. The skeptical prosecutor charged her with premeditated murder, but as the trial began, he surprised everybody by dropping the case. After that, Alana Shannon disappeared from sight.

Bill examined the Google images of Alana Shannon. He focused on one in particular, a formal portrait of her as the owner, with her husband, of the North Raleigh Real Estate Development Corporation. Bill covered the middle of the picture using his index finger, blocking out Alana Shannon's nose, focusing on her eyes, mouth, and chin. It gave him a chill. With the nose blocked out, the face looked like Cheryl's. Next he blocked the eyes and mouth, examining the nose.

Alana Shannon had a thin and finely sculptured nose, while Cheryl's had a bump on the bridge and wider nostrils. Last he examined the eyes. The curve of the eye sockets, their placement on the face, and their shape matched Cheryl's; but again, the eye color was different. After much further examination, Bill concluded that the resemblance was too uncanny for them to be unrelated.

Many of the articles sensationalized Alana Shannon's hidden past. As a young woman in Los Angeles, she had gone by the name of Rebecca Blaze and had appeared in numerous men's magazines like *Penthouse* and *Hustler*. The articles also mentioned prior arrests for drug possession and prostitution.

Bill started to google *Rebecca Blaze*, but paused. Something told him he should go back to bed. He started to turn off the computer but stopped. His curiosity got to him. He hit the return key and a flood of images filled the screen, showing an exceptionally beautiful young woman with bright-red hair and amazing green eyes. In most of the pictures she was striking sexy poses for the camera, wearing a bikini or some other revealing outfit. In each picture it seemed as if she were looking directly at him, as if they were alone together in the room.

A message at the top of the page required him to enter his birth year to view her nude photos. A new array of pictures filled the screen. Images of Rebecca Blaze topless, smiling at the camera, sticking her tongue out playfully, and then suggestively through the corner of her mouth. Images of her fully naked, lying on a chaise longue by a pool. Pictures of her on her knees, viewed from behind, her face turned back with an enticing smile.

Bill riveted his attention on one picture in particular. Rebecca Blaze was staring into the camera with a sexy pout, her incredible eyes beckoning him. Her hands cupped her breasts upward and her index fingers touched her nipples. Bill zoomed in on the exposed underside of her raised right breast, focusing on a small crescent-shaped birthmark.

70

He swallowed hard. He knew that birthmark well—he had kissed it hundreds of times.

"Are you looking at pornography?" Bill jumped and quickly turned to see Cheryl standing in the door frame.

"No, I was surfing the Internet and some nude pictures came up."

"Don't lie to me. I've been watching you—you've been staring at the pictures of some naked redhead for the past few minutes. You were so engrossed you didn't even hear me come in." She shook her head. "I'm going back to bed. Don't stay up all night." She walked away.

Bill sat shaken. His wife had just caught him viewing nude pictures of a beautiful young woman, except she didn't know that he was looking at her.

CHAPTER TWENTY-THREE

BILL RETURNED QUIETLY to the bedroom, lying next to Cheryl, unsure whether she was asleep, hoping to avoid a confrontation. He pulled up the covers and turned over.

She immediately sprang up, tearing the covers away. "Don't you turn your back to me," she shouted, climbing over him, naked. "You don't have to look at other women. I can give you everything you want." She reached down between his legs.

Bill had never seen her like this. She sat above him, straddling his hips. "You can fuck me however you like." She flicked her tongue to the side of her mouth and pursed her lips into a come-on pout. Bill had just viewed the same expressions on the Internet, on Rebecca Blaze's face. He was confused but excited. He surprised himself by grabbing her by the waist and turning her over until she was on her knees.

They went at it for over an hour. In the past their lovemaking had been tender and warm, but this was animal lust and savage abandon. She screamed and moaned as Bill plowed back and forth. She turned to face him and dug her fingernails into his back. All restraints vanished and all inhibitions evaporated. They were lost in a frenzy of wild, primal lust. She gradually took control, telling him what to do, guiding him to different positions, even calling out their names: "Let's do cowgirl." "Let's do scissors." "Let's try sidesaddle." All the time Bill noticed her crescent birthmark.

Finally spent, they lay together panting, covered with sweat, the sheets torn off the bed. Bill's body tingled as Cheryl reached over and kissed him good night. "See, I told you I could please you. You don't need to look elsewhere. Sweet dreams, darling."

Bill stared at the ceiling in the dark, trying to comprehend what had happened. She had shown a side of herself that he had never seen or even imagined. He wondered if this was how they'd made love before the accident. Then a terrifying thought struck him, sending shivers through his body. *Maybe there wasn't an accident. Maybe we really don't have a past together.* He squirmed uncomfortably, trying to recall his first memory of her. They were walking through the door of their new beach house on the island. She turned to him and smiled, filling him with an overwhelming sensation of love and warmth—a sensation that had never ebbed during their time together on the island.

Cheryl was fast asleep as he climbed out of bed and moved to the bathroom, there to sit on the edge of the bathtub, deep in thought. He wondered whether their past was a fiction. He had no doubt that she was Alana Shannon, and Rebecca Blaze. *Then who am I?* he wondered. None of the articles on Alana Shannon had mentioned his name. *How do I fit in?* A sudden bolt of terror struck him. *What if I'm the only one with amnesia? What if Cheryl is playacting?*

CHAPTER TWENTY-FOUR

BILL AWOKE TO the smell of bacon. Sunlight streamed through the blinds. He heard Cheryl singing cheerfully like a songbird in the kitchen. He put on his bathrobe to find her.

"Morning, sleepyhead," she said, smiling warmly. "I thought I should cook you a real breakfast to replenish your strength. How about some eggs, bacon and coffee?" She came over and put her arms around him. Bill thought she was going to kiss him, but instead she bit him lightly on his earlobe. "I think we should pick up where we left off last night—real soon. Maybe out on the deck of the sailboat this afternoon." She gave him a mischievous grin.

Bill poured coffee and sat down at the kitchen table, observing her. She glowed. "What was that song you were singing?"

"I don't know…some old Hawaiian melody I heard on the radio."

"We need to talk about last night."

Cheryl brought over a plate of eggs and bacon and sat across from him. "There's no need to talk about anything. We did plenty of talking with our bodies last night."

"Where did all that come from? It's like you became a different person."

"I'm not sure. When I saw you looking at that redhead and all her sexy poses, something snapped inside. I guess it was part anger and part jealousy. I wanted to show you that you didn't need to look at her."

"But where did you learn all of that? You knew all those positions and even their names. And you've never talked dirty like that before."

She blushed. "I was as surprised as you were…It all bubbled up…It seemed natural. Maybe we had a different sex life before the collision?"

"I need to tell you about the girl I was looking at on the Internet."

She frowned. "Why? Let's forget about that. Didn't I make you happy last night?"

"It's not what you think. The girl I was looking at…"

"I don't want to know. Why are we even talking about her?"

"Did you get a close look at her face?"

"No. And from what I saw it wasn't her face you were staring at." Her voice was caustic. "Do you have a thing for redheads…Is that it? Do you want me to dye my hair?"

The sound of a vehicle pulling fast into their driveway and screeching to a halt interrupted them. They ran to the front window and saw two people bounding quickly out of a black SUV: a young stocky man in a gray business suit and a tall skinny woman with long black hair in black slacks and a dark jacket. Cheryl gasped when she recognized the woman. "It's my aunt Janet!"

Bill recognized her too, but it didn't make sense. What would she be doing here, and how could she have arrived so fast?

Cheryl opened the door as their visitors reached the top of the stairs. "Aunt Janet," Cheryl squealed, and opened her arms to hug her.

The woman stopped, abruptly extending her arm straight forward. "Stand back," she ordered in a deep authoritative voice.

Cheryl withdrew in shock and confusion.

"I'm not your aunt—I never have been. I'm Agent Garibaldi with the CIA. You need to come with us, now." She flashed a CIA identification card.

"What are you talking about?" asked Bill, inserting himself between Cheryl and the woman.

"Your identities have been compromised. We need to get moving."

"Moving where?" asked a bewildered Cheryl.

"You'll know soon enough. You need to get dressed. Let's go!"

"We're not going anywhere until you tell us what this is all about," said Bill.

The man opened his jacket to reveal a firearm. "You can either cooperate or we can take you by force. Your choice."

Agent Garibaldi copied the gesture. "It will be much easier for all of us if you comply." She grabbed Cheryl by the arm and pulled her toward the living room. "Now go get dressed."

Bill froze, unsure what to do. He wanted to resist, but he knew it would be futile against two armed CIA agents. He figured he'd better do what they said until he knew what was happening.

The agents followed them into their bedroom.

"What should we wear?" asked Cheryl.

"It doesn't matter," said Agent Garibaldi.

Bill put on shorts, a Hawaiian floral shirt, and white running shoes. Cheryl put on a bright-yellow pullover, white shorts, and jogging shoes, and started to apply some makeup.

"We don't have time for that," snapped Agent Garibaldi.

. . .

A few moments later they were all in the SUV, Bill and Cheryl in the back. They swerved out of the driveway onto the road, taking off at a high speed.

"Where are we going?" asked Cheryl.

"To the airport; a jet's waiting," answered Agent Garibaldi.

"A jet?" repeated Bill, astonished. "Why would there be a jet?"

"You'll find out once we're in the air."

"When will we be coming back?" asked Cheryl.

"You won't be," said the man, who was driving. "You're being moved."

"What does that mean?" shouted Cheryl.

"Exactly what it sounds like," responded Agent Garibaldi.

"This is our home," pleaded Cheryl. "We don't want to leave."

Bill had a foreboding feeling, almost a premonition. "You're going to kill us, aren't you?"

Agent Garibaldi turned and stared into his eyes. "Nobody's going to harm you."

Immediately Bill knew she was lying. Just as she finished speaking, a flicker of discomfort flashed across her face. She snapped her head away and gave the driver a quick sidelong glance.

Cheryl was enraged. "So everything you told me about being my aunt and our accident in Colorado was a lie?"

"Yes."

"And those stories you told me about my father and the ranch where I grew up. Those were all lies too?"

"Shut up," screamed the driver. "No more questions until we take off."

...

As they approached the airport, they took a detour from the main entrance, turning onto a side road marked "Private Aircraft Only." The road looped around the airport to the other side of the runway, opposite the main terminal. They stopped at a gate, the driver handed a security guard some paperwork, and they proceeded onto the tarmac. The SUV pulled behind a small, sleek, unmarked white jet. Steps led from the side of the aircraft, and a man in a pilot's uniform paced at the bottom.

"Wait in the car," ordered the driver as he and Agent Garibaldi exited. Agent Garibaldi walked over to the pilot as the driver stood guard by the SUV.

Bill surveyed the scene. The main terminal was a quarter of a mile away on the other side of the runway. Planes were alternately taking off and landing. He grasped Cheryl's trembling arm and whispered into her ear, "We have to escape."

She looked at him wide-eyed. "How?"

"When I say go, take off to the terminal. Run as fast as you can. Don't look back. Don't worry if they have me. You have to make it across the runway and get help. It's our only chance. Do you understand?"

"Yes," she said, with wet eyes.

"Trust me."

They waited in the car for a few minutes until Agent Garibaldi, still talking to the pilot, signaled to the driver. The driver opened the door of the SUV. "Out—this side."

Cheryl exited and Bill followed her over the tarmac.

"This way," said the driver, pointing to the steps of the jet.

"Go!" yelled Bill as he slammed his body headfirst into the driver's chest, smashing him against the hood of the SUV. The driver immediately rebounded. Bill kicked him hard in the groin and sprinted toward the terminal, chasing Cheryl. She was twenty feet in front and turned to look back.

"Keep going! Run!" yelled Bill.

The driver sprang to his feet and raced after them, joined by Agent Garibaldi.

Bill and Cheryl were both in great shape and worked out daily. Still, the driver and Agent Garibaldi were gaining. As they approached the runway, a plane accelerated for takeoff. Cheryl hesitated. "Don't stop!" yelled Bill, calculating that she could make it across the runway before the plane. She darted ahead.

Bill glanced back. The driver was only eight feet away. He lowered his head and charged forward just as the plane lifted off the ground. As he crossed the runway, he felt the swoosh of the aircraft's wheels a few feet over his head. He didn't look back; he kept running until he caught up with Cheryl.

Sirens blared and two airport security guards charged toward them with weapons drawn. Bill and Cheryl headed toward them.

"Stop where you are—stop where you are," yelled the security guards. "On the ground."

Bill and Cheryl fell to their knees, raising their arms over their heads. As the security guards approached, Bill glanced back to the runway. The two agents were retreating to the jet.

CHAPTER TWENTY-FIVE

"**WHY WERE YOU** running across the airport?" demanded the chief of airport security when he finally arrived at the windowless airport holding room. Bill was relieved to see him. For the past fifteen minutes he had been trying to convince the security officer to stop the white jet from departing. The officer had shrugged as he said he didn't have the authority and they needed to wait for the chief.

The chief was clearly Hawaiian, but appeared awkwardly out of place dressed in a dark suit and a black tie, sporting a thin mustache. He was all seriousness. "According to your driver's licenses you live on the island."

"You have to stop that white jet from taking off," Bill begged. "The people on it tried to kidnap us. They abducted us from our house. They claimed they were CIA agents. We escaped when they tried to force us onto the jet—that's why we were running across the airport."

"What jet are you talking about?"

"A private one, a Lear or something. It's all white except for some black lettering."

The chief scratched his head. "You're saying the people who tried to abduct you claimed they worked for the CIA? Why would the CIA want to kidnap you?"

"I don't know," yelled Bill in exasperation. "If you stop them from taking off, you can find out."

The chief picked up the phone and dialed a number. A voice came over an intercom. "Control tower."

"This is the security chief. Is there a white jet parked in the private aviation area?"

"There was—it took off five minutes ago."

Shit, thought Bill.

"It was strange," said the tower voice. "We had to hold all incoming and outgoing flights to give them clearance—same as when they landed."

"Why?" asked the chief.

"They carried special flight codes—they get automatic priority."

"Where are they headed?"

"Their flight plan says Indonesia, but our radar shows them flying east. We've been trying to raise them on the radio, but they're not responding."

The chief turned to Bill and Cheryl. "That's bizarre. And you have no idea why they would abduct you?"

Cheryl thought about telling him that one of the agents had previously posed as her aunt, but decided to stay mum.

"Here's what will happen," said the chief. "You're in violation of FAA regulations and federal law for unauthorized trespass on airport property. I'll take your statements, but you will have to appear for a formal hearing before a US magistrate judge in Honolulu—we don't have a courtroom here since the quake. The judge will decide whether to dismiss charges or schedule you for a court date. In either case, they will likely release you after the hearing. Now please excuse me for a few minutes while I make the arrangements."

After the chief left, Bill studied Cheryl's distraught face. She was struggling to hold back tears. He marveled that he'd ever suspected her of playacting. She had risked her life running across the runway. He knew they were in this together, their lives inextricably bound to each other's.

After twenty minutes the chief returned, shaking his head. "Bad news. I can't get a hearing scheduled until tomorrow morning. In the meantime I'm required by federal law to hold you in secure custody."

"You mean jail?" asked Cheryl.

"I'm afraid so. The Molokai Police Department is sending over an officer to pick you up."

"But we didn't do anything wrong—we were abducted. We're the victims," cried Cheryl.

"I'm only doing my job. I have to follow the law. It's only one night. Your hearing is set for ten o'clock tomorrow. I've scheduled you on the first commercial flight to Honolulu at seven. One of our security staff will escort you to the hearing and back. Now I need to take your statements."

CHAPTER TWENTY-SIX

A SUBDUED BILL and Cheryl gave their statements, omitting only their past relationship with Agent Garibaldi. As they were wrapping up, the officer arrived from the Molokai Police Department. Cheryl and Bill immediately recognized him.

Sergeant Keahi's jaw dropped when he saw Cheryl and Bill. "Hey, I know these people. They're not criminals—they live on the island. They were friends of Uncle Eddie. Why do you want me to take them to jail?"

The chief raised his eyebrows. "Really? Uncle Eddie?"

A half hour later they were in the back of Sergeant Keahi's squad car, pulling out of the airport terminal and heading to Kaunakakai, to the jail.

"That's really weird," said Keahi. "I didn't know it was a crime to be abducted."

"Neither did we," said Cheryl.

. . .

Sergeant Keahi pulled the car over to the side of the road. He turned around to face them. "The feds are always so serious. I don't understand why they didn't let you go. You live on the island—you're not going anywhere. I didn't want to tell the airport chief, but we don't have room at the jail. We only have four cells and they're already doubled up. We're repairing the others due to quake damage. So I don't have anyplace to hold you without having to make all kinds of special arrangements." He lowered his voice. "Let's do this the Molokai way. I'll drop you off at your house and pick you up tomorrow morning around five thirty. That will be plenty of time to get you on your flight to Honolulu, and the airport chief will never know the difference. Otherwise it's going to be an administrative nightmare and a lot of extra work for me. We don't want that, do we?"

Bill and Cheryl agreed.

"We need to keep this between ourselves," continued Keahi. "It's the Molokai way—we look out for each other and keep everything informal."

Bill wasn't sure that going back to their house was a good idea, as he feared the CIA might be waiting for them. "Could you drop us off in Kaunakakai? We need to get some supplies at the market…Our car is in the shop and our Jeep is still at the lookout."

Cheryl looked at Bill with surprise.

"Sorry, I can't do that. I can't wait for you to go shopping and then take you home. I'm not a taxi service."

"You don't need to wait for us. We'll take the island bus back to our house."

Sergeant Keahi thought for a few moments. "I guess that will be all right."

Keahi dropped them off in front of the market. They thanked him, and he reminded them that he would pick them up at 5:30 a.m. Bill and Cheryl walked to the back of the store, searching for a quiet corner.

"What are we doing?" asked Cheryl.

"I don't feel comfortable going back to the house—the CIA may be waiting."

"I agree."

"I had this horrible feeling that if we got on that jet we would end up dead."

Cheryl took a deep breath. "I had the same feeling—I don't understand what's happening."

"Neither do I, but we need to find out. We can't stay on the island; they might come back for us at any time."

"So where can we go?"

Bill checked his watch. "It's twelve forty-five. The ferry for Maui leaves in fifteen minutes. It's a ten-minute walk to the dock. We should leave now."

"Are you sure?"

"I've never been surer of anything in my life."

"Okay, but what happens when we get to Maui?"

CHAPTER TWENTY-SEVEN

CHERYL WATCHED THE verdant cliffs of Molokai shrink in the distance as the ferry to Maui entered the channel between the two islands. From the stern, a path of white foam stretched outward. Her heart sank. It felt as though she were awakening from a long, blissful dream. "We're never going home again, are we?"

"I don't know," said Bill, looking at his watch and calculating how much time they had until Sergeant Keahi was to pick them up. "We have sixteen hours until the feds realize we're gone."

"How about the CIA?"

"Let's hope they think we're in police custody."

"What did they mean when they said our identities were compromised?"

"I think it's clear that we're not the people we think we are."

"Then who are we?"

Bill didn't answer at first. "Sit down," he said, motioning to a bench near the back of the ferry. "I started to tell you about the woman on the Internet, the redhead."

Cheryl's face turned sour. "I told you I don't want to talk about her. Why are you so obsessed with that woman?"

Bill took her hands in his. "Because that woman is you."

She immediately pulled her hands away. "What? Me? How could that be?"

"Remember the crazy reporter—she called you Alana Shannon and she called me Ryan Butler."

"So?"

"Last night I decided to search for the name Alana Shannon on the Internet. There were tons of articles on her. They charged her with the murder of her husband in North Carolina. Later the prosecutor dismissed the case and she disappeared. It all happened one month before our supposed accident. There were many pictures of Alana Shannon, and she looked very much like you, the same mouth, the same chin, the same figure…even the shape of her eyes. Only her nose and eye color were different. Other than that, she could be your twin."

Cheryl breathed deeply. "Maybe she is my sister?"

"I don't think so. The reason the murder trial drew so much attention was that Alana Shannon had a secret past; she had been a porn star when she was younger. She went by the name of Rebecca Blaze. I was searching that name when the pictures of the redhead appeared on the screen. That's whom I was looking at when you walked in. I'm sure I was looking at you."

"Are you saying I was a porn star? That's impossible." Her raised voice attracted the attention of several people. Bill and Cheryl moved to an emptier area of the vessel.

"Look, Cheryl. I examined the pictures of Rebecca Blaze. In a couple of the poses, I saw under her right breast. She had a small birthmark, a crescent moon with a slight backward curve at the bottom. I know that birthmark well; so do you."

"I don't believe it," she said in a low, defiant voice.

"Who else could it be? She had your face, your body, and your birthmark—only her nose and eye color were different. She was listed as five foot seven, same as you. I can show you the pictures when we get access to the Internet. You can see for yourself."

Cheryl remained quiet for a long time. "Well, if I really am that woman, what am I doing on Molokai? Why do I think I'm from Colorado? Why would the CIA be involved? And who the hell are you? It doesn't make any sense."

"No, it doesn't. But we need to find the truth."

"How?"

"We're going to fly to the mainland and meet with that reporter who came to see us."

"I don't even remember her name."

"I kept her business card." He reached into his wallet, pulled out the card, and handed it to Cheryl. It read, "Connie Blythe, Investigative Reporter, the *Beltway Insider*, Rosslyn, Virginia."

"Where's Rosslyn?"

"It's next to Washington, DC. That's where we need to go."

END OF PART 1

PART 2

CHAPTER TWENTY-EIGHT

JAMES LAMONT WAS still reeling from yesterday's meeting. On his desk lay several drafts of his resignation letter, with many more balled up in the trash. He couldn't decide whether to go out quietly or with a bang. Part of him wanted to turn his resignation into a scathing indictment of the new CIA leadership, to rail against its politicizing of the agency, its cooking of intelligence, and its wanton mismanagement. He fantasized about leaking the letter to the press, but he was too much of a professional for that.

It had all started three days ago when Bruce Marko told him that William and Cheryl Parker's identities had been compromised. The Parkers had called their handler, Agent Garibaldi, who they believed was Cheryl's aunt, with questions concerning their past. They also mentioned that a reporter had come to visit them and had called them by the names Ryan Butler and Alana Shannon.

The revelation that they were beginning to question their identities came as a surprise. Initially Lamont had sent two agents to Molokai to test the power of the drug. Posing as Cheryl's aunt Janet and uncle Doug, the agents subtly questioned them, probing for any signs of recognition from their past lives, even mentioning the name Ryan Butler. Neither showed any hint of recognition. Subsequent visits and phone calls revealed no changes.

After huddling with Marko and Kronig, Lamont decided to pull them back from Hawaii—the risk of their exposure was too high. At all costs his team had to protect the secret of the drug. Together they prepared a plan. Agent Garibaldi and a security agent would immediately fly to Molokai and bring them back to the mainland. There the CIA would provide new identities and a new home.

Six hours later the new director called Lamont into his office. "What's this about a jet and two agents to go to Hawaii?" With the director was Special Assistant Arnie Crowder.

The question surprised Lamont. "It's within my operational authority to requisition the jet. There's no reason this should concern you."

"It used to be within your authority," said Crowder, "but things have changed. This has the smell of an intelligence operation all over it. It needs to be approved by me."

"Then go ahead and approve it," snapped Lamont. "There's no need to involve the director."

Director Goodwin sat behind an immense, shiny, empty desk. The ceiling lights reflected off his bald pink head. His muscular body filled a dark business suit. He twirled an empty Coke can in one hand. "Why the hell do you need a jet and two agents?"

Lamont knew he was trapped; they weren't going to approve the request without an explanation. "It's to bring back two associates under deep cover. We fear their identities may have been blown and we need to pull them in as a precautionary measure."

"Why would they be in deep cover on the island of Molokai? Is there a secret operation going on there?" asked the director, mockingly.

Lamont grimaced. "I'm not at liberty to tell you the details. There's a certain protocol involved—it relates to a Black Box operation."

The director frowned. "The president briefed me on Black Box operations." He turned to Crowder. "They're extremely covert operations that only the president can verbally approve. The president's never told the details, only the objective and the risks and rewards involved."

"We shouldn't be discussing this in front of Mr. Crowder," stated Lamont firmly. "He doesn't have clearance."

"He does now," shouted the director, slamming the Coke can against the desk. "I should have been briefed on this Black Box when I came on...Why wasn't I?"

"It was long over when you arrived. We're wrapping up some loose ends, nothing more."

"So are you going to tell me what this Black Box operation was about?"

"Not with Crowder in the room."

Crowder sneered. "Perhaps it was an aborted plan to use a secret hypnotic drug to find and kill Osama bin Laden?"

"How do you know that? You've never been cleared for that information."

"I have been now."

"Things have changed," said the director, leaning back in his swivel chair and folding his arms smugly over his chest. "We know about your secret drug. We also know that you have two people hidden on Molokai. It's a foolish operation that never should have been launched in the first place."

"Who told you?" demanded Lamont, the muscles tightening in his neck.

"Bruce Marko."

"Marko?"

"You are so out of it," said Crowder. "Did you really believe you could keep it secret? Did you really believe you could continue to manufacture the drug right under our nose? And those two on the island—they should have been erased a long time ago. Marko says that's what he recommended, but you and Kronig concocted this risky scheme to use the drug to distort their memories and hide them on Molokai...a reckless plan given their knowledge of the drug and Alana Shannon's notoriety."

Lamont couldn't believe that Marko had spilled everything. He'd never liked the man, but he had always trusted him. "It wasn't just us—the president's security adviser approved it."

The director perked up. "Scotty Olds? Well, he's out of his job, isn't he? This is just another example of the poor judgment shown by the previous regime."

Lamont shook. "Back to my requisition. Are you going to approve it or not?"

"It's approved," said Crowder. "But we won't be bringing them back to the States."

"What do you mean?" asked Lamont as the blood thumped through his veins.

"We're doing a handoff. You're familiar with those, aren't you?" Crowder smirked.

Lamont felt sick. A handoff was a way of getting rid of a bad asset. They would drop the Parkers off in a foreign country and turn them over to a rebel or opposition group, usually one covertly funded by the CIA. The couple would quietly disappear.

"Look, we made a deal. There's a contract in my safe. The CIA promised to protect them—it's all in writing."

"Signed by whom?" asked the director.

"Signed by me."

"Well, I guess they made a mistake in trusting you. As far as I'm concerned it's a contract between them and you, not the CIA."

"You don't know the full story…Ryan Butler has a long history with us…He's risked his life for us in the past. We owe him."

"Well, I think *past* is the operative word. Things have changed. You act like you haven't noticed." The director slowly crushed the Coke can into a ball in front of Lamont's face.

"Where's the handoff?"

Crowder answered flippantly. "We're flying them to Indonesia and turning them over to the Free Papua Movement along with some cash. Problem solved. We won't have to worry about them being recognized or exposing the drug."

Lamont trembled with rage as he glowered at them.

Director Goodwin stood up, stuck his jaw out, and stabbed a finger at Lamont. "I've had it with you. Coming in here with your demanding, whining, bleeding-heart attitude. You've let your emotions cloud your judgment. The drug is the greatest weapon we have and you've been selfishly keeping it hidden. A deplorable act in direct defiance of the best interests of your country. Your work for the agency is finished. I want your resignation on my desk by tomorrow morning. You can take a few days to complete your administrative duties, but you better stay clear of intelligence matters."

CHAPTER TWENTY-NINE

BILL AND CHERYL landed at Chicago's O'Hare Airport a few minutes after two in the morning. It had been a long and exhausting day, and they arrived drained and apprehensive.

After debarking from the ferry in Maui, they'd stopped at the First Hawaiian Bank and each withdrawn $9,000 in cash. Bill wanted to take out more, but vaguely remembered that cash withdrawals of $10,000 or more triggered special reporting. He didn't want to draw scrutiny, knowing that tomorrow the authorities would list them as fugitives.

From the bank they took a taxi to the airport in Kahului, stopping at airline counters, searching for flights to the mainland. Only one had availability, a nonstop to Chicago. Bill plunked down $3,200 in cash for two coach tickets. The airline couldn't seat them together, so they flew the nine hours stuffed uncomfortably between strangers, twelve rows apart.

As they exited the terminal to hail a taxi, a stiff fifteen-degree wind nearly flash-froze them. The driver gazed at them in wonder as he opened the cab door, smiling at their tropical shirts and shorts.

Although Bill was tempted to go to a hotel near the airport, he thought it would be safer to go into the city. He reasoned that if the CIA traced them to Chicago it might check the airport hotels, but couldn't check everywhere in the city.

The taxi dropped them off at the Downtown Marriott, a huge high-rise on Michigan Avenue, a few blocks north of the Wrigley Building and the Chicago River. They dashed through the cold into the lobby.

The desk clerk eyed them warily, two haggard individuals dressed in Hawaiian clothes in the middle of winter, checking in late at night without luggage. Since they weren't carrying credit cards, the clerk required them to leave a $900 cash deposit for two nights.

They fabricated a story that the airline had lost their luggage. Listening to their plight, the clerk softened and gave them a small package of bathroom accessories, and promised to send up complimentary robes.

They entered the business-oriented room and collapsed on the bed. Bill started to drift off to sleep, but Cheryl forced herself into the bathroom to wash her face and brush her teeth. Bill noticed the clock radio on the nightstand flashing "12:00." Annoyed, he pulled the plug. He was too tired to mess with resetting it. When Cheryl returned from the bathroom, he was snoring.

...

The sound of knocking jolted Bill from a deep sleep. For a second he wasn't sure where he was, and then it all rushed back. The knocking grew louder, along with a muffled voice. Cheryl was awake too. "They're coming to get us," she hissed.

Bill quickly turned on the light and checked his watch; it read 5:12 a.m. He heard the sound of a key in the door. He grabbed the clock radio and ran to the door just as the knob twisted. Still in his underwear, he raised the radio over his head, holding it like a rock, ready to smash the intruder. The door swung open and Bill started to strike but quickly pulled back. Beneath him cowered a small woman in a striped housekeeper's uniform.

"Don't hit please. I clean room. I knock but no answer."

"Why in hell are you cleaning at this hour?" roared Bill.

The frightened woman peered up at him. "It is morning."

Cheryl placed her hand on Bill's back. "It's the time change. Your watch is still on Hawaiian time. It's much later here."

They profusely apologized, closed the door, and embraced. Their hearts beat loudly. They went to the window and pulled open the dark drapes. The light outside was muted and listless. From their room on the thirty-second floor they faced across a side street to stacks of tall buildings. Falling snow wrapped everything in a sheer white gauze. Below, people scurried back and forth like bundled dots darting between snow-covered vehicles. After Hawaii, it felt as though all the color had drained from the world, leaving behind a bleak black-and-white existence.

"Hold me," said Cheryl.

They climbed back into bed and snuggled together, their bodies tight. Bill felt her tears against his face. They made love, but not like the last time. Now it was soft and tender healing. Afterward they fell back to sleep.

...

They awoke several hours later, roused by hunger, and ordered sandwiches from room service. Outside the snow was falling harder, obscuring the facing buildings. It was early afternoon, but it was so dark it seemed like late evening.

"What are we doing here?" asked Cheryl.

Bill kissed her forehead. "We're here to find out who we really are."

"You already told me who I am—a porn star and a murderer." She shrugged her shoulders and sat down on the edge of the bed. "I can't believe I'm that horrible person. Do you know what it's like to find out that everything you thought was true is a lie? I didn't grow up on a ranch; I didn't meet you at the University of Colorado; I wasn't a schoolteacher; I never lived in a house that looked out to the Rockies. For all I know, I didn't even meet you until we arrived on the island."

"That's occurred to me too...that maybe we never knew each other before. Yet I don't see how that could be. I know I love you. I have no doubt about that."

"And I love you too."

"At least you know who you were. The name Ryan Butler isn't mentioned anywhere in connection to Alana Shannon or Rebecca Blaze. There are pictures of you all over the Internet, but none of me. So who am I?"

"How about that baseball player from Pennsylvania?"

"He was three years older than me."

"Do you really know that? Maybe your birth certificate from Kansas is a fake. Maybe you are that baseball player. Maybe you're older than you think. Maybe you are Ryan Butler."

Bill sat next to her. "I never really thought of that—you could be right."

She put her arm around his neck. "Then why are we together?"

CHAPTER THIRTY

LAMONT WAS PACKING up his desk when Marko knocked. "Come in," he said coldly.

"I wanted to say good-bye. I know you're mad, but I had no choice. If it had only been Crowder I would have kept quiet, but the director asked me right to my face if the CIA was manufacturing a drug that enhanced hypnosis. You know me…I'm a straight shooter. I couldn't lie."

"But you also told them about Ryan Butler and Alana Shannon in Hawaii."

"Well, once I told them about the drug, I had to come clean. I think they already knew. They didn't seem surprised by any of it. I think the information has already leaked…but I didn't mention anything about the drug being skimmed."

"Good."

"Anything new on Patrick O'Brien's investigation?"

"No. Everybody on the sixth floor of the apartment building checks out, so we're at a dead end." Lamont angrily shoved a file into his briefcase. "So I guess by now Ryan Butler and Alana Shannon are in shallow graves somewhere in Indonesia."

"You don't know?"

"Know what?"

"They escaped. We thought they were in police custody but they released them. We didn't know they were missing until a few hours ago. The Justice Department just issued warrants for their arrest."

Lamont sat down in his chair. "So they're alive."

"We've started tracing their credit card and banking transactions. Somehow they got to Maui and withdrew a lot of cash. There's been no activity since. We suspect they are either still on Maui or caught a flight out. We've started searching the passenger lists, beginning with flights to the mainland."

"What will you do if you find them?"

Marko looked blankly at Lamont. "The director wants them erased. Once we find them, we'll bring in a contractor to do the job."

Lamont angrily shook his head. "We had an agreement, they trusted us."

"This is what we should have done in the first place. I know you didn't want to—nobody wants to kill innocent people, but sometimes it's necessary. I advised you that Kronig's plan was too risky, and now we have this mess on our hands."

"So how many innocent people are we going to kill to keep the drug secret?"

"As many as it takes," said Marko icily. "What choice do we have? If the drug's exposed, it will compromise all our operations against al-Qaeda and set us back years. If we have to sacrifice Ryan and Alana, so be it."

"So how are you going to find them?"

"We think they'll try to contact the reporter who confronted them in Hawaii. We don't know for sure, but we suspect it was Connie Blythe with the *Beltway Insider*. She's the obvious candidate, given her history with them. We're bugging her phones as we speak."

Lamont sighed. "You know, I'm almost glad I'm getting out of this business." He stared at Marko. "Don't let them corrupt you. I never particularly cared for you, but you always did your job well. These new guys are vicious sharks, and if you submit to their methods, they will destroy you and the agency."

"I'll take that under advisement," said Marko, extending his hand. "Good luck, James."

"Good luck to you. You'll need it more than me."

CHAPTER THIRTY-ONE

HEADS TURNED AS Bill and Cheryl walked off the elevator into the busy hotel lobby. Blasts of frigid air accosted them from the outside doors. People trudged in, stamping their feet on the marble floor to dislodge snow from their boots. *We're a long way from Hawaii*, thought Cheryl.

The concierge suppressed a giggle as they stood in front of her, looking like two people who had just walked off the beach. "You know there's a blizzard outside."

They explained that the airline had lost their luggage and they couldn't wait any longer; they needed to buy new clothes. The concierge spread open a map of downtown Chicago and the Magnificent Mile, the high-end shopping district on Michigan Avenue. The closest department store was a Nordstrom three blocks away. They took the map, thanked the concierge, and headed to the doors.

"You can't go out dressed like that, you'll freeze to death," said the concierge. She invited them to take a seat in the lobby. She reappeared carrying two large overcoats. "This is the best I can do. They belong to staff, so you'll have to give them back. Sorry I don't have anything for your feet," she said, looking down at their running shoes.

A few minutes later they were outside with the snow biting into their faces. A cold knee-deep accumulation covered their skimpy shoes. Pedestrians in burka-like wrappings passed by, their bodies slanted against the howling wind. Lines of cars crawled up and down Michigan Avenue with their tires spinning wildly.

When they finally reached the department store, their faces were stiff and their feet numb. It felt like an arctic version of hell. As they entered the store, a welcome rush of warm air greeted them. They brushed the snow off their hair and shoulders and began shopping.

. . .

Two hours later they returned to the hotel carting several bags of winter clothes: pants, shirts, shoes, boots, hats, and socks. They'd also bought toiletries, underwear, and two small suitcases. It had set them back close to $4,000. The speed with which their cash stockpile was dwindling alarmed Bill.

They returned the borrowed coats, changed in their hotel room, and headed to the business center, searching for a computer with Internet access. Sitting together in front of a monitor, they viewed the articles on Alana Shannon and the accompanying photographs. Cheryl carefully read the articles and studied the pictures.

"She's much prettier than me."

"No, she isn't," said Bill, although he knew it was true.

Cheryl indicated that she wanted to see the photographs of Rebecca Blaze. They scanned the area. The only other person in the room was the business center manager, who was fixated on his computer. Bill typed in *Rebecca Blaze* and entered his birthday, and the nude pictures popped up. Cheryl examined them closely, zeroing in on the crescent birthmark. Finally she sighed. "That's me, unless I have a twin sister."

"Do twins share the same birthmark?"

They jumped when the business center manager tapped them on the shoulder. "I'm sorry, you're not allowed to view pornography here. This is a public place."

"Oh, it's not what you think," said Cheryl. "It's me when I was younger."

The manager stared at her with disgust. "I don't care. You can't look at naked pictures in here."

They immediately closed the page, and the manager returned to his desk, but continued to eye them.

Their next question was how to get to Washington. Bill knew they couldn't fly; the airlines would want identification. He feared that the CIA or the feds might have added their names to a no-fly list or to some other fugitive screening program ready to snag them. He reasoned their best bet was to travel by bus or train.

They checked the Amtrak schedule on the Internet. The Capitol Limited left for Washington every evening at 6:25. The trip was an eighteen-hour overnight ride through Cleveland and Pittsburgh. Neither of them was up for that. They had already paid for an additional night, and outside a blinding snowstorm raged. They decided they would take the train the next day.

CHAPTER THIRTY-TWO

A FEW HOURS after walking out of CIA headquarters, James Lamont sat in the basement of Wilhelm Kronig's house in McLean, Virginia. They were in a room within a room that Kronig had built when he was deputy director of the CIA back in the 1980s. Made of solid concrete and covered with soundproof padding, it was as secure as any room at Langley. Kronig had it continually swept for electronic bugs. He recognized that he was fanatically careful, but it gave him comfort.

The blood rushed to Kronig's face as Lamont relayed the story of his meeting with Director Goodwin and Crowder, and his good-bye conversation with Marko.

"Those sons of bitches," said Kronig, shaking his fist with uncharacteristic fury. "We had an agreement."

"They don't give a shit. Worse, they know about the drug. Imagine what they'll do with it," said Lamont.

"My greatest fear is coming true. Next they'll be using it for political purposes. I wonder if they've told the vice president."

"Possibly, Goodwin and the vice president are close. Maybe it's time to brief the president," said Lamont. "I argued for that from the beginning, but Scotty Olds talked us out of it."

"But back then we had the Black Box operation in play. It's different today, and if the vice president knows about the drug, then the president should too. Let's give Olds a call," suggested Kronig.

"What good would that do? He's been fired."

"He's still at the White House. The president made him liaison to the Justice Department on security matters."

"I didn't know…I guess I've been out of the loop."

"I'm sure the president didn't want to fire him, but succumbed to the pressure from Congressman Luke," said Kronig.

"And privately from the vice president," added Lamont.

"My guess is that the president wants to keep Olds close, as a closet adviser."

"Okay, I'll call Olds—see if I can set up a meeting," said Lamont.

They stayed quiet for a few minutes, thinking of the ramifications.

"Maybe I should talk to that reporter, Connie Blythe," said Kronig.

"Why?"

"You just told me that the CIA thinks that Ryan Butler and Alana Shannon may try to contact her—the CIA is tapping her phone and possibly bugging her office. I could warn her and keep Ryan and Alana safe."

"You don't want to put yourself in the way of the new CIA leadership. You could end up like Wolaski."

Kronig laughed. "They wouldn't kill an old dog like me. Besides, I can take care of myself." He opened his jacket to point to the Glock pistol in his shoulder holster.

"If you say so, but I'd be careful."

Kronig changed the subject. "As for the skimming of the drug, it looks like we're at a dead end. All we have is Patrick O'Brien's report and the names of the twelve people on the sixth floor."

Lamont exhaled loudly. "We know there's a traitor in our midst, and we're helpless to do anything."

"We're not helpless; we just don't know which of the twelve it is."

"Even if we did, what could we do? We're no longer part of the CIA. We don't have the money or resources to follow up."

"Don't be so sure. I've been around a long time—I know some tricks," said Kronig, revealing a wry smile.

CHAPTER THIRTY-THREE

CONNIE RETURNED FROM lunch and checked her phone messages. There was a puzzling one, a few seconds of silence and then a woman's voice in the background saying, "Hang up," then nothing. The log indicated that the call had come from area code 812. Connie knew that was Chicago. During her years as a journalist, she had memorized the area codes for many major cities.

She turned her attention back to the rape cases. Annie Weaver had agreed to the paternity test and the results were in, but without a sample of the congressman's DNA, they were no help. The Weavers thought that if they brought a criminal complaint against the congressman, a judge might order a blood test, but Connie was doubtful it would go that far. That would require a formal filing of rape charges, and there wasn't sufficient evidence for a prosecutor to act. They needed somebody else to come forward. Jason was watching to see if Luke met with any new female interns, but there had been none. Apparently the warning from his chief of staff had put him on good behavior.

The receptionist rang. "There's a man here to see you. He says you will know who he is. His name is Robert James."

"That name doesn't ring a bell," said Connie.

She walked out to the reception area and spotted an older, somewhat overweight, bespectacled bald man wearing a dark overcoat and gray scarf. He was holding a fedora and examining the paintings on the wall. He turned as Connie appeared and offered a friendly, reassuring smile. "Hello, Ms. Blythe."

"Do I know you?"

"I believe you do," he answered in a soothing voice. "I'd like for you to take a walk with me," he said, and handed her a note:

"My name is Wilhelm Kronig, but call me Mr. James. We can't talk here, your phone is tapped and your office may be bugged."

Connie stiffened. She knew who Wilhelm Kronig was, the former deputy director of the CIA and the man Ryan Butler had gone to see on the day he disappeared.

Connie put on her heavy red overcoat and matching scarf, and they took the elevator to the lobby without speaking. Exiting the building, they headed down the street toward the Potomac River. They crossed the Lee Highway into Gateway Park and found a bench to share under a bare oak tree. With temperatures in the midforties under a gray sky, few people were in sight.

"I know who you are. What can I do for you, Mr. Kronig?"

"I want to know if you were recently in Hawaii. The island of Molokai, to be exact. And if so, did you happen to visit two friends of mine, William and Cheryl Parker?"

Connie turned to face him, noticing his gentle hazel eyes. "You mean Ryan Butler and Alana Shannon, don't you?"

Kronig smiled. "We invested a lot of effort and money to set them up in Hawaii and to keep their identities secret. How did you find them?"

"I saw a news clip on CNN, covering the earthquake. I thought I recognized her on the screen."

"Even after the nose surgery and the eye color change?"

"Her nose was different, but facial recognition software revealed strong matches for her other features, and we were able to confirm that the man with her was Ryan Butler. Alana's former lawyer in North Carolina recognized him."

"So he knows too. That's not good."

"Tell me what you want."

Kronig leaned forward on the bench, looking into Connie's eyes. "I'm not here to give you a news scoop. You can't write about what I tell you."

"I'm a reporter. It's my job to write articles."

"This isn't about selling papers or winning awards, this is about national security and the lives of two innocent people."

"Their lives are in danger?"

"Yes, thanks to you."

Connie pulled back. "What do you mean? When I spoke to them on the island, they pretended that they had no idea what I was talking about. They told me they were Cheryl and William Parker and demanded that I get off their property. They were very convincing."

"That's because they were telling the truth. They honestly believe they are Cheryl and William Parker. They believe they survived a car wreck in Colorado, had brain damage, and suffered amnesia."

"How did you get them to believe that?"

"I'm sure you can figure that one out, my dear."

Normally Connie would have winced at the term *my dear*, but there something so grandfatherly and gentle in his voice and manner that she took no affront.

Kronig continued. "It was you who investigated the drug experiments in Wisconsin. It was you who made a public records request of the CIA regarding those experiments. You, Ryan, Alana, and the lawyer from North Carolina were on the verge of exposing a deep secret; that's why we had to step in."

"So you used the hypnosis drug on them."

"I know you understand the power of the drug. I reviewed the draft article your boss sent over for comment. I suspected you were the author. You were correct on a number of things, and wrong on some. Of course, the CIA would never have let the article be published."

"My boss wasn't going to publish it anyway; he only wanted to gauge the CIA's reaction. He said there were too many gaps and unidentified sources."

Kronig nodded. "I want you to understand that the drug is critical to the security of this nation. We are using it against the terrorists. The information we have obtained has saved countless lives. We have averted three major terrorist attacks in this country and in Europe. Using it, we are running operations that are tearing al-Qaeda apart from within. Exposure of the drug would compromise everything we have done and are doing. It would mean the resurgence of al-Qaeda and the death of many innocent people. Now our secret is threatened because of your visit to the island."

"I don't understand," Connie said, tightening her scarf against her neck. She wasn't sure whether the sudden chill she felt was from the wind or his words.

"After you visited them on the island, they began to ask questions. They began to doubt the veracity of their past. They made disturbing inquiries hinting that they were on the verge of discovering their true identities. We had to move in. Our initial intent was to bring them back, snap them out of their hypnotic hold, and relocate them somewhere under new names."

"So you were holding them prisoners by stealing their memories, making them believe they were someone else. That's appalling." Her eyes were daggers.

"No, we didn't force them—they agreed to relocation and submission to the drug. We signed a contract—they knew what they were doing."

"Why would they agree to that?"

"Honestly, my dear. They didn't have much in the way of options. There were forces in the intelligence community who wanted them erased."

"You mean killed?"

"Erased, eliminated, killed, it's all semantics. They would no longer be a problem. I pressed for relocation, got my higher-ups to agree, and convinced Alana and Ryan that it was in their best interests. It wasn't to be permanent, only until certain operations were completed and al-Qaeda destroyed."

"So why are you telling me this? You already said that I can't write about it."

"Because the new CIA leadership nixed the agreement and has other nasty plans for them. Alana and Ryan sensed they were in danger and managed to escape; nobody knows where they are—but they may try to contact you."

Kronig reached into his pocket and took out two small devices, a hand-size voice recorder and a cell phone. He turned the recorder on, a green light appeared, and he placed the device on his lap.

"From here on I'm going to record our conversation."

"Why?"

"Because of a question I think you will ask me, later. If they call you, you need to get them off your phone as fast as you can. Tell them to call you right back on your cell phone—not your current one—this one." He handed her the cell phone. "If you don't feel comfortable using this one, buy your own, but make sure it's one of those cheap no-contracts that can be easily discarded and can't be traced. When they call you back, make sure you take the call outside of your office."

"I don't understand. Who is tapping and bugging me? I assume we're talking about the CIA, but aren't you working for them?"

"Not anymore. As you know, there is new leadership at the top. These people don't care about agreements, contracts, procedures, or laws. They will do anything to achieve their objectives. If they find Alana and Ryan, they will erase them. I'm the only one who can save them."

Connie breathed hard. "Killing of American citizens is illegal."

"It certainly is."

"So what should I do if they make contact?"

"I want you to set up a meeting with them, somewhere, and then call me on my cell. Here's my number." He handed her a card. "Then the four of us will meet. You can interview them if you want, although you can't publish anything now—it would only be for the future. Then, if they agree, I will take them somewhere safe."

Connie shook her head. "And why in the world should I trust you? Maybe you're using me to get to them. I could be leading them right into the lap of the CIA."

Kronig turned off the recording device and held it in front of her face. "This is why you should trust me. I've just told you that the CIA is planning to assassinate US citizens, which, as you noted, my dear, is clearly illegal. If anything happens to them, you have your scoop. I trust you, however, not to use anything on this tape unless you honestly believe that I have deceived you." He pressed it into her hands.

Connie examined the cell phone and the tape recorder.

Kronig gently touched his gloved hand to hers. "Please, my dear, their lives are at stake."

She stayed silent for a few minutes, debating whether to trust him. She wanted to say no, but his face was so compelling and so honest that she acquiesced. "Okay, I'll do it."

"Good," said Kronig, patting her again on her gloved fingers.

"But you're wrong concerning the drug; I don't think it's a secret anymore."

"What do you mean?" asked Kronig, sitting up straight.

"I'm working on a story about Congressman Steven Luke. You've heard about his tea sessions?"

"Of course."

"I think he's putting some kind of drug in the tea. Maybe the same drug from the Wisconsin experiment or something similar. Everybody's behavior changes after drinking the tea. They shift their positions to mirror Luke. I also have two young women, interns in his office, who claim he tried to rape or molest them under the influence of the tea. One is pregnant."

Kronig's face went distant, suggesting he was struggling to invoke a memory. His brow furrowed. "Does the name Laura Jansen figure in your investigation?"

Connie was aghast. "Yes she does. How would you know that? She's Congressman Luke's chief of staff."

"My God, you're right—they're using the drug."

. . .

They continued talking excitedly, sharing information, oblivious to the black sedan parked a few hundred feet away on the road that looped through the park. Inside, the driver aimed a zoom-lens camera with the shutter clicking continuously.

CHAPTER THIRTY-FOUR

"**WE'VE GOT THE** target," said Kronig on his cell phone to Lamont, driving back to his house after meeting with Connie. "It's Congressman Luke's chief of staff, Laura Jansen. She's on O'Brien's list—she lives on the sixth floor of the apartment building. I'm pulling in O'Brien and some others. Can you make a meeting at my house this evening? We need to move quickly."

"Are you sure she's the one?"

"Got to be, ninety-nine percent sure. That's enough to give it a go."

"Give what a go?"

"You remember the old *bait, trap, and release* sting?"

"It's been a long time, and those are tricky—they usually backfire."

"I know, but it's worth a shot. We've got Patrick O'Brien to lead it— he's a master at this."

"How will we pay for the setup?"

"I'm financing this from my own pocket."

Kronig hung up. It gave him chills to think that a man like Congressman Luke was using the drug. Kronig had met with him once and was familiar with his background.

As a basketball player for the University of Missouri, Luke made the game-winning basket in the third round of the 1976 NCAA tournament. Although he was never a star and never played professionally, that shot made him a local hero. After graduation he married the daughter of the owner of a large auto dealership and, capitalizing on his basketball fame, became the advertising face of the franchise. Bankrolled by his right-leaning father-in-law, he successfully ran for Congress.

Kronig's meeting with Luke was an attempt to dissuade him from calling for preemptive nuclear strikes against North Korea and Iran. The intelligence community believed that Luke's saber rattling was undermining diplomatic efforts to rein in both nations' nuclear ambitions.

When they were introduced, Congressman Luke towered over Kronig. Although his height was given as six foot six, he appeared taller. Rumors circulated that he wore elevator shoes to make himself look even more imposing. Like the rest of his body, his face was lean, and it was punctuated by a prominent hawk nose.

During the meeting, Luke was cordial and polite and listened intently as Kronig outlined the CIA's concerns. However, his final words left Kronig rattled. "You and I have different perspectives on the world. Mine are based on God's will, so if I were to agree with you, then we'd both be wrong."

CHAPTER THIRTY-FIVE

DIRECTOR GOODWIN CALLED Marko into his office. Crowder was also present.

"Look at these pictures," said Crowder, handing him six large photographs. Crowder's ruddy face was more flushed than usual, almost matching the color of his ginger hair.

"It's Wilhelm Kronig and some woman I don't recognize," said Marko.

"We do. It's Connie Blythe, a reporter for the *Beltway Insider*. Kronig's talking to the press."

"Look, I know him well, he would never reveal anything secret—he plays by the rules."

"Well, we can't ignore what's before our eyes," said the director.

"How did you get the pictures?"

"Pure luck," said Crowder. "We had some plumbers scouting the building where she works—trying to figure out the best way to bug her office, coming up through the freight elevators. One of our men happened to recognize Kronig leaving with the mark. He followed them, just out of sight, and called his superiors. It came up to us and we sent out an operative to take photos."

Director Goodwin stared at Marko. "Did you tell Kronig that we were tapping Connie Blythe's phone?"

"Of course not."

"How about Lamont?"

"Yeah, I told him."

"Shit," yelled Crowder. "Why the hell would you do that?"

"It was his operation, and his last day in the office, so I mentioned it."

"You fucked up, Marko. We know Lamont and Kronig are close. He probably tipped him off and Kronig's out there warning Ms. Blythe that Ryan and Alana may contact her."

"I don't think Kronig would do that."

"I don't give a damn what you think. We need to watch Kronig," said Goodwin.

"How?"

"Put a tracer on his car, so we can monitor his movements on GPS," said Crowder.

"That will be hard to do. Kronig's very guarded and always on the alert for bugs."

"I don't want to hear your excuses. Get it done," shouted the director.

CHAPTER THIRTY-SIX

FIVE MEN CONVENED in Wilhelm Kronig's basement. In addition to Kronig, the group included James Lamont, Scotty Olds, Patrick O'Brien, and ex–FBI agent Alex Sandoval. They couldn't all squeeze into his secure room, so they stretched out on couches and chairs in the den.

The planning went into the night, with Kronig's live-in housekeeper, Maddie, bringing sandwiches and coffee. In reality, Maddie was more than an employee. She and Kronig had shared a close and affectionate relationship ever since the death of his wife years earlier.

They broke the operation into three parts. First they had to lure Laura Jansen into a private meeting. Second they had to work out a strategy to win her over and convince her to cooperate. Third, if successful, they had to confront Congressman Luke. O'Brien, with the help of Sandoval, would handle the first two parts. Lamont and Olds would handle the third part, if it got that far.

Setting the bait, Kronig researched Jansen's family tree. She had been born and raised in Missouri. However, her grandmother and great-grandmother had hailed from Oklahoma. Kronig decided that was the key. He zeroed in on the Oklahoma secretary of state's unclaimed-property website, searching for a large bank deposit that would expire within the next week. He spotted a good one, Eleanor Spearman of Tulsa with an unclaimed account of $223,334. Checking other sites, he learned that she had died fifteen years earlier at the age of ninety-seven. The short death notice listed no family.

Kronig guessed it was a sad case of an elderly woman without children outliving her spouse and siblings and forgotten by the younger generation. As she aged, her memory had declined until she lost all recollection of the account.

The time to initiate a claim for the money had passed. Under Oklahoma statutes, funds unclaimed for fifteen years automatically reverted to the state. However, it was the start of a fiction for setting the bait.

. . .

Laura Jansen sounded skeptical when Patrick O'Brien called, giving his name as Wellington Tyman, president and CEO of Asset Reclamation Inc., a firm specializing in recovering unclaimed assets. He spoke with a smooth Southern accent as he explained that her late great-aunt in Oklahoma, Eleanor Spearman, had left a bank deposit worth $223,334. Absent immediate action, the money would revert to the state. He described his company's business model: identifying expiring unclaimed property, tracking down rightful heirs, initiating a claim on their behalf, and recovering the money minus a 30 percent commission. He explained that he had identified seven legitimate heirs in the Washington, DC, area and each was legally entitled to a share of $37,166, before his cut. He advised her that she could verify the information by checking the Oklahoma website.

"I don't remember the name of Spearman," she said, "but I know my family traces back to Tulsa on my mother's side. But there must be many other relatives."

O'Brien knew he had her. The deception depended on the target's not knowing the names and relationships of ancestors from generations earlier, but recognizing a place of origin. As for the number of relatives, O'Brien breezily indicated that there were hundreds of qualified relatives spread over the country, but he'd contacted only those in the Washington area because that's where his business was located and it would be impractical and unprofitable to find all of them. Then O'Brien lowered the boom:

"After my commission, you are entitled to $26,016. You will have to meet me in person to sign paperwork transferring your claim to me. I give you the money up front from my company's account, and later I secure the payout from the state. I can have the check ready for you this Saturday, or if you would prefer I can give it to you in cash. It's that simple."

"What's to prevent me from making the claim myself, without your help?"

"The submission deadline is over; you're too late. However, I've already submitted a claim with the required legal documentation, and all I need is your signature. It's a win-win for both of us. You receive an unexpected monetary windfall without any effort on your part, and I receive thirty percent. I make a good living doing this."

When O'Brien got off the phone, Laura Jansen had agreed to meet him on Saturday morning at ten in the John Adams Room of the Willard InterContinental Hotel on Pennsylvania Avenue, near the White House, only a few blocks from her apartment.

With the trap set, they had to procure the necessary equipment, create false documents, and rehearse the pitch.

CHAPTER THIRTY-SEVEN

CHERYL AND BILL took the overnight train from Chicago to Washington. They booked a roomette, using cash, but had to show their driver's licenses when purchasing the tickets, which heightened their anxieties.

Before checking out, they called Connie Blythe from their hotel room, but immediately hung up when the call went to voice mail. On reflection, Bill thought it would be smarter to use a cell phone. Not theirs, they had thrown those away in Hawaii realizing that their names were on the contract and their calls were traceable. A no-contract phone would give them anonymity, so they bought one at an electronics store on Michigan Avenue before taking a cab to the train station.

By the time they boarded, it was late evening, so they decided to wait until the next morning before calling Connie again.

The screeching of brakes awoke them as the train pulled into the station in Pittsburgh. Bill checked his watch; it was just after eight. They had slept soundly through the night, lulled to sleep by the rocking rhythm of the rails. They ventured out to the club car for breakfast, bringing coffee and muffins back to their room. As the train rolled across the snow-covered hills of western Pennsylvania into Maryland, they called Connie. She answered on the second ring. Bill put the call on speaker.

"Connie Blythe, *Beltway Insider*."

"Hello, Ms. Blythe. This is Bill and Cheryl Parker. You left us your card when you visited our house on Molokai…"

"Hang up and call me back at 202-666-8412. Do it right now. It's 202-666-8412. Got it?"

"Yes," said Bill as the phone disconnected.

"What the hell?" said Cheryl.

Bill dialed the new number and Connie answered immediately. "Where are you?"

"On a train heading for Washington. We were hoping to meet with you. Maybe you can tell us why you called us Ryan and Alana. We think you may know who we really are."

"You're Ryan Butler and Alana Shannon—and you're in danger."

Cheryl gripped Bill's hand.

"What time does your train arrive in DC?"

"One twenty-five at Union Station."

"I'll call you back to give you instructions. Give me your phone number."

...

Arriving at Union Station, Bill and Cheryl followed Connie's directions, proceeding down Louisiana Avenue past crowds of people and right onto D Street to the Hyatt Regency Hotel. As instructed, they took the glass elevator to the eighteenth floor and knocked on room 1854. The door opened and they immediately recognized Connie from her visit to Molokai.

"Come in," she said. They halted as they entered the room, eyeing an older man in a gray jacket perched on one end of a bed. "This is Wilhelm Kronig. He's the former deputy director of the CIA."

They stiffened at the mention of the CIA, fearing they had walked into a trap.

"You're safe with me," said Kronig, sensing their alarm. "I know you don't remember me, but I set you up on Molokai. Although Alana, my dear, you do look quite different with your dark-brown hair and your cosmetic surgery."

"So I really was Alana Shannon, the woman who killed her husband?"

"Yes, my dear," said Kronig with a sympathetic nod.

"I read all the articles on the Internet, but I still can't believe it's me. And I was once Rebecca Blaze—a porn model."

"That was a long time ago, when you were young and foolish."

"Who am I?" asked Bill.

"You were a lawyer in Arizona working for the EPA. In reality you were much more, but since you don't remember, it's better that I don't tell you—you're safer that way."

It was Cheryl's turn. "If I was Rebecca Blaze, how did I end up as Alana Shannon?"

"It's a long story. You turned your life around, got off drugs, went to college, got a job, married Steve Shannon, and became rich investing in real estate in North Carolina. You were the bad girl turned good."

"Then why did I shoot my husband?"

"You legitimately believed he was going to kill you—it was self-defense."

"Why was he going to kill me?"

"It's complicated, but you did nothing wrong, my dear. I would like to tell you more, but again, that would put you in danger. The less you know the better off you are."

Bill's frustration burst forth. "None of this makes any sense. How did Cheryl and I meet, and why were we on Molokai?"

"You were lovers; you had been for a long time. After the murder trial, we feared for your safety—you knew too much."

"About what?"

"National security secrets—that's all I can tell you. I worked out an agreement for you to enter our protection program. You signed a contract with the CIA. You agreed to submit to a top-secret drug that enhances the effects of hypnosis—one that can block memories and influence behavior. That's all I can tell you about the drug." He turned to look at Cheryl. "And you agreed to surgery—we reshaped your nose and changed your eye color. You also dyed your hair dark brown."

"But I like my hair that color."

"Of course you do, my dear, you were told to like it that way. We gave you a backstory about an auto collision in Colorado and resulting amnesia. We also instructed you not to question your past and to avoid people. We put you on Molokai because of its remote location and tiny population. However, when Ms. Blythe went to see you it aroused your curiosity and you started looking where you shouldn't have. We were concerned that the drug might be wearing off, so we decided to pull you back in so your real identities wouldn't be compromised."

"So we were safe…We should have boarded the jet?"

"No, you did the right thing. There are people at the CIA who want you erased—dead people tell no tales. Your instincts to escape were prescient. So tell us exactly what happened on Molokai and how you got here."

As Connie took frantic notes, Cheryl and Bill related their story: the abduction by the CIA, the waiting jet, their dash across the runway, the escape on the ferry, the flight to Chicago, and finally the train to DC. When they were finished, Cheryl looked up. "What happens now, shouldn't we go to the police?"

"That's not a good option. The police can't protect you. They can listen to your story, but they won't believe you and they won't act. They will just let you go—which leaves you a ripe target for those who want to get rid of you."

Connie interrupted. "They said they skipped a court hearing in Honolulu. Won't the authorities be searching for them? Won't that come out if they go to the police?"

"Possibly," said Kronig. "But the authorities will likely release you again. I doubt they want the expense of transporting you all the way back to Hawaii for running across a runway. They'll probably transfer the case here, hold a quick hearing, fine you, and maybe require that you spend a few days in jail. And then you'll be set free—once again sitting ducks."

Cheryl looked to Connie. "What should we do?"

Connie placed her hands in the air. "That's totally your decision, I'm only a journalist."

"I will protect you," said Kronig in a strong confident voice. "I'll move you to a secure house I have at the beach. Nobody knows about it. You will be safe there."

"For how long?" asked Bill.

"That's the hard part. I don't know…but if you don't come with me, you will likely end up dead—or, in the parlance of the CIA, erased."

CHAPTER THIRTY-EIGHT

BRUCE MARKO CLUSTERED with Director Goodwin and Crowder at Langley listening to the conversation in room 1854. An hour earlier the CIA's tracking of Connie Blythe and Wilhelm Kronig's automobiles had shown them converging at the Hyatt Regency. A team quickly moved in. They were too late to catch Kronig or Connie arriving, but they recognized Ryan and Alana when they entered the lobby. An agent followed them up to room 1854. When they disappeared into the room, the agent affixed a tiny listening device to the door. The device picked up all the sounds from the room, but also passing conversations in the hallway, and at times from other rooms. Soon sophisticated software back at Langley separated the voices and neutralized extraneous noise.

At first the discussion in the room sounded muffled and difficult to understand, but as the software learned to recognize and separate voices, the conversation became clear and distinct. They listened as Kronig convinced Alana and Ryan to leave with him rather than go to the police.

. . .

Shortly after the conversation ended, agents in the lobby observed Kronig, Ryan, and Alana exiting the elevators. An agent discreetly followed them to the parking garage and watched them climb into Kronig's silver Cadillac Escalade. Connie Blythe left a few minutes later, after settling a bill at the front desk.

Crowder turned to Marko. "What do you know about Kronig having a beach house?"

"Nothing. I know he talked about vacationing at the beach, but he never said where."

Crowder frowned. "Is the contractor on call?"

"He's awaiting instructions in Bethesda."

"Can Kronig's GPS tracking location be transferred to the contractor?" asked the director.

"It's just a matter of providing him the link and the password for his laptop. That's easy," said Marko.

"Then activate him. Tell him to follow them."

"Okay," said Marko.

"Who are you using?" asked Crowder.

"The motorcycle man."

"Good. He's the best."

"So what do I tell the contractor? To keep us updated on their location?" asked Marko.

Director Goodwin pounded his hand on his desk. "No. You tell him to kill them when he gets a clean shot—the sooner the better."

"But they're with Kronig. What about him?"

"Tell the contractor to kill him too. That's the cleanest way."

"But you're talking about a former deputy director of the CIA."

"We're talking about a traitor," screamed Goodwin. "He's conspiring behind our backs, revealing government secrets, talking to a reporter, for Christ's sake. The man's out of control. Take him out and good riddance."

Marko hesitated. "There's an agency rule…We don't harm our own."

"We're wasting time," said Goodwin. "I don't want to argue. Just do as you're told. Get on the phone to the contractor."

Marko just stood there.

The intercom on the director's desk buzzed and his administrative assistant came on.

"I told you not to bother me," yelled Goodwin.

"I know, but it's the vice president on the line."

Goodwin glared at Marko. "I have to take this."

"What the fuck are you waiting for?" shouted Crowder. "You heard the director. Get going."

CHAPTER THIRTY-NINE

ON THE TRIP down Interstate 95, heading south, Kronig told Bill and Cheryl that his beach house was in the town of Duck, North Carolina, on the northern tip of the Outer Banks. He confided that the house was his refuge, where he could escape the stress of work. There he would become Martin Henley, a prosperous lawyer. He assured them that nobody at the CIA knew about the house or his alter ego.

On the road he called his housekeeper, Maddie, and told her to meet him at the beach. He said he was bringing Bill and Cheryl Parker and instructed her to stock the house with groceries for a week. He also indicated that if anybody asked, she was to say that Bill was his nephew visiting from Hawaii and Cheryl was Bill's wife.

Bill and Cheryl bombarded Kronig with questions, but he stayed vague. He kept telling them that the less they knew the safer they were.

"Were we ever in the Caribbean?" asked Bill unexpectedly.

Kronig tilted his head sideways. "Why would you think that?"

"I have this dream…I'm on a boat somewhere on the ocean and I'm shooting a gun into the chest of a big blond man. There's blood everywhere. In the dream, I think I'm in the Caribbean. There's also a woman on the boat, a redhead. I never realized it before, but I think it's Cheryl."

Kronig kept his eye on the road, but a trace of a smile crossed his face. "It's not a dream, it happened. That's all I can tell you."

They exited Interstate 95 in Richmond for Interstate 64 heading southeast toward the coast. An hour later they were on a lonely two-lane road, Route 17, between Norfolk, Virginia, and Elizabeth City, North Carolina. The road sliced across the Great Dismal Swamp, a large area of uninhabited wetlands on the eastern coastal plains of North Carolina, a web of marshes, bogs, and tidal streams.

It was almost dark, but Kronig knew the route well. The road was elevated so it wouldn't flood in high tides. On either side, thick walls of mulberry, myrtle, sumac, and black gum trees concealed the marshes beyond.

Cheryl sat in the front passenger seat and Bill in the back. Both of them were drifting in and out of sleep. Kronig's eyes focused ahead, scanning for the white-tailed deer, possums, and raccoons that frequently crossed the road at night.

There were few cars in either direction. Kronig noticed a single headlight in his rearview mirror approaching at a high speed. As the motorcycle neared, it shifted into the other lane to pass. He inched the car over to give the cycle a wide berth. The loud roar of the approaching engine stirred Cheryl and Bill.

It all happened in a few seconds. The motorcycle abruptly slowed as it approached the Cadillac, until it pulled even. Kronig turned his head to look, staring at the barrel of a gun. He was skilled in evasive maneuvers, but it was too late. As he applied the brakes, a shot rang out, penetrating the side window with a hollow circle, entering his left cheek, and exiting on the other side, just missing Cheryl's head, splattering her face with Kronig's blood. The Cadillac veered violently to the right, off the road, plowing through the vegetation and taking out trees and shrubs on the way. For a few seconds it was airborne before it landed in a marsh, skidding forward ten feet and shuddering to a stop in the grassy muck. The passenger side of the car lodged against the trunk of a cypress tree. The headlights illuminated a foggy vista of tall trees with thick tangled roots rising up from misty green sludge.

Bill and Cheryl flew back and forth. Their seat belts burned into their chests, but the air bags didn't deploy.

Blood spurted from Kronig's mouth. "Get out. Get out. Run," he grunted.

Cheryl tried to open her door, but the tree blocked it. Bill opened the back driver's side door and Cheryl crawled over the seat and followed him out. Immediately they sank into a half foot of soggy mud. They looked back toward the road and saw the dim silhouette of a man heading toward the car carrying a gun.

"Go!" moaned Kronig. They ran away from the car and the approaching man, farther into the swamp, but it was hard to make progress through the wet mire. They finally reached a cluster of trees on higher ground. Crouching low, they watched the motorcycle man walk to the car. He finished smashing the driver's side window and then pointed the gun at Kronig's chest, firing twice. He reached in through the window and switched off the engine. The headlights went out and everything turned dark except for the faint glow of a crescent moon diffused through thick clouds. The moonlight was sufficient to create shadows through the murky fog, but not much more.

Suddenly a bright light appeared, a flashlight, scanning back and forth. They flattened their bodies on the ground, tasting the dirt, breathing heavily. The man began moving toward them. They knew he was coming to kill them.

"We can't stay here," whispered Bill. "We need to separate. You head back to the highway and I'll try to draw him the other way." The flashlight beam was getting closer. Cheryl squeezed Bill's hand and took off. Bill immediately sprinted in the opposite direction.

The flashlight swept from side to side in a widening angle. They tried to keep their bodies low, recognizing that the swamp fog was thicker close to the ground. Bill ran for several minutes until the earth gave way and he sank into a pool of cold water. His head surfaced as he trod water, looking back at the man aiming the flashlight. The light shone in the other direction toward Cheryl. For a split second she was visible, caught in a strobe-like flash, slogging through the mud. Bill yelled out, trying to draw the shooter's attention away from Cheryl, but he ignored him. Suddenly the marsh reverberated with the sound of a single gunshot, followed by the flapping sounds of hundreds of birds rising from the trees. The flashlight quickly turned back toward Bill. He held his breath and plunged his head beneath the frigid water. *She's dead*, he thought.

CHAPTER FORTY

CHERYL LAY FACEDOWN in the mud, breathing hard. She felt the bullet whiz over her head, making a sharp hissing sound. She realized that the man must have thought he had hit her, because the beam of the flashlight swung away. She waited a second, caught her breath, and rushed toward the Cadillac. The muck slowed her progress, but she ran with all the strength she could summon. The motorcycle man didn't hear her or decided to ignore her, as he continued his hunt for Bill, moving away from the vehicle.

She dove in through the back door of the Cadillac and slid over the seat to the front. Next to her, Kronig slumped over the steering wheel, smeared in warm sticky blood. She reached in and peeled back his jacket, searching for the shoulder holster she had noticed at the hotel. She groped around until she felt the gun grip. She slid it out and wrapped her hands around it. It felt slippery with blood. Through the windshield she saw the dim shadow of the motorcycle man in front. His back was to her as he swept the flashlight across the marsh, creating spooky patterns on the trees. She reached over and blasted the car horn.

The man turned around, hesitated, and began moving back toward the Cadillac, aiming the flashlight in her direction. Cheryl crouched down in her seat, occasionally peeking over the dashboard and ducking back down, trying to gauge the shrinking distance between the approaching man and the car. She continued to pound the horn.

Surprisingly, the gun felt natural in her hands. Now came the hard part: she had to wait until the man was within range. Her heart raced and her breathing accelerated. She let go of the horn and wrapped both hands around the weapon. Everything was eerily quiet. The beam from the flashlight brightened as it shone directly on the windshield. She peeked out again, carefully, over the dashboard. The man was twenty feet away. Immediately the piercing sound of gunfire broke the silence and the windshield exploded into a thousand shards. It was time for action.

She switched on the headlights. Seen through the shattered windshield, the man was lit up like a stage actor. He stopped abruptly, dropped the flashlight, and brought one hand up to shield his eyes from the blinding headlights. Cheryl wasted no time. She fired repeatedly. The first two bullets missed, but the third hit him in the shoulder and he stumbled backward. Another shot missed, but the next bullet exploded into his head with a burst of red. He dropped backward to the ground.

Cheryl climbed quickly out of the car and ran to the fallen man. In the distance she saw Bill running toward her. In a few moments they were standing over the lifeless body, looking down at the red gaping hole above his left eye, both of them in shock. Cheryl trembled. "Oh my God, I killed him! I killed him!"

Bill took Cheryl in his arms, trying to calm her. "It's okay. It's okay. We're alive. Where did you get the gun?"

"From Mr. Kronig. I noticed his shoulder holster back at the hotel…inside his jacket."

"I didn't know you knew how to use one."

"Neither did I," she sobbed, gasping for air. "You're soaking wet."

"I know. I was in the water."

Still in each other's arms, they surveyed the scene. In front lay the dead motorcycle man. Behind them was the Cadillac holding Kronig's bloodied body. To their left was the highway.

"How do we get out of here?" asked Cheryl.

"We need to flag a motorist."

"We just killed someone. We're wet and muddy…I'm covered in blood—nobody will pick us up."

"Maybe a highway patrol car will pass."

"And how do we explain the bodies?"

"We tell the truth."

. . .

As they climbed up the bank to the highway, they noticed something shiny in the shrubs. It was the chrome fender of the motorcycle. The key was still in the ignition.

Bill straddled the seat. "Get on."

"Do you know how to ride it?"

"I think so," he said, turning over the ignition and revving the throttle on the handle grip.

Cheryl hesitated. She still had the gun in her hand. "What should I do with this? Throw it away?"

Bill thought for a second. "Your fingerprints are on it, and we may need it. Put it in the motorcycle saddlebag." Cheryl unlatched the bag and dropped it in. She mounted the cycle and wrapped her arms tight around Bill's chest. They took off, fishtailing as the tires slid from the muddy bank onto the highway.

As the cycle accelerated, a cold, cruel wind blasted into their faces. Their bodies shivered in their icy, wet clothes. Bill's hands on the throttle throbbed, and his wet hair began to freeze.

"Where are we going?" yelled Cheryl over the roar of the engine.

"Elizabeth City, North Carolina. The last sign said it was seventeen miles away."

. . .

Approaching the outskirts of Elizabeth City, they passed a small old motel with a neon vacancy sign. Bill spun the cycle around and pulled into the parking lot. "Hidden Pines Motor Court" read the ancient signage. The office was straight ahead, with a semicircle of six tiny separate bungalows on either side. Behind the office was a residence. It looked like something out of an old Hollywood movie.

"I'm freezing," said Bill. "Let's get a room for the night and then figure out what to do next."

CHAPTER FORTY-ONE

THE MAN BEHIND the counter eyed Bill suspiciously. Mud covered Bill's body and caked his hair and face. Cheryl lurked outside the door to the office, not wanting the light to illuminate the red stains on her clothes.

"What happened to you?" asked the man, looking up from a television. He appeared to be in his fifties, unkempt, with a two-day whitish stubble, scraggly greasy hair, and crooked teeth.

"Our cycle spun out and we went into a ditch."

"Looks like you went all the way into the swamp. That your girlfriend by the door?"

"That's my wife."

The man yelled out to her. "Come here, miss."

Cheryl walked to the door, and the man examined her.

"You've got blood all over you. Seems you got injured in your accident. You should go to the hospital."

"No, I'm all right," said Cheryl.

The man raised his eyebrow. "The room's forty-five dollars a night, but I can't rent you one. You'd track mud all over."

"Please," said Cheryl. "We're soaking wet and freezing. We're supposed to go all the way to the Outer Banks tonight, but we need to get out of these clothes and get warm."

A heavyset woman with long gray hair entered through a side door.

"These two want a room for the night, but they're filthy," said the man.

She looked them up and down. "Let's charge them a cleaning fee."

Bill immediately took the hint. He opened his wallet and pulled out three fifties. "This should cover the room and any cleaning."

"That will work," said the woman, grabbing the bills. "You got identification?"

Cheryl gasped at the question, realizing that her purse was still in the back of Kronig's Cadillac in the swamp.

Bill handed the woman his driver's license.

"Hawaii? You're a long way from home. Here on vacation?"

Bill couldn't tell if she was serious or being cynical. "No, were just visiting some relatives."

The woman glanced out to the motorcycle. "Got luggage?"

"No. We didn't expect to be spending the night."

"I'll see if I can scrounge up something."

. . .

They entered the dingy motel room, stripped off their shoes and clothes, and threw them into a pile on the floor. Naked, they dashed to the bathroom and squeezed into the small shower. The hot water felt comforting as they embraced, trying to get warm, still trembling from their ordeal. Streams of brown and red trickled down their bodies, circling their feet before disappearing down the drain. They remained in the shower, holding on tightly, not wanting to let go, in disbelief that they had escaped certain death.

They jumped when they heard a loud rapping at the door.

Bill darted out of the shower and wrapped a towel around himself. He wished he had the gun, but it was still with the motorcycle. He moved cautiously toward the door, pulling back the window blinds. The woman from the office stood in front holding a stack of clothes. He opened the door.

"These look about your size—some old sweatshirts and sweatpants. I also brought some men's underwear and socks. Can't do anything about your shoes. You don't have to return them—I should have given them away years ago. They belonged to my son in high school. She hesitated, shaking her head. "You know, we're not buying your story. Your clothes are soaked in blood." She glanced at the pile on the floor. "Anybody losing that much blood should be dead."

Bill didn't say anything but felt the tension mounting. Cheryl's head peeked out from the bathroom.

"It's none of my business, but I suspect that you're in big trouble. I convinced my husband not to call the cops. You're safe for tonight, but we want you out of here first thing in the morning."

Bill nodded.

"I brought you something." She handed him a bottle. "It's vodka— the cheap stuff, but it works for me. You two look like you could use it."

. . .

After the woman left, they put on the clothes and ordered pizza from a local delivery joint. Bill ventured outside, barefoot, to get ice and retrieve the saddlebag. They washed the gun in the sink and wrapped it in a hand towel to erase the fingerprints.

Sitting in bed, they gulped pizza and sipped vodka from cheap plastic cups. The warm glow from the booze helped to soothe their nerves. They switched on the television, scanning channels for any mention of the shootings. There wasn't any. The radiator clanked, but the heat was welcome.

After finishing the pizza, they spread out the contents of the saddlebag on the floor. They recognized binoculars, handcuffs, ammunition clips, a large folder, and a laptop computer, but the other items, mostly small electronic devices, were foreign to them. Inside the folder were three US passports, all showing the same face, but with different names. The pictures showed a clean-cut white man with a short GI Joe haircut wearing a dark suit and a tie. There were also numerous driver's licenses from various states. There were business cards showing different names, and occupations ranging from private investigator to insurance agent. There were official-looking IDs and badges from police and probation departments, and even one from the FBI. There was also a small blue case holding four tiny tubes with needlelike points, resembling darts. They closed the case and opened the laptop. The screen showed a small red circle on a satellite map. Next to the circle was a road. Bill zoomed out from the map, and the outline of the Great Dismal Swamp and Route 17 came into view. They realized they were looking at the location of Kronig's Cadillac.

"There must be a tracking device on the car," said Cheryl.

Bill immediately closed the laptop. "This guy's a professional hit man."

"So what should we do? Take all this to the police?"

"If we go to the police, we're at their mercy. They'll probably put us in jail. We're fugitives, and they might think we killed both of them. I'd rather hold on to our freedom for now."

Cheryl's face collapsed. "They're still going to try to kill us."

"I know. Let's take our chances. I trusted Mr. Kronig. I think we should track down his house in Duck. He said his assistant would be waiting for us…Maddie. She may be our only hope. If not, we go to the police."

CHAPTER FORTY-TWO

THE RINGING OF the phone startled Bill and Cheryl out of a deep sleep. Their exhaustion and the vodka had put them out for the night.

"It's seven o'clock and you need to get going," said the woman from the motel office.

"We'll be gone shortly," said Bill.

"By the way, your stay here is off the books. We're not keeping any records, and if I were you I would dump your old clothes in the trash bin behind the office before you leave." She hung up.

...

Twenty minutes later they were on the motorcycle heading toward Duck. Bill wore a tight red sweatshirt with "Elizabeth City High School Football" emblazoned across the front. His too-short sweatpants exposed his shins. An oversize pale-blue University of North Carolina sweatshirt engulfed Cheryl. They wore their muddy, damp shoes from the previous day.

The ride from Elizabeth City to the Outer Banks took an hour and fifteen minutes, across the Wright Memorial Bridge. They paused for breakfast at a small diner in Kitty Hawk, periodically scanning the corner television for news. There was no mention of any shootings or dead bodies in the swamp.

At the Outer Banks Visitor Center, they told a cheerful clerk that they were heading to visit their cousin, Mr. Martin Henley, in Duck, but had lost his address and phone number. The smiling clerk wrote "334 Atlantic Drive" on a map and wished them a good visit. After they left she called the Duck Police Department advising that there were a couple of suspicious persons on a motorcycle heading their way.

Soon Bill and Cheryl were hopelessly lost. They had traveled up and down Atlantic Drive, past huge expensive beachfront homes, but none of the numbers corresponded to Henley's address. As they started to head back to the visitor center, a police car pulled behind them with lights flashing. Cheryl tightened her arms around Bill. He pulled the motorcycle over and waited for the cop to approach.

"Hello, I'm Officer Tom Clifford with the Duck Police Department." He stood about half a foot shorter than Bill, and was flabby, with a paunch hanging over his belt. As he neared he sucked in his stomach and pushed out his chest. "I've been watching you driving up and down Atlantic Drive. What are you looking for?"

"A house," said Bill, handing the officer the address. "We must have the wrong street number."

Officer Clifford examined them, his stare dwelling on their clothes. "You're in the wrong part of Duck. You're on South Atlantic. You want North Atlantic. The roads don't connect. It's another mile or so up the island, almost to the town of Corolla. May I see your identification, please?"

Bill handed him his license.

"Hawaii? You sure are a long way from home." He walked to the back of the motorcycle, noticing the Maryland plates. "This your cycle?"

"No. A friend loaned it to us."

"So you've driven all the way here from Maryland?"

"Yes."

"Wearing those clothes? Not a very good choice for the weather."

"We had a spill and landed in the mud, so we had to buy new stuff at a thrift store in Elizabeth City," offered Cheryl.

Officer Clifford stared at her skeptically. "You got a registration card for the motorcycle?"

"Our friend forgot to give it to us," said Bill.

The officer stared at the saddlebag. "Why don't you check in there, that's where most people keep them."

Bill stood frozen, not sure what to do. Cheryl interrupted. "We've double-checked. It's not in there."

The officer frowned. "I'll have to call your plate in. We've had a lot of break-ins around here during the winter, so I have to check out anyone who looks suspicious. I'm also going to write you a ticket. You're required to wear a motorcycle helmet in North Carolina."

"Can't you just show us the way to the address?" pleaded Cheryl. "We're supposed to meet Mr. Henley there."

Officer Clifford perked up. "You know Mr. Henley?"

"Yes. His housekeeper is probably there now, waiting for us. I'm sure she's worried. We're very late."

"The black woman?"

Cheryl hesitated. "I didn't know she was black; I haven't met her before."

"I've known Mr. Henley and his housekeeper, Aida, for a long time. Haven't seen them much in recent years. How do you know Mr. Henley?"

"I'm his nephew," offered Bill.

"They're probably worried sick about us," added Cheryl.

"Okay, why don't we do this? I'll show you the way to the Henley house and see if you check out."

They followed the police car a few miles up the coast and through myriad winding roads, ending up at a large isolated home, built on stilts, right on the beach. Parked in front was a late-model Buick LeSabre with Virginia plates.

The three of them walked up the steps to the entrance. As they started to ring the bell, the door opened and a well-dressed older black woman stepped out and enthusiastically hugged Bill and Cheryl. "I've

140

been so worried about you—I expected you much earlier. Is there a problem, Officer?"

"Not as long as you know these two. I found them down the road—they were lost."

"Bill here is Mr. Henley's nephew."

"So you've seen them before?"

She caught the slight shake of Bill's head. "Well, not in person, but I've seen a zillion pictures of them. They've come all the way from Hawaii to visit us."

"Where's Mr. Henley?

"Oh, he's on his way. He's caught in traffic."

Officer Clifford politely removed his hat, revealing a shock of white hair. He turned to Bill and Cheryl. "I apologize for the inconvenience. I'm only doing my job—you can't be too cautious with all the break-ins. Enjoy your visit." He started to walk away, but then turned back to Bill. "I'll let it go this time, but get a helmet before you take the motorcycle out."

. . .

The three of them watched as Officer Clifford drove off. As soon as he was out of sight, she ushered them inside and closed the door.

"Where's Wilhelm?" she asked in a panicked voice.

Bill took a deep breath. "He's dead. A man on a motorcycle shot him—tried to kill us too."

Her knees buckled as she brought her hands to her ears. "Oh no…," she sobbed. Bill and Cheryl steadied her and led her to a sofa. She collapsed, covering her face with a pillow, drowning it in tears.

. . .

A half hour of weeping later, Bill and Cheryl told Maddie what had happened.

"I can't believe it," she kept repeating. Streams of tears flowed down her dark cheeks. "Why would anybody kill Wilhelm?"

"Because of us. Somebody wants us dead, and he was in the way. I think we should go to the police," said Bill.

Maddie looked up through tears. "Wilhelm wouldn't want you to do that. He said it was important to keep you here. I've brought enough food for a week. He wanted to keep your whereabouts secret. There's something going on. He's been meeting the last few days with many people at our house in Virginia. They're planning something big—I think for today. It was very important to him. That's why he asked me to come here—he said he had to get right back to Washington. He was so excited, more so than I've seen him in years. I have this feeling that if you go to the police it will ruin everything."

"So we stay here?"

"Please, at least for a day or two, until whatever they were planning is over. That's what he would want."

"Are we safe here?" asked Cheryl.

"Nobody knows about this house. Wilhelm was always so careful to keep it secret. When he was younger, he would bring his wife and kids here using the name of Henley. He loved walking on the beach, but he never stayed long. He always had to rush back to Washington for some crisis."

"We have his gun," said Bill. "It's in the motorcycle. Should I get it?"

Maddie's face turned very serious. "Yes, go get it. I have my Smith & Wesson in the kitchen. I keep it there during the day and take it to bed with me at night. I'm a very good shot. Wilhelm taught me well."

CHAPTER FORTY-THREE

THE WILLARD INTERCONTINENTAL Hotel's meeting board indicated that Asset Reclamation Inc. had booked the John Adams Room from nine in the morning to three in the afternoon. The company had also reserved the adjoining Thomas Jefferson Room, but that booking wasn't on the public schedule.

Inside the Adams room Patrick O'Brien and Alex Sandoval paced back and forth, awaiting the arrival of Congressman's Luke's chief of staff. The small boardroom held an oblong table and eight chairs. Portraits of John Adams and eighteenth-century sketches of Washington, DC, lined the walls. Hidden next to one of the sketches was a tiny camera that would provide a live feed to James Lamont's laptop—in a room on the third floor. The adjoining Thomas Jefferson Room contained a video camera and a stenograph machine, in case it was needed.

For the meeting Patrick O'Brien had morphed into the impeccably dressed and flawlessly mannered Chase Wellington, the descendant of a high-society Boston Brahmin family. His upper-crust New England accent hinted at Phillips Exeter Academy, Harvard University, and Yale Law School. His six-foot height, angular jaw, and deeply cleft chin gave him an air of authority. His black hair was smoothed back, with a touch of gray added to provide additional dignity. He wore a sharply tailored charcoal Brooks Brothers suit and a blue silk tie.

Sandoval was the counter, with a no-nonsense edge and a working-class demeanor. Small, with a round face and close-set brown eyes, he went by the name of Agent Palmer.

The door to the room opened and a woman peered in, of medium height, thin, with straight blonde hair parted in the middle, showing just a hint of dark roots. Bright-red lipstick on a small mouth offset a pale face. O'Brien guessed her to be in her early forties.

"Am I in the right place?" she asked. "I'm Laura Jansen."

"Come on in," said O'Brien, flashing a friendly smile. "We've been expecting you."

"You sound different than on the phone."

"Oh, you spoke to Mr. Tyman. He won't be here today."

"Why not?"

"Because Mr. Tyman doesn't exist."

Her eyes opened wide and she tilted her head quizzically sideways. "What do you mean?"

Moving quickly before she fully processed what he had just told her, O'Brien flashed an identification card. "My name is Chase Wellington, from the United States Office of the Attorney General. My colleague is Agent Palmer with the Federal Bureau of Investigation." Sandoval gave her a half smile and held up an FBI badge.

"Please have a seat," said O'Brien, gesturing to a chair at the table. His voice was authoritative but nonthreatening.

"I don't understand," she said, still standing.

"We are investigating a leak of extremely sensitive top-secret information that threatens the security of the United States, and we need to have a chat with you."

"Why didn't you tell me that over the phone? Why this charade about an inheritance?" Her face knotted in frustration.

"Because, Laura…Can I call you Loraine?"

"If you wish," she answered nastily.

"Because we were concerned that you might not be willing to meet with us if we told you our real reason, and besides, we couldn't reveal the purpose over the phone, owing to national security protocols."

"Why wouldn't I be willing to meet you?"

"Because, Laura, you are a target of the investigation."

She took a slight step backward. "Shouldn't I have a lawyer?"

O'Brien laughed her off. "Oh, we're nowhere close to that. We just want to share the status of our investigation and give you reasonable warning. The time for lawyers is later—if we decide to proceed with prosecution. As you can see, this is an informal meeting. We're not taking notes…We're not recording anything. As I indicated, this is an opportunity for an informal talk—a very preliminary phase of our investigative process. Now please sit."

She took a seat.

"I am going to show you some photographs. You are not required to make any statement. I want to go through the evidence to see if there is anything we may have missed or misinterpreted."

"Okay," she said in a low voice.

Sandoval placed an eight-by-ten color photograph in front of her.

Laura looked up, surprised. "That's the lobby of my apartment building."

O'Brien waved her off. "You don't have to volunteer any information. As I said, this is informal. Let me do the talking—and you are right, it is the lobby of your apartment building, 802 Pennsylvania Avenue."

Sandoval put down the next photograph, side-by-side images of a man in the lobby, labeled with different time stamps: one from 9:52 in the evening and one from three minutes after ten. O'Brien watched as her eyes widened and her face flushed. "This man has been seen entering and leaving the lobby of your apartment building on consecutive Thursdays. His name is Dr. John Cameron, and he's the chief chemist for the CIA's central lab."

She sat rigid, her lips tightening.

Sandoval pulled out another picture, side-by-side close-ups of the case the man carried, with accompanying time stamps.

O'Brien studied her as she briefly glanced at the photos. Her expression showed no reaction, but he noticed beads of perspiration forming on her brow. "In each of these pictures, you can see that Dr. Cameron is carrying a small brown case. At first we assumed it was the same case, but our spectrographic analysis indicated they are different. It appears an exchange took place somewhere in the apartment building."

She glanced at her watch and then at the ceiling. "I don't see what any of this has to do with me." She stood up. "You're wasting my time."

"Please," said O'Brien in a calm, reassuring voice. "Give me a few more minutes to explain. We know from our video surveillance that Dr. Cameron took the elevator to the sixth floor. We have a list of those living on that floor."

"I live on that floor. So what!"

O'Brien sensed the need to reassure her. "As I previously indicated, you don't need to confirm or deny anything. Until a few days ago we didn't know to whom Dr. Cameron was making the delivery…but now we have his statement." O'Brien reached into a briefcase and slapped a two-inch-thick document on the table. The cover read, "Sworn Statement of Dr. John Cameron." It was entirely fabricated. O'Brien flipped to the back page of the document and pointed to the signature in blue ink. "I can't let you read the statement, but it's signed and dated by Dr. Cameron."

"I don't know this man."

O'Brien noticed her rapid blinking. "Again, Laura, you don't have to confirm or deny anything, but I thought you'd want to know that Dr. Cameron claims he delivered the case to you. He further contends that the case contains a top-secret drug of critical importance to national security. He stated that he has been siphoning it off from the CIA lab."

Laura staggered backward. "I'm leaving." She turned for the door.

O'Brien raised his voice, formal and commanding. "You are free to leave at any time, but if you walk out of that door we will charge you with multiple counts of felony violations of United States espionage and secrecy laws. With the video surveillance of your apartment building and the statement by Dr. Cameron, a conviction is certain. We will arrest you this evening and take you straight to federal prison. Because of the nature of the crime, you won't be eligible for bail. After you're convicted, you will spend anywhere from forty years to life in prison. You can leave if you want, but if you do, the next few hours will be your last taste of freedom."

Her face became bright crimson.

"Are you really sure you want to walk out that door? Once you leave, there's no coming back—ever."

"I demand to see an attorney," she yelled.

"Fine, you will have the right to an attorney when you are arrested." O'Brien shook his head slowly and lowered his voice. His face softened. "But you see, Laura, we really don't want to charge you at all; we just want your cooperation. Please come back and let me explain." He opened his hand and gestured to her chair, as if inviting her to sit down for dinner.

She slowly returned and took her seat. "So you want me to become an informant? Well, I have nothing to inform. If you expect me to incriminate Congressman Luke, you're mistaken."

"I don't remember mentioning Congressman Luke."

Her face reddened again.

"But you are right. We're not interested in you. We're after your boss. We suspect that he has been using the drug to influence other congressmen as part of his tea sessions. We are prepared to charge him with offenses that are even more serious than we have slated for you. In addition to grievous violations of federal espionage laws, we will charge him with felonious restraint, fraud, coercion, and other crimes. He will spend the rest of his life in prison. But we don't want that to happen. That's why we're having this conversation."

"What do you want, then?"

O'Brien opened his arms as if he were parting the sea. "We want all this to go away. Obviously there is a reason the drug is classified top secret. I have only limited knowledge, but I understand the intelligence community is adamant that it remain secret. My understanding is that its exposure would cripple the war on terror and irrevocably damage the safety and security of the American people. Therefore, if we file charges against the congressman, we will have to reveal the existence of the drug. We don't want to do that. Instead we want Congressman Luke to voluntarily resign, and we need your help in convincing him to do so."

O'Brien moved to the other side of the table. "There are two scenarios before us, Laura. Scenario one, you refuse to cooperate. In that case you, the congressman, and Dr. Cameron will spend many decades in prison, quite possibly the rest of your lives."

O'Brien placed his hands on the table in front of Laura, leaned in, and stared into her face. "Scenario two, you cooperate and Congressman Luke resigns. The bottom line is that he isn't charged, you're not charged, and Dr. Cameron is not charged. You are all free to go on with your lives. For this second scenario to become a reality, we need your cooperation. We need a videotaped and sworn statement as to what you know, just like the one we obtained from Dr. Cameron."

"What if I make a statement and the congressman still refuses to resign. What then?"

"We will file charges against the congressman, but not against you."

Sandoval placed a sheet of paper on the table.

"This is a letter signed by the assistant attorney general," said O'Brien. "It promises you immunity from prosecution if you fully cooperate." He pushed the forged letter in front of her.

148

She read it and her face pointed to the ceiling. O'Brien could tell she was debating everything in her mind. Her eyes darted back and forth, and she shifted her position uncomfortably. He had expected her to cave by now.

"I need a cigarette," she said, reaching for her handbag.

"You're not allowed to smoke in here," said Sandoval.

"It's okay," said O'Brien. "Go ahead."

She lit a cigarette and inhaled slowly.

O'Brien quietly and patiently watched her, unable to read her face. He caught himself rubbing his index finger along the cleft of his chin, an unconscious mannerism that surfaced when he became nervous.

Finally she took a long last draw on the cigarette and blew the smoke defiantly out of her nostrils. "Here's what I think…This is a setup. You already told me you don't want the drug exposed. You're badgering me to help you get rid of the congressman, but my hunch is that if I refuse to cooperate, nothing will happen. I'm going to call your bluff—I'm leaving."

O'Brien signaled to Sandoval, who quickly blocked the door.

"What?" she shouted when she saw Sandoval. "You're going to hold me in here against my will? That would be a big mistake. Congressman Luke is very powerful—you don't know who you are dealing with."

O'Brien knew the time had come to play his ace, thanks to information provided to Wilhelm Kronig by Connie Blythe. "On the contrary, we know exactly who we are dealing with. In addition to being a traitor and a liar, we are dealing with a pervert and a rapist."

She stopped cold.

"We know the congressman has been drugging and raping interns in your office, and we know you are well aware of his behavior. We have two young women, Aubrielle Blake and Annie Weaver, who are prepared to testify. We have Jason Cassidy from your office, who claims he heard you tell the congressman that the drug wasn't meant to satisfy his dick. That's a quote."

She stared back in disbelief.

"Did you know that Annie Weaver is pregnant? We have the paternity test for her, and I'm sure when charges are filed the judge will order a blood test for the congressman. I think we both know what the results will show. You, Loraine, are an accessory to rape and sexual assault, a crime that carries many years in prison. Oh, and did I mention that if you ever do get out of prison, you will have to register as a sex offender?"

O'Brien waved his hand at Sandoval. "Step aside and let her leave." His voice dripped with contempt.

Sandoval moved away from the door, but Laura stood frozen. "Are you offering to drop the sex charges against me as well?"

"Yes. Same terms as before. We are authorized to grant you immunity from prosecution."

O'Brien knew he had turned her. She was white as a ghost.

"What do you need me to do?"

"As I previously said, give us a signed statement on camera."

She looked around the room. "I don't see how I have any choice."

CHAPTER FORTY-FOUR

LAMONT WATCHED THE interview on his laptop in his hotel room. His stomach churned as the meeting progressed and he feared they were going to lose her. Her fierce resistance until the end unnerved him, as Kronig had assured everybody it would go smoothly. Now Kronig was missing. He'd phoned Lamont two days ago, indicating he had to make an unexpected trip out of town, but would return in time for the interview. Since then Lamont had heard nothing. He'd called Kronig's cell phone several times, but the calls went to voice mail. He'd also called Kronig's home, hoping that Maddie could fill him in on his whereabouts, but nobody answered. Lamont agonized over calling the operation off in light of Kronig's absence, but decided to proceed, given all the time, preparation, and expense they had put into the plan.

O'Brien, Sandoval, and Laura Jansen moved to the adjoining Thomas Jefferson Room. Laura sat in a chair in front of a video camera. O'Brien explained that she was to talk directly and clearly into the camera, relating her story—how she'd learned about the drug, how it had been transferred to her, and how Congressman Luke was using it. Next to her chair was a voice-recognition stenography system. It would translate her words into text and print out the pages. O'Brien explained that when she finished her testimony she could review the transcript, make any changes, and sign the document.

In a clear but halting voice, Laura explained how one afternoon Congressman Luke had asked her to check out the background of a Dr. John Cameron who had been calling the office asking for a meeting. Cameron claimed he had inside knowledge of illegal CIA activities. Laura was able to verify his credentials and set up a private meeting.

Later Congressman Luke summarized to her what Cameron had told him. He claimed that his lab was manufacturing a secret drug and distributing it to Guantánamo and to other CIA interrogation sites in Uzbekistan and Poland. He had never been told the purpose of the drug, only the formula and the production steps. However, he knew from another source that it was an extremely powerful, behavior-modifying, hypnotic drug. The CIA had covertly developed it the 1960s at the University of Wisconsin. In addition to aiding in the interrogation of prisoners, it was being used in extremely risky and illegal covert operations. Furthermore, he claimed that the CIA had kept the existence of the drug hidden from the president, the vice president, and Congress.

She related that Cameron said he had learned the truth about the drug from a close friend named Alfred Wolaski who had been his colleague at the CIA and later a national security adviser to the vice president. He claimed that the CIA had engineered Wolaski's firing for attempting to inform the president about the drug. Cameron alleged that the CIA leadership had threatened to kill Wolaski if he ever disclosed anything about the drug. Wolaski had disappeared eighteen months earlier, and later his decomposing body had surfaced in Montana.

Laura cleared her throat and asked for water. Sandoval handed her a glass. She took a sip and continued. "Cameron said he wanted to help the congressman take down the CIA leadership. He said they were recklessly out of control. In his opinion they were undermining the president's foreign policy and lying to Congress. Congressman Luke suspected that his real motive was revenge for his friend's death."

"Did Congressman Luke really believe that the CIA killed Wolaski?" asked O'Brien.

"He was skeptical, but shared Cameron's contempt for the CIA leadership."

"What did Cameron tell Congressman Luke about the drug?"

"It worked by enhancing hypnosis. A small dose could influence an individual's perspectives and thought processes. Larger doses could have extreme effects, forcing people to do things that would harm themselves or others and violate their own moral codes…something not possible under normal hypnosis. Even greater doses could block or change people's memories. In its extreme, Cameron claimed the drug could reduce people to slaves."

"So how did Congressman Luke start using it in his tea sessions?"

"After their initial meeting, Cameron and the congressman met several times in secret. Then Congressman Luke told me that Cameron would be delivering a case to my apartment on Thursday nights after nine. He said it would be best if Cameron was not seen coming to the Capitol. He told me to bring the case with me to work the next day. That established the weekly exchange.

"I told him that I didn't want to be involved unless I knew what was in the case and what he was planning to do with it. He was reluctant to include me, but finally capitulated, telling me he was going to use very small dosages to help persuade other congressmen to support his positions on national security and the CIA. I was appalled at first, but he convinced me that the drug was simply a means to get attention. He made it sound innocuous. He used the analogy that it was like using a bullhorn to amplify his voice—that's all. I should have known better, but I went along.

"Congressman Luke would invite another congressman over to his office for an informal chat. I would prepare the tea, putting five eyedrops of the drug into the visitor's teacup—that's all it took. After drinking some of the tea, the visitor would become very relaxed, even euphoric. It wasn't like hypnosis you see in the movies. Congressman Luke would tell the visitor to relax and request that they give him thirty minutes of their undivided attention to explain his views. By the end of the meeting, he had them eating out of his hand, pledging their support and acknowledging that the meeting had been a revelation, although they couldn't recall any specifics. They would turn one hundred and eighty degrees on policy issues."

…

As the videotaping continued, O'Brien asked additional clarifying and explanatory questions. When satisfied that she had fully documented the tea sessions, he switched gears to the meetings with the interns and the sexual relations. Her face and posture dropped.

"I heard the rumors that Congressman Luke had a roving eye, and several times I noticed him ogling women in the office. It isn't public, but he is estranged from his wife in Missouri. I wasn't aware of any overt sexual indiscretions, only murmurings that he liked the ladies. So I was surprised when one of the staff told me that he met alone with some of the female interns when I was away. I asked the interns about the meetings, and they told me that he wanted to hear their perspectives on national issues. When I questioned them further, they were very vague about what had transpired. I should have been more suspicious, but I looked the other way, at least in the beginning. Then I noticed that we were running out of the drug much faster than we should. I put two and two together and confronted the congressman. At first he denied it, but I knew by his face that he was lying. He ended up confessing on his knees crying. He told me it was some touching and oral sex, not intercourse. He begged me to forgive him for his weakness. I agreed if he promised it would never happen again. I didn't believe he was raping them."

…

After Laura finished her testimony, she reviewed the printed transcript, making small corrections with a blue pen. In each case O'Brien reviewed the changes. They were mainly to spelling and grammatical errors. When finished, she lifted her head to O'Brien.

"May I leave?"

"As soon as you sign the document."

He held her stare as her face shifted from a look of defeat to one of satisfaction, suggesting some new insight had crossed her mind. In a panic O'Brien feared she was going to refuse to sign it. Again he rubbed his finger along the cleft of his chin.

She smiled. "You really don't know the full story, do you? What's happening is much bigger than you think."

O'Brien started to ask her what she meant, but she immediately started signing the document, except she didn't stop after completing her signature. She added something handwritten at the bottom of the page. When done, she quickly flipped the document over and stood up.

"I've given you everything you asked for. I'm leaving."

"Can I see what you just wrote?"

"After I leave," she said, gathering her purse and quickly heading for the door.

"I advise you not to communicate with Congressman Luke for at least thirty-six hours," said O'Brien. "We will be paying him a visit in the meantime."

"Are you serious? After what I just did? I'll never talk to him again in my life." She shook her head. "I'll tell you what I'm going to do. I'm going to stop by a liquor store on my way home and buy the biggest bottle of Jack Daniel's they have. Then I'm going back to my apartment, lock the door, and disconnect my phones." She marched quickly out of the room.

O'Brien turned over the document and read what she had written after her signature. Immediately his cell phone rang. "What just happened?" asked Lamont.

"You better come here and read this. It changes things."

CHAPTER FORTY-FIVE

AFTER LAURA JANSEN departed, Lamont walked the two blocks from the Willard Hotel to Scotty Olds's office in the Eisenhower Executive Office Building adjacent to the White House. Sitting at a mahogany desk in front of a large map of the world, Olds slowly and carefully read the transcript. When he reached the last page, he quickly lifted his head. "What the hell is this at the end?" Beneath her signature Laura had drawn an arrow to the bottom of the page and written, "Congressman Luke has kept the vice president informed about the drug every step of the way."

"She's implicating the vice president?" asked Olds.

"It appears so, although it may be a tactical ploy, a red herring. She knows that we don't want to go after Luke publicly; we only want his resignation. By mentioning the vice president, she makes it much harder for us to threaten to release her testimony to the press. We would be accusing the vice president of treason, and we have no evidence to support that. It would escalate the whole matter to a constitutional crisis. It may be her insurance that she and Congressman Luke will never be exposed."

"Is she really that clever?" asked Olds.

"I don't know. Or the other possibility is the vice president really is involved."

"Actually, it might help us when we show the transcript to Congressman Luke. If it's true, that would put more pressure on Luke to resign. He wouldn't want to finger the vice president."

"But if it is a fabrication, we're sunk."

"It's a chance we have to take. I've had some suspicions about the vice president, especially given his close ties to Luke and the new CIA director, Goodwin. It's a gamble."

Lamont shifted the conversation back to their plan. "Are you still sure Congressman Luke will be at the dinner tonight?"

"I checked again, it's on his schedule, and it would be an insult to the State Department for him to be a no-show. I'll take him aside during the reception and let him read the transcript—convince him that he has to resign or we're going to the press."

"And if he calls our bluff?"

"Then we lose. We're not going to release it—it contains top-secret information." Olds thought for a few moments. "I wish we had another way to ratchet up the pressure—make him believe that we really will go to the press."

"What about that newspaper reporter that Wilhelm mentioned? Connie Blythe. She's the one who told him about the rapes. What if I call her and offer her a scoop?"

"That's risky," said Olds.

"Hear me out. We tell her that we have a written confession from Congressman Luke's chief of staff concerning the sex crimes, nothing more. We indicate that we are trying to convince him to resign. If he refuses, we promise to give her the testimony, but only the parts related to the rapes—we redact everything else. If he resigns, we withdraw the offer."

"I'm not following you."

"It's leverage. We tell Congressman Luke that we have a reporter lined up to run the story. We give him the name of the reporter, so he's less likely to call our bluff."

"Will Ms. Blythe cooperate?" asked Olds.

"Probably not, but you never know."

"See if you can find her, but you have to act fast. I'll be seeing Congressman Luke sometime between six and seven."

Lamont's watch read 1:20 in the afternoon.

CHAPTER FORTY-SIX

AT FOUR IN the afternoon, Connie Blythe met James Lamont in the hotel lobby of the Key Bridge Marriott, a few blocks from her office in Rosslyn. They moved to a secluded couch in a far corner.

Connie read the heavily redacted copy of Laura Jansen's transcript without emotion. "Most of this is blacked out. All that's here is confirmation that the congressman was raping female interns. I already knew that."

"The rest involves national security."

"Like how he has been using the drug in his tea sessions to influence other congressmen—now that would be a real scoop."

"The rapes aren't enough for you?"

"As I said, it just confirms what I already know. What do you really want from me?"

"We want the congressman to resign, and, quite frankly, to keep this out of the papers."

Connie raised her eyebrows. "If that's the case, why are you talking to a reporter?"

"We were hoping to use you as leverage to increase the pressure on Luke to resign…by mentioning your name when we confront him. I know you're already working on the rape story—Wilhelm Kronig told me."

The mention of Kronig rattled Connie. "Are you a friend of Mr. Kronig?"

"Yes, an old friend."

"Have you spoken to him lately? He was supposed to call me."

Lamont stared at her, his eyebrows furrowed. "I don't know where he is; he's missing."

"Shit," murmured Connie. "Anyway, I can't use this testimony."

"Why not?"

"Because the two women who were raped are my confidential sources. I can't release anything without their permission, and they don't want to come forward. So this is no help."

Lamont went quiet, his face narrowing in disappointment. He folded the transcript into his suit pocket and stood up. "I understand. Thank you for your time, Ms. Blythe. One last question, however. Why were you expecting a call from Wilhelm Kronig?"

"I'm not at liberty to tell you," she said.

"Does it have anything to do with Ryan Butler and Alana Shannon?"

Her eyes tilted upward. "Again, I'm not at liberty to tell you."

Connie stayed seated as Lamont stood above her, immobile, his face distant, rubbing his chin. He appeared so upset that she felt sorry for him. "There is something I could do—I could call his office and ask him to comment on an article I'm working on about a secret drug and his tea sessions. If he comes on the phone, I'll ask him if he's using drugs to influence congressmen and molest interns. That should get his attention."

"You'll do that?"

"Yes, but on the condition that if he talks, and reveals anything, I'm free to use it."

Lamont knew that Luke would never spill to a reporter. "I'll agree to that because I know he won't tell you anything."

"But I bet it will shake him up. I assume that's the kind of leverage you're looking for."

"Exactly."

CHAPTER FORTY-SEVEN

BRUCE MARKO PULLED his Chevy Malibu onto the shoulder of Route 17 in North Carolina, close to what his laptop indicated was the location of Kronig's car—still transmitting its GPS signal. Through a drenching downpour, Marko could barely discern the tire tracks crossing from the road into the trees and shrubs. He knew that in a few hours the rain would wash them away.

He continued to seethe over his assignment to track down Kronig's Cadillac. Director Goodwin and Crowder had celebrated when they learned that Kronig's car had come to a stop off the highway in a remote part of eastern North Carolina. They assumed that the motorcycle man had completed his mission and Ryan and Alana were dead, as well as Kronig. They became increasingly concerned when the motorcycle man didn't check in after the job, as required by the contract and necessary for payment.

Marko wanted no part of it, believing they had crossed the line when they ordered Kronig's assassination. Nevertheless, he needed to stay in their good graces to keep his job.

He exited the car and followed the tracks. He cleared his way through a thick wall of shrubs until the swamp came into view. In the distance he spotted the Cadillac partly submerged in mud. Twenty feet beyond lay the dark figure of a man. Marko assumed it was Ryan Butler's body. He looked around for Alana Shannon's body, but it was nowhere he sight.

He returned to his car and donned a pair of hip boots and rain gear. Once dressed, he began slogging through the swamp, heading for the body in the mud. As he approached he observed boots sticking up. The dead man wore a dark motorcycle jacket, and his face was a mess of raw, swollen flesh. Although he had never seen him in person, Marko knew it was the motorcycle man. He waded over to the Cadillac. A seat belt held up Kronig's blood-soaked body, but his head was slumped over his chest. Marko reached through the window and felt along Kronig's jacket, searching for his firearm holster. It was empty. Next he reached into Kronig's side pocket, searching for his wallet. It was right where he'd expected it. He felt farther down along the jacket lining until he detected another pocket, this one zippered. Inside he found a thinner wallet with a different driver's license. The face belonged to Kronig, but the name was Martin Henley, 334 North Atlantic Drive, Duck, North Carolina. He knew he had discovered the location of Kronig's secret beach house.

Marko tried to patch the sequence together. The motorcycle man had shot at the car, hitting Kronig and forcing him off the road. As the motorcycle man approached the vehicle, the injured Kronig shot and killed him through the front windshield. Kronig later died of his injuries. However, if that was the case, where was the weapon? He searched the inside of the car but found no trace. All he found was Alana's handbag and two suitcases in the trunk. He spent an hour trekking through the swamp, searching for the gun and for Alana and Ryan's bodies. It slowly dawned on him that maybe Ryan and Alana had escaped. There was no sign of any motorcycle. As improbable as it seemed, he wondered whether they had killed the motorcycle man and taken off on his cycle. He kept rejecting that theory, but finally concluded there was no alternative explanation.

It took two round-trips for Marko to lug Ryan and Alana's possessions from the Cadillac to his car. He wanted to remove any trace of them. He knew that in a few more weeks the car and the motorcycle man's body would completely sink into the swamp. In the meantime, if someone discovered the car, the authorities would find evidence of only two people at the scene.

Marko dialed Crowder over his secure cell phone line.

"What did you find?" asked Crowder.

"Is the director there?"

"I'm here," grumbled a voice in the background.

"Kronig is dead. Shot in the face and the chest. The motorcycle man is dead too, a bullet through his head."

"Where the hell are Alana and Ryan?" yelled Director Goodwin.

"I don't know. There's no sign of them or the motorcycle."

"Shit. How could have they escaped?" asked Goodwin.

"I don't know."

"You have to find them. Do you have any idea where they are?"

"Not really. Kronig was taking them to his beach house. I found the address—it's in the town of Duck on the Outer Banks. They could be heading there, or maybe they've gone to the police. Who knows? Perhaps they're trying to get as far away as possible."

"We're unaware of any police reports," said Crowder. "We need to find them before they ruin everything."

Now it was the director's voice. "I want you to check out Kronig's house in Duck, see if they're holed up there. Let's hope they haven't gone to the authorities or split."

"And if I find them, then what?"

"Kill them," ordered the director.

Marko took a deep breath. "I'm sorry, sir, I took an oath. It's against the law to kill citizens."

The director scoffed. "But you're okay hiring a contractor to do the job for you."

"That's different. I don't directly participate in the killing."

"I don't have time for your semantic games, and we don't have time to bring in another contractor. You'll have to do it."

"I can't do that."

"You listen to me and listen well. Everything is at stake here. If you refuse to obey, I will bury you. These orders are coming from high up—understand?" His voice oozed with menace.

"You're giving me a direct order to kill US citizens?"

"Don't play games with me—just do as you're told."

Marko waited a long time before responding. "I'll get back to you."

CHAPTER FORTY-EIGHT

SCOTTY OLDS ARRIVED at the State Department Building in Foggy Bottom at six in the evening for the cocktail reception preceding the formal awards dinner. The annual event recognized State Department staff, deployed around the world and at home, for diplomatic accomplishments and for other achievements.

Olds sported a formal black dinner jacket with a bright white shirt and a black bowtie, as did most of the men. In contrast, the women wore evening dresses in a rainbow of glittery colors. Waiters in white jackets glided among the guests carrying silver trays of hors d'oeuvres and crystal glasses of champagne.

Olds sipped only water, wanting to keep his mind clear and sharp. The reception spilled outside to a large patio overlooking the National Mall. Several dozen propane heaters warmed the patio, and the mall glowed majestically, lit up in white floodlights all the way from the Jefferson Memorial to the Lincoln Memorial. Olds moved back and forth from the outside to the inside, making small talk, but all the time searching for Congressman Luke. He wasn't there.

When the reception hour ended, everyone moved into the elegantly gilded Benjamin Franklin State Dining Room. Huge red marble Corinthian columns lined the banquet room, which was adorned with elaborate gold moldings. Large cut-glass crystal chandeliers hung in rows. The Great Seal of the United States looked down from the ceiling in bas relief. Gold-backed chairs circled stylishly set tables. Those in the front were reserved for the vice president, the secretary of state, and other high-ranking dignitaries.

Olds had viewed the seating chart and knew exactly were Congressman Luke would be, close to the front table, grouped with representatives and senators from key foreign relations and intelligence committees. Olds sat a few tables away, joined by representatives from the Justice Department. He eyed Congressman Luke's empty seat. He worried that Laura Jansen might have changed her mind and alerted him.

Olds exchanged pleasantries with his colleagues as everybody waited for the arrival of the vice president and the secretary of state. All the while he kept checking Congressman Luke's empty chair.

The guests stood and applauded when the vice president and the secretary of state entered through a side door. Olds breathed easier when he saw Congressman Luke trailing the vice president into the dining room and taking his assigned seat.

Although it wasn't the most opportune time, he had to make his move. The waitstaff were beginning to serve salads as he walked over to Congressman Luke's table. He came from behind and put his hand on the congressman's shoulder. Luke glanced up, scowling.

"Hello, Scotty," said Luke, with thinly disguised contempt.

"I need to talk to you."

"Fine," said Luke. "Call my office and my administrative assistant will set a meeting." He immediately turned his attention back to his salad, ignoring Olds.

"I mean right now."

"Can't you see I'm eating?" His raised voice attracted the stares of the others at the table.

"It's about your chief of staff." Olds placed a typed notecard in front of Luke, angling it so only the congressman could see it.

"I have with me a signed confession by your chief of staff, Laura Jansen, documenting your use of a top-secret drug, illegally obtained from the CIA, for purpose of drugging and influencing other congressmen during your tea sessions."

The blood rushed to Luke's face. He stood up and slapped his napkin down on his plate. "Please excuse me," he said to the other guests, and huffily followed Olds out of the banquet room, down a small hallway, and to a side room, the Walter Thurston Gentlemen's Lounge.

Inside the lounge Olds closed the door. Colonial furniture and early American landscape paintings filled the room, and they sat down on an uncomfortable hard-backed yellow couch with an antique table in front. Olds handed Luke a copy of Laura Jansen's testimony. The muscles in Luke's neck tightened as he read the first few pages. His face bristled. "This is all crap, there's not a word of truth in here. How did you get this?"

"You'll note it's signed by your chief of staff. Look at the last page."

Luke grumbled under his breath when he read the handwritten note. "This is clearly a forgery."

"We have the entire testimony on videotape, including her signing of the document."

He gritted his teeth. "Then she is obviously a deranged woman. I had no idea she was psychotic."

"There's no point in denying it. You know it's true. The *Beltway Insider* is going to run the story on Monday."

Luke slammed his fist hard on the antique table and pulled it back in pain. "Fuck you! You have no idea who you are dealing with. If you try to drag the vice president into this, we will crush you." He immediately stood up, and Olds sprang to his feet.

"Step aside, you little asshole," Luke shouted, towering over Olds.

"There's a way out. If you resign by six o'clock tomorrow afternoon, the story won't run. It will all disappear."

"You can't prove anything. It's only the pathetic testimony of a disgruntled employee."

"Even if we can't prove everything, the release of the document will ruin you. All those who had tea will be suspicious and will avoid you like the plague. The media will go berserk. Your political career will be trash."

"Get out of my way," demanded Luke, shoving an arm into Olds's chest, almost knocking him over.

Olds raised his voice. "Then there are the rape allegations and the intern you impregnated under the influence of the drug, Annie Weaver. It's all in the transcript, read the last few pages."

Luke stopped and swung around, his face ghostly. "You bastard," he screamed, and charged toward him, his fists flying.

Olds ducked beneath a wild punch and rushed past him to the door. "You have until six o'clock Sunday—think about it." He exited the lounge and headed back to the banquet.

For the remainder of the evening, Olds stared at Luke's empty seat, wondering what he would do.

. . .

Congressman Luke stayed behind in the lounge, reading the entire testimony carefully, cursing under his breath. He took out his cell phone and dialed Laura Jansen. He heard a recorded message indicating the phone was out of service. "Stupid cunt," he screamed. He started to compose an e-mail message to her, but noticed a long string of texts from his press secretary. Each indicated that a reporter named Connie Blythe with the *Beltway Insider* was trying to reach him for comment on a story she was planning to run on Monday—something about the illegal use of a top-secret drug.

Congressman Luke heaved his phone across the room, smashing it against the opposite wall, just missing a revered Western landscape by Charles M. Russell.

CHAPTER FORTY-NINE

RAINDROPS PELTED THE picture window as Bill and Cheryl looked out on a gray and gloomy ocean. Thick, dark clouds obscured the horizon.

"We're in a house by a beach again," said Cheryl in a tone of despair.

"Wrong house and wrong beach," said Bill.

They had spent the night there. Maddie had cooked dinner and breakfast, but they ate without enjoyment, saying little, shrouded in gloom. Maddie kept busy, but the lines of pain and grief on her face were obvious. After breakfast she'd retreated to her bedroom.

"I'm not sure about this," said Bill. "I feel helpless waiting here, doing nothing. I know she asked us not to go to the police, but I'm afraid waiting will just make matters worse."

"We promised her we wouldn't contact the authorities until tomorrow," said Cheryl. "We owe her that."

The sound of a car pulling into the driveway startled them. Maddie quickly bolted out of her bedroom, clutching her Smith & Wesson. "Get your weapon," she shouted to Bill. They heard the car door slam shut.

Bill grabbed Kronig's gun and the three of them moved to the front entrance. Through the side glass panels they watched a dark figure quickly climb the stairs. The doorbell rang. Maddie slowly opened it until the safety latch caught. Bill stood behind her with his gun raised. Cheryl watched from the kitchen.

"Maddie," said the voice on the other side of the door. "It's me, Bruce Marko. Please let me in."

"Oh, Bruce, I'm so glad you're here." She lowered her gun, undid the latch, and opened the door. She rushed to hug him.

Marko stepped back, surprised by the warm greeting. He awkwardly patted her on the back, looking very uncomfortable.

Bill and Cheryl watched with suspicion as the man entered the hallway.

"Wilhelm is dead!" cried Maddie.

"I know," said Marko, making eye contact with Bill and Cheryl, noticing the pistol in Bill's hand. "You won't need that...I'm here to protect you."

"Marko is an old colleague of Wilhelm's," said Maddie. "I've known him for years. Wilhelm always trusted him—you can too."

Bill laid the gun on the kitchen counter.

"I know you don't remember me, but I know you. I helped Wilhelm set you up on Molokai." He turned to Cheryl with a disapproving gaze. "They really did a hack job on your face, didn't they? You used to be so beautiful."

Maddie glared at Marko.

"Oh, you're still good-looking, just not the knockout you once were."

"Forgive Marko," said Maddie. "His people skills are terrible."

Marko changed the subject. "I've just come from Wilhelm's car in the swamp. There's another body there—the motorcycle man—a contract killer for the CIA."

"What? The CIA wouldn't harm Wilhelm," said Maddie.

"There are new people in charge who don't give a damn about anything or anybody. They have no respect." Although Marko's words were emotionally charged, his facial expression stayed like granite. He looked to Bill and Cheryl. "It was you he was after—Wilhelm was in the wrong place at the wrong time."

Maddie doubled over, sobbing again.

"How did you know where to find the car?" asked Bill.

"I didn't. Wilhelm told me he was taking you to his place in Duck. He said he would call me when he got to the beach house…that I might need to come down and guard you after he assessed the situation. I got worried when he failed to follow through, so I decided to investigate. The CIA taught me to be very observant. As I drove down Route 17, I saw tire tracks heading off the road. Most people wouldn't have noticed, but I stopped to check it out."

"Wilhelm told you about the beach house?" asked Maddie, looking up through streams of tears. "He's never told anyone before."

"It was just two days ago. He said these were special times."

Maddie seemed satisfied with his response. "Are you sure we're safe here? If he told you about the house, maybe he told somebody else."

"I don't think so. He only told me because he wanted me to protect Bill and Cheryl." He looked at them. "I don't think anybody will find his car, at least for a while. In case they do, I removed all evidence that you two were there. I have your handbag and luggage with me. Did you kill the man on the motorcycle?" Marko asked Bill.

"Cheryl shot him…in self-defense."

"I don't know how you managed to pull that off. I couldn't find any trace of Wilhelm's gun…Is that it there?" He pointed to the firearm on the counter.

"Yes," answered Bill.

"Somebody must be a great shot. Anyway, I'll go get your luggage." He turned around and walked down the steps back to his car.

"What's wrong with him?" Cheryl asked Maddie.

"He doesn't relate well to people; he rubs everybody the wrong way. Wilhelm thought he might be borderline autistic, but he always told me that he was straight as an arrow and one hundred percent trustworthy. They worked together for a long time." Just as Maddie finished, Marko walked back in carrying Cheryl's handbag over his shoulder and a suitcase in each hand.

Bill and Cheryl took the bags to their bedroom, wanting to change out of their crummy sweat clothes. They showered, dressed, and returned to the living room. Maddie put on coffee, and they all settled around the kitchen table.

"Wilhelm indicated that something big was going to happen in the next few days," said Maddie. "He was very upbeat and optimistic. They've been meeting about it for the past few days."

"Who has?" asked Marko.

"James Lamont and some others. You didn't know?"

"I knew something was up, but Wilhelm didn't share the details with me. It's all about the need to know."

"So what are we going to do?" asked Bill. "Cheryl and I thought we should go to the police, but Maddie asked us to wait."

"She's absolutely right. You shouldn't go to the authorities. Let's wait and see what happens with whatever Kronig had in the works. If you go to the police, they can't guarantee your safety. These people are vicious. If they were willing to kill Wilhelm, a few police officers wouldn't mean much. He asked me to make sure you're safe, and that's what I'm going to do."

"So we just stay here?" asked Maddie.

"No. I think you should go back to your house in Virginia. Make everything seem normal. We need to keep his murder a secret for now."

"So I'm supposed to pretend that nothing has happened?" asked Maddie, her lips quivering.

"I know that will be hard, but yes, at least for a few more days. You go home and I'll stay here with Ryan and Alana."

CHAPTER FIFTY

WHILE MADDIE PACKED, Cheryl, Bill, and Marko sat at the kitchen table.

"I apologize for what I said earlier, about your looks," said Marko. "Sometimes I don't think before I speak. I didn't mean any offense."

"None taken," lied Cheryl.

"It's just that I thought you were so gorgeous. Before you were given the drug, I would notice how you two looked at each other. You'd smile and hold hands. I remember thinking that's what being in love must be like."

"You've never been in love?" asked Cheryl, widening her eyes in sympathy.

"No. I'm incapable. There's something lacking in me. Oh, I've had sex with plenty of women. They seem to find me attractive at first, but I always end up disappointing them. They want something from me that I can't give them."

"I'm sorry," said Cheryl. She reached over and patted his hand. Marko placed his other hand over hers.

Bill cringed. He didn't like the way Marko was staring at Cheryl or how she was looking back doe eyed. He hated that Marko was touching her fingers. His eyes narrowed at Marko. "We're going to take a walk on the beach," he said curtly, breaking off the conversation. The rain had stopped and the sun peeked through gray clouds, focusing a large spotlight on the ocean.

"It would be nice to get out of the house," said Cheryl, looking at Marko. "Is it okay for us to take a walk?"

Bill resented her asking him for permission.

"Don't go too far. I'll watch you from the window."

. . .

They meandered down the beach arm in arm. The clouds were clearing fast and the midday sun felt good on their faces. The temperature was in the low sixties and the air crisp and clean. Being outside by the ocean lifted their spirits.

"He gives me the creeps," said Bill. "I don't like the way he was talking to you, telling you how beautiful you were, staring at you and touching your hand."

"I think he's pathetic." She abruptly stopped. "Are you jealous?"

"Maybe. He's very handsome. Reminds me a little of George Clooney, but without any warmth."

"He's attractive, but he's not my type. I go for tall, blue-eyed, brown-haired ex–professional baseball players."

They both laughed for the first time since fleeing Molokai. It felt good.

"So you think we should stay at the house with Marko for a few days?" asked Bill.

"Yes. I trust Maddie, and Maddie trusts Marko, so I think we should too."

"Well, we trusted Mr. Kronig, and look where that got us. What I'd really like to do is jump back on the motorcycle, maybe head south to Florida and try to reestablish our lives somewhere. Change our names and escape this mess."

"That would be nice, but it's wishful thinking."

. . .

From the big picture window, Marko watched Cheryl and Bill strolling down the beach. He knew he had won their trust; they had left the gun on the counter. He couldn't believe he had opened up to her. He never, ever talked about himself, but something in her kind smile had brought it out. He felt torn. He preferred his world black and white, devoid of all

174

nuance. Everything was so much easier to comprehend that way. Now he was in a quandary. He didn't want to kill her, or Ryan, but he didn't see a way out.

CHAPTER FIFTY-ONE

BILL AND CHERYL helped carry Maddie's luggage to her car. Marko joined them to say good-bye. They waved as she drove away. Bill and Cheryl returned to the house, but Marko remained outside, indicating he needed to get some things from his car. He opened the glove compartment of his Chevy, reached past his handgun, and pulled out a small penknife. He opened the trunk and grabbed a duffel bag. He moved into the garage, cut a small incision in the front tire of the cycle, and watched it slowly deflate. Next he rifled through the contents of the saddlebag. He knew that a contractor would be carrying all kinds of electronic equipment, weaponry, and other tools of the trade, but he was surprised when he saw the small blue box containing the tranquilizer darts.

When Marko returned to the house, Bill was watching a football game and Cheryl was upstairs in the bedroom. "Can I bother you for a moment, Bill? I want to show you something." Bill followed Marko down the inside steps to the garage. As they passed the motorcycle, Marko pointed at the tire. "You've got a flat."

Bill knelt to examine the tire. "It looks like it's been sliced." His eyes tilted up to Marko. "Who could have done that?"

"I did—you weren't thinking of escaping, were you?"

Bill felt a lump in his throat. His muscles tightened. Marko stared down at him impassively.

"You're deranged!" Bill shouted, baring his teeth and jumping to his feet, lunging at Marko.

Marko was fast and jumped out of the way. As Bill went by, Marko wrapped his right arm around his throat in a choke hold, tightening his bicep against Bill's carotid artery. Bill struggled helplessly as his face turned red and then blue. Marko slowly increased the pressure until Bill went limp.

Marko knew the choke hold maneuver well. Over the years he had learned how to apply the right amount of pressure to either kill or incapacitate an enemy. He released his hold and Bill fell to the floor. Marko knew that he would be out for about twenty seconds as his body struggled to resume pumping oxygen to his brain. He quickly opened the duffel bag and duct-taped Bill's mouth. Next he flipped him over, pulled his arms behind his back, and taped his wrists together. Bill roused as Marko gripped his ankles. Suddenly Cheryl's voice was at the top of the stairs. "Is everything okay?"

"We'll be up in a minute," yelled Marko, but he heard her footsteps descending the stairway. Just as he finished taping Bill's ankles, she came into view.

"What are you doing?" she screamed, and ran back up the stairs. Marko let go of Bill and sprinted after her, busting into the living room.

Cheryl stood in the kitchen, the gun in her hands, pointed at Marko.

"Put it down," ordered Marko, calmly moving toward her.

"I'll kill you if you come any closer."

"No, you won't."

"I will. I shot the man on the motorcycle and I'll shoot you too!"

"Give me the gun," Marko said, stretching out his hand.

She squeezed the trigger, but heard only a clicking sound. She continued squeezing as Marko lunged at her, smashing the gun out of the way, grabbing her arms, and twisting her around, placing a chokehold around her neck.

"I removed the bullets when you were on the beach," he whispered into her ear. He pressed hard against her neck, noticing the softness of her skin. She went limp. He hoisted her over his shoulders and carried her to the garage.

A few minutes later Bill and Cheryl were flopping on the garage floor like fish on land, struggling to break free. Marko pulled out the box of tranquilizer darts. "This will put you out for a few hours," he said, and punctured the backs of their necks. The squirming stopped and they fell silent. He pulled them by their legs to his car and lifted them into the trunk. After shutting the lid, he went back into the house to clean up.

CHAPTER FIFTY-TWO

MARKO GATHERED BILL and Cheryl's belongings, wiped away evidence of fingerprints, and vacuumed for stray hairs that could reveal DNA. All the while he felt a growing sickening sensation in his gut. Things were usually simple for him; there were the good guys and the bad guys. He had no problem killing the bad guys, or even eliminating innocent people for the greater good. He wasn't sure why he hadn't finished the job on Ryan and Alana; he'd just needed to apply a little more pressure. Maybe it was her sweet smile and the soft touch of her skin.

He knew he still had to kill them, but he wanted to arrange it so he didn't have to look into their faces, especially hers. He decided to take an alternative route back to Washington, crossing the Virginia Dare Memoria Bridge to the mainland and then cutting over to the Alligator River National Wildlife Refuge. He recalled a remote picnic area by the water. He would pull their slumbering bodies out of the trunk, shoot them in the backs of their heads, and dump them in the river. It was impersonal that way—they would die painlessly in their sleep. Once they were in the water, their fresh blood would attract alligators. If someone finally found their remains, they would carry no identification. It would take a lot of forensic work to link their remains to two missing persons from Hawaii.

. . .

Marko had just finished vacuuming when the doorbell rang. He ran downstairs and opened it, staring into the badge of a police officer.

"Hello, sir. I'm Officer Tom Clifford with the Duck Police Department. I'm doing routine house checks. Is Aida here?"

"She left a while ago to go home."

"What about the other two who were staying here, Bill and Cheryl?"

"They left too."

"Who are you?"

"I'm Vince Avery, I'm a friend of Mr. Henley. He told me that he would be coming here this weekend, so I stopped by to see him, but he wasn't able to make it. That's why everybody left."

Through the doorway Officer Clifford scanned the living area. Next to the stairway, on the shiny wood-paneled floor, sat a large plastic trash bag and two small suitcases. "I thought I heard a vacuum running when I rang the bell. Are you here alone?"

"Yes, Officer. I was tidying up before I left. I'm compulsive that way."

"So you're leaving now?"

Marko noticed the officer staring at the suitcases. "Yes, I've just finished packing; I'll be on my way in a few minutes."

"When did you get here?"

"Last night."

"I drove by last evening and earlier this morning making my rounds. I didn't see your Chevy, only the Buick."

"I went out a few times to the store; you must have stopped by then."

Officer Clifford cocked his head and raised his eyebrows. "Can I see your driver's license, please?"

Marko started to reach into his back pocket but stopped when he realized that the license in his wallet carried his real name and he had just told the officer that he was Vince Avery. "I don't have it on me; it's in my car, in the glove compartment."

"Why don't you go get it and I'll look around."

"Don't you need a search warrant for that?"

Officer Clifford frowned. "Is there something you don't want me to see?"

"Of course not, it's just that this isn't my house. It belongs to Mr. Henley."

Officer Clifford pulled out his cell phone. "Why don't we call him? Do you know his telephone number?" He stared at Marko.

"Not off the top of my head."

"I'll dial directory assistance. I just need to know where Mr. Henley lives. What city?" He stood waiting, one finger hovering over the phone's keypad.

"I don't recall."

"I thought you said you were a close friend?"

Marko said nothing.

Officer Clifford put down the cell phone. "You just gave me probable cause." He pushed past Marko into the house and over to the plastic bag and the suitcases. He pulled two sweatshirts from the bag. He recognized them immediately…one reading "Elizabeth City High School" and the other "University of North Carolina." Next he opened a suitcase stuffed with women's clothes crumpled into balls. That was all he needed. He drew his weapon and pointed it at Marko. "Put your hands up."

. . .

After a quick perusal of the house, Officer Clifford marched Marko to the Chevy with his gun pointed at Marko's back. "I'll need to check out your car."

Marko didn't resist and kept his arms over his head, awaiting his opportunity.

Officer Clifford peered in the front and back seats and then ordered Marko to open the trunk.

Marko quickly spun around, kicked the weapon away from Officer Clifford, and tackled him to the ground. Once again he used the stranglehold to subdue him. He opened one of the rear doors of the car and reached into the duffel bag for the tranquilizer darts—they weren't there. He remembered they were still in the garage by the cycle. He sprinted back to the house to retrieve them.

Officer Clifford started to stir, staggering to his knees, disoriented. Marko dashed out of the house and pounced on him, quickly jabbing a dart into the officer's shoulder. He watched him collapse. He dragged Clifford's body to the police car and propped him up in the driver's seat.

He raced back to the house, grabbed the suitcases and the trash bag, threw them into the backseat of his Chevy, started the engine, and peeled out of the driveway, speeding past the squad car with Officer Clifford slumped over the steering wheel.

CHAPTER FIFTY-THREE

MIDAFTERNOON ON SUNDAY, James Lamont again joined Scotty Olds in his office. All they could do was wait. An NFL playoff game was on the television, but they were barely watching. Half-eaten containers of Chinese food, with chopsticks sticking out of the tops, sat neglected on a small conference table. Occasionally Olds switched to CNN for news. He had assigned a staffer to monitor the Associated Press and other outlets for any announcements regarding Congressman Luke.

Lamont fidgeted as Olds reviewed paperwork. The window in Olds's office overlooked the South Lawn of the White House, but there was no activity. The grandfather clock in the corner of the office moved impossibly slowly. Breaking the tension, Lamont's cell phone rang. He hoped it would be the good news they were waiting for, but instead it was Maddie.

"James, I'm on the road, but I just checked the voice messages at home and noticed that you've been calling."

"I'm trying to reach Wilhelm; do you know where he is?"

Immediately the sobbing commenced, spilling from Maddie as from a burst dam.

"What's wrong?"

"I'm not supposed to tell anybody, but Wilhelm's dead. He was shot by a man on a motorcycle."

A chill ran down Lamont's spine. He knew the motorcycle man—a contract killer for the CIA. "I'm here with Scotty Olds. I'm going to put you on speaker."

Her crying continued in torrents.

"How do you know that Wilhelm is dead?"

"Cheryl and Bill Parker told me," she said through sobs. "They were with him when he was shot."

Lamont and Olds shared astonished stares, as Maddie, in a quivering voice, reconstructed the events: the call from Wilhelm indicating he was with Cheryl and Bill, his instructions to meet him at the beach house, his failure to show up as planned, and the arrival of Cheryl and Bill on the motorcycle. However, the emotional impact was greatest when she relayed the story of the deadly encounter in the swamp as told by Cheryl and Bill.

When she finished, Lamont exhaled hard. "Where are you?"

"I'm at a rest stop on Interstate 95, just north of Richmond. I'm on my way home."

"Are Cheryl and Bill with you?"

"No, they're still at the beach house."

"Where is the beach house, Maddie?"

"I can't tell you. Wilhelm made me promise never to reveal the location."

Olds said, "Maddie, this is Scotty. In this situation, I'm sure Wilhelm would have wanted you to tell us, for Cheryl and Bill's safety."

"Oh, don't worry, they're safe. I wouldn't have left them if they weren't. Bruce Marko is there. Wilhelm sent him to protect them."

Lamont and Olds simultaneously threw their hands into the air. By the time the conversation ended, Maddie was a basket case. "I don't know who to trust anymore," she cried.

The call had been an ordeal for all of them. Lamont and Olds had tried everything to convince her to give them the address of the beach house, without success. She was adamant, insisting she couldn't renege on a promise she had made to Wilhelm many years earlier. She argued that the location of the beach house was his most closely held secret and that to divulge it would be a betrayal of his memory. When they told her they didn't believe that Wilhelm had really sent Marko to protect Cheryl and Bill, she broke down in cries and moans. She hung up when they told her that Marko might kill them.

...

Lamont and Olds exhaled hard after the call. Without the location of the beach house, there was nothing to do.

"Do you think the CIA ordered Kronig killed?" asked Olds.

"The CIA doesn't kill Americans, you know that."

"Oh, that's right, you just arrange for other people to do the dirty work for you."

"I know you don't approve, but the use of contractors allows us to skirt the law—to do what has to be done—whether you like it or not."

"I'm not a lawyer, but I doubt that flimsy technicality would hold up in a courtroom."

"It will never come before a court. Too many important people know what's going on, including you."

Olds grimaced.

"Despite my distaste for Goodwin, I can't believe that he would order Wilhelm killed. That would be stepping over a bright line in the agency."

"And what will Marko do with Ryan and Alana? Will he kill them?" asked Olds.

"I don't think so. He knows that's illegal, but he may be setting them up, waiting for another contractor to arrive. Or he may be delivering them to someone else to do the job."

"How do you think Marko found the beach house?"

"I have no idea, but I'm sure that Wilhelm never told him to come protect them."

"Do you have Marko's phone number?" asked Olds.

"Yes, in my cell phone contacts."

"Why don't you call him?"

"I doubt he'll answer, but I'll give it a try." Lamont left a message on Marko's phone.

The ticking of the grandfather clock grew louder and louder. Olds checked his Rolex against the clock; they both read twenty-one minutes after five, and there was still no word from Congressman Luke. The suspense mounted as the clock crept closer to the six o'clock deadline.

Olds's assistant barged into the room. "Here it is," he shouted. "Just released a few minutes ago by Congressman Luke's press secretary. It hasn't hit the media yet, but it should break in a few minutes." The staffer put the press release on Olds's desk and left.

"With a sad heart, I announce my resignation from the United States Congress, effective immediately. God moves in mysterious ways, and I am now called upon to devote my full attention to a difficult family medical matter. I ask you to respect my privacy during this trying time. I am exceedingly grateful to the good people of Missouri for the confidence they placed in me as their elected representative, and I have striven to honor their trust. It is up to others to carry forward my cause to ensure the safety of our great nation and to preserve the American way of life. God bless you.

"Steven Luke"

"We got him," shouted Lamont, raising a fist in triumph. Olds walked over to a walnut cabinet and took out two crystal glasses and a bottle of Crown Royal. He poured two inches into each glass.

At that moment CNN broke in with the news. Next Lamont's cell phone rang; it was Patrick O'Brien offering congratulations. However, at the end of their brief conversation, O'Brien asked if they had heard anything from Kronig. It brought them back to earth. Their victory was bittersweet. They had stopped Congressman Luke and his use of the drug, but they had lost a friend in the struggle.

"Here's to Wilhelm Kronig," offered Lamont, raising his glass. "We won't see the likes of him again." They both took a long, deep swallow.

CHAPTER FIFTY-FOUR

DRIVING TOWARD THE Alligator River, Marko took stock of his situation. The likely scenario was that the police officer would wake up in a few hours and call for help, or others would show up looking for him. He wondered whether the officer had recorded the DC license plate on his Chevy. If so, he was sure the local police would issue an APB for his vehicle.

His thoughts gravitated to his contempt for Goodwin and Crowder. In the past he had arranged for killings in the United States, but always using an outside contractor. Although he knew it was a hollow technicality, it put distance between him and the killings. This was different; there was no wiggle room; killing Alana and Ryan would violate the law. However, disobeying orders would end his CIA career, and possibly his life. The director's threat had hardly been veiled. The nauseating feeling in his gut continued to grow, inflamed even more by his confrontation with the police officer. His neat and tidy world was unraveling.

Marko crossed the bridge to Roanoke Island onto the mainland. He took a turnoff down a rural two-lane side road to the Alligator River, eleven miles away. He switched on the radio, hoping to distract his thoughts. Religious broadcasts and country music faded in and out. Through heavy static he picked up the public radio station in Norfolk, hoping to catch the news at six.

Fiddling with the radio, he nearly missed the turnoff for the Alligator River picnic area, but quickly swerved into the entrance. He pulled the Chevy into a secluded spot next to the river. Picnic tables lined the area, but there were no people. He was reaching to turn off the ignition when the news came on:

"In a surprise announcement this afternoon, Steven Luke of Missouri resigned from Congress, citing an unspecified family medical emergency. Congressman Luke was chair of the influential House Intelligence Committee and a close friend of the vice president. He had been a vocal critic of the CIA and the State Department. In other news…"

Marko switched off the radio. He wondered what the resignation meant for Director Goodwin and Crowder. He wondered if they were on the way out. If that was the case, he had aligned himself with the wrong people.

He got out of the car and opened the trunk. Bill and Cheryl were asleep. He reached in and shoved their legs to the back, clearing space. He pulled back the mat, revealing a small door. He retrieved a large envelope and a black case and closed the trunk.

From the envelope he pulled out a Delaware license place, a registration card, and a screwdriver. He replaced his current plate and returned to the front seat with the case. He removed his pistol from the glove compartment. After opening the case, he lifted the suppressor and screwed it onto the gun barrel. Holding the weapon in his hands, he leaned back in his seat, feeling paralyzed. He knew he was postponing the inevitable, but he couldn't bring himself to move. As he waited, the sky turned dark and stars appeared.

The red flashing light of his cell phone broke his trance. Earlier, to avoid distraction, he had muted the phone and left it in the cup holder on the door. The flashing meant there were new voice messages. He checked the recent calls: three from CIA headquarters and an unexpected one from James Lamont.

Lamont's name on his cell phone conjured up the image of Kronig's bloodied body in the swamp. Marko thought back to the last time he had seen him alive. It had been with James Lamont back at Langley, before all the changes. They were reviewing Patrick O'Brien's report on the surveillance of the apartment building.

It struck him like a thunderbolt—Congressman Luke's chief of staff lived on the sixth floor of the building. Suddenly it all made sense. Maddie had talked about a secret operation, and now Congressman Luke had abruptly resigned. He guessed that Dr. Cameron had been delivering the drug to Congressman Luke's chief of staff. That would explain the mysterious tea sessions.

Marko picked up his cell phone and listened to the messages. The first two were from Crowder, demanding that he immediately call back. The third was from Goodwin, two hours ago. Marko had to move the phone back a few inches from his ear—the director was screaming. "Marko, answer the fucking phone. Where are you? Did you find Ryan and Alana? Have you killed them yet? You better not cross me unless you want to end up like Kronig."

Last he listened to James Lamont's call, from only forty-five minutes before. "Marko, this is James. Please call me back. I know you have Alana and Ryan. Please don't do anything stupid."

He made up his mind and dialed Lamont's number.

CHAPTER FIFTY-FIVE

JAMES LAMONT AND Scotty Olds watched the unfolding coverage of Congressman Luke's resignation. The pundits were already spinning the story. One talking head stated there were rumors that Congressman Luke had skin cancer. An unidentified source indicated that the congressman had recently had a small growth removed from his neck. The fact that the report was unconfirmed didn't dampen the speculation. Olds wondered how long it would be before they were interviewing some medical expert about the spread of melanoma. It was all padded news, filling the hours with endless talk and conjecture, but little substance.

Lamont's cell phone rang. He looked at the display and then to Olds in disbelief. "Hello, Marko," he answered in a slow, cool voice.

"I got your message. How did you know I had them?"

"Maddie told me."

"Listen, James, I need your help."

"How?"

"I want to bring Alana and Ryan in."

"In where?"

"To the Justice Department. Did Maddie tell you that Kronig is dead?"

"Yes."

"The director ordered the hit. He also ordered me to kill Alana and Ryan. I have the evidence—a voice message from the director saved on my cell phone."

"What do you want me to do?"

"I'm heading directly for the Justice Department headquarters—I'm not going to risk taking them to any way station. I need you to get me access through the guardhouse into the courtyard. I need somebody there from Justice to meet me and take possession of Alana and Ryan and the phone."

"We can't let the Justice Department know about this."

"Well, I'm going to tell them unless you can get somebody higher up to intervene. Maybe Scotty Olds can pull some strings."

"He's with me now. I'll see what I can do. When will you be there?"

"Between midnight and one, depending on traffic."

"How are Alana and Ryan? Can I speak to them?"

"They're sleeping."

"What?"

"Never mind. Just get me into the Justice Department."

CHAPTER FIFTY-SIX

BILL AWOKE FIRST, unsure where he was, feeling groggy. It was pitch black. He tried to talk but his mouth was sealed. His wrists hurt behind his back. He couldn't move or see them. He felt rumbling and constant vibration all around and deduced that he was in a moving vehicle. Through the noise he vaguely heard garbled voices, as if from a radio.

The last thing he recalled was lying on the garage floor next to Cheryl, bound and gagged, with Marko looming above. He guessed they were in the trunk of Marko's car. He had no idea how much time had passed.

He wondered what Marko would do to them. At least they were still alive, he thought, as he felt Cheryl's slowly breathing body next to him, his front to her back, spoon-like. He scrunched his face downward along Cheryl's arm until he felt the masking tape that bound her wrists. Something hard protruded above the tape. He realized it was her watch. Despite the discomfort of his position, he rubbed the side of his face against it, catching the edge of the duct tape. As he rubbed, some of the tape peeled away, slowly and painfully.

It took a while for Bill to strip the tape halfway off his mouth. In the process he scraped skin from his cheeks. His blood tasted salty on his lips.

He straightened his body and put his face against the back of Cheryl's neck. He had removed enough of the tape to form words. "Cheryl. Can you hear me?" She didn't respond.

He reached his face over to hers, feeling for the side of her mouth where the duct tape met her cheek. He bit into its edge, catching the tattered end in his teeth. He also caught some of Cheryl's flesh in his bite. He snapped his head back hard and the tape ripped off. She flinched and grunted.

Bill waited as Cheryl slowly awoke. At first she made small, almost imperceptible movements accompanied by low moans. She started to stretch. The stretch evolved into panic. She violently shuddered, struggling to move her hands and legs.

"There's no use, Cheryl. Your wrists and ankles are bound."

"Where are we?"

"I think we're in the trunk of Marko's car. I don't know where we're heading, but it feels like we're moving at a good clip. Do you remember how we got here?"

"No," she said, and turned quiet. Bill wondered if she had fallen back to sleep.

Bill stayed patient until Cheryl stirred again. "What did you ask me?"

"What happened at the beach house...with Marko?"

"I came down to the garage looking for you and saw him wrapping your ankles. I ran upstairs to get the gun. He came after me and I shot at him—but there were no bullets. Then he grabbed me by the neck. That's all I can remember. Where do you think he's taking us? Somewhere to be executed?"

"I don't think so. He could have killed us before. He must have other plans."

"My mouth is bleeding."

"I bit the tape off, I'm sorry if I hurt you."

"This is a nightmare."

"At least we're alive and together. We're going to get out of this."

"How?"

"I don't know...somehow."

She began thrashing again, trying to free her hands and legs, and then belted out a series of screams.

"It won't do any good, nobody can hear you. We must be on a highway…I can hear vehicles passing."

"I was such a stupid fool to trust Marko. I should have listened to you—we should have jumped on the motorcycle to Florida."

"We wouldn't have got far. We're running out of money and we don't have helmets…We would have been stopped in no time."

"Better than this."

"Our mistake was not going to the police—letting everybody talk us out of it."

"We never should have left Hawaii in the first place," she said, sniffling.

"I know…It's all my fault—I'm sorry." He nuzzled his face against the back of her neck.

They remained silent, feeling the bumps and the rattles and hearing passing vehicles and occasional horns. The car alternately slowed and sped up, suggesting they were hitting heavier traffic.

Bill listened to her shallow breathing, wondering what she was thinking. She stayed quiet for a long time.

"Our luck's finally run out," she whispered.

"I don't believe that, but if it has, I wouldn't trade the past two years with you for anything."

"I wouldn't trade one minute."

He softly kissed her on her tearstained cheek.

CHAPTER FIFTY-SEVEN

SCOTTY OLDS AND James Lamont waited in the interior courtyard of the Robert F. Kennedy Department of Justice Building, continually checking their watches. Using his White House credentials and his Justice Department contacts, Olds had arranged for the smooth entry of Marko's Chevrolet through the security gate. He'd also discreetly secured an office and a meeting room in the bowels of the building. Fortunately it was late at night, so there were few witnesses.

Olds's cellphone rang, and he turned to Lamont. "Marko's at the gate. They're waving him through. He should be here any minute."

They waited on the curb as car lights approached. Lamont recognized Marko in the driver's seat, but there were no other passengers. "Shit—he's alone."

Marko pulled the Chevy next to them and sprang out of the car. "Here it is," he said, handing the cell phone to Olds.

"Where the hell are Alana and Ryan?" shouted Lamont.

"Oh, they're in the trunk," said Marko, almost as an afterthought.

At that moment they heard muffled cries from the back of the car.

. . .

The courtyard floodlights blinded Bill and Cheryl as the trunk opened. Through squinting eyes, they looked up at a mustached man.

"You're safe now—you're at the headquarters of the United States Department of Justice. Let's get you out of there." Lamont pulled out a set of keys and used the edge to cut the masking tape from their wrists and ankles. He helped them to their feet as their legs wobbled.

Bill surveyed the courtyard. To his right was a large entranceway with the words *United States Department of Justice* engraved above and a statue of a blindfolded woman holding scales. However, they headed in the opposite direction to a smaller door.

They entered a hallway and proceeded down a flight of stairs, along a wide corridor, and into a massive office. At one end sat a large walnut desk next to an American flag. Behind the desk hung pictures of the president and the attorney general. The US Department of Justice seal occupied another wall—an American eagle over a red-white-and-blue shield, both encircled by a golden braid. A small table, chairs, and a couch filled the remainder of the office. Although large and elegant, it appeared unoccupied.

Lamont invited them to sit down on the couch. "Until recently I was the deputy director of the CIA. I can assure you that you are safe. I know you don't remember me, but I helped Wilhelm Kronig hide you on Molokai. Try to relax in here as best you can. We are meeting down the hall and will bring you in later to get your story, but first we have some urgent matters to take care of. I'll come back for you in an hour or two. In the meantime I'll get you some food and medical attention. This office also has a private bathroom." He pointed to a door next to the desk and departed.

Alone together, Bill and Cheryl embraced. Soon a nurse appeared and treated their reddened mouths and the irritation on their wrists and ankles. The nurse spoke sparingly and never asked how they'd received the wounds. Next a young, cherub-faced man brought sandwiches, soft drinks, and small bags of snacks.

They welcomed the food, but were agitated and apprehensive, wondering what was happening. They paced around the office, stretching out their legs and arms after the hours bound in the trunk.

At two in the morning Lamont reappeared and led them to a large conference room. They were surprised to see only three people, all clustered at one end of a long table. At the head sat a dapper man in a blue blazer and gold tie. Bill hesitated when he saw Marko. He pointed at him: "That's the man who kidnapped us and tied us up in the trunk. What is he doing here? I thought you said we were safe."

The dapper man cleared his throat. "You are safe. Although Mr. Marko's methods are unorthodox, he did deliver you to us mostly unharmed. Now please take a seat."

Marko's face showed no expression.

They sat together across from Olds and Lamont.

"Introductions are in order. My name is Scotty Olds. Until recently I was the president's national security adviser. Currently I serve as the White House liaison to the Justice Department. To my right is James Lamont, the former deputy director of the CIA, and you already know Bruce Marko."

Marko didn't look at them.

Olds continued. "We know you have been through a frightening ordeal, but we need you to describe the events leading up to and following William Kronig's death. Please begin with your first meeting with Mr. Kronig, and tell us what happened from that point on. Don't leave out any details, even if you think they are unimportant."

Bill and Cheryl retold their story. The men listened intently, occasionally asking follow-up questions, especially about Kronig's murder. Marko said nothing.

When they finished, Lamont spoke. "Your lives have been endangered because of your knowledge of extremely sensitive government secrets that bear directly on the safety and security of the United States. Do you know what those secrets are?"

They shook their heads. "We don't know anything," said Cheryl. "Maybe we did once, but not now. We have no recollection of anything before Hawaii."

"Has anybody said anything to you about a drug?"

"Mr. Kronig did," said Cheryl. "He told us we had agreed to submit to a powerful drug and to change our identities. He said I agreed to cosmetic surgery and signed a contract with the CIA. He didn't want to tell us more…He kept telling us that the less we knew the safer we would be."

Olds straightened his tie. "It appears that in your current state, you cannot reveal any secrets, but you still remain assassination targets."

The words chilled Bill and Cheryl.

"Did Mr. Kronig indicate you were in danger?" asked Lamont.

"Yes," said Bill. "He told us that there were people who were trying to kill us. That's how he convinced us to go with him. He said he'd keep us safe at his beach house."

"Did he indicate who was trying to kill you?" asked Lamont.

"Yes, the CIA."

Olds stood up from his chair. He placed his hands on the back of his chair, looking at Cheryl and Bill. "We are in a difficult predicament. In order to ensure your safety, we must keep you in our custody. Obviously you cannot stay here. Therefore, we will be moving you to a special unit at the Federal Correctional Complex in North Carolina, commonly known as Butner. I know you can't remember, but you've been there before."

Cheryl panicked. "You're going to put us in prison?"

"It's not a prison, but it is secure, meaning your movements will be restricted—but you will be together. We can legally hold you because there's a warrant for your arrest—for failing to appear at a court hearing in Honolulu. However, we need to keep all knowledge that we have you suppressed—for your protection—so we will be playing it close to the vest."

"What does that mean?" asked Bill.

"It means mistakes are going to be made; papers will be lost and proper procedures will not be followed."

"Whatever you call it—you're still taking away our freedom," said Cheryl.

"You won't be able to come and go, if that's what you mean," said Lamont.

Cheryl burst into tears. "I just want to go back home, to Hawaii…please."

Olds waited for her outburst to subside. "As I said, it's not really a prison. There's no other way. I don't believe you will be there for long—just time enough for us to work out some plans. Besides, it's your only hope of restoring your memories."

Bill and Cheryl fell silent, stunned by the implications.

"You do want your memories back, don't you?" asked Olds, studying the uncertainty on their faces.

Bill and Cheryl gazed at each other, unsure of their answer.

CHAPTER FIFTY-EIGHT

THE PRESIDENT GREETED Olds with an annoyed scowl. "This better be good, Scotty, I just canceled a meeting with the Ohio congressional delegation…not a smart move, considering I need their support on the war resolution."

"I wouldn't have asked for this meeting if it wasn't urgent. I have two matters to discuss. First, Congressman Luke didn't resign for health reasons."

"No?" asked the president, who was sitting behind his desk in the Oval Office.

"He resigned because he was about to be exposed for the use of a top-secret drug to brainwash legislators during his tea sessions. He was also using the same drug to rape and molest female interns."

The president sprang forward in his chair. "What drug are you talking about? I don't know anything about a top-secret drug."

"It was developed by the CIA years ago. They've been using it to interrogate enemy combatants and for covert operations against al-Qaeda. All under the guise of enhanced interrogation."

"Why the hell don't I know about this?" He gave Olds a withering glare.

"It was my decision—I thought it best you didn't know. We've been bending the law here…operating outside of congressional oversight. I didn't want to involve you—to keep you politically insulated."

The president continued glaring.

"Do you remember the Black Box operation against Osama bin Laden that you approved?"

"Yeah, it got called off because of that idiot, what was his name—Wolaski?"

"The drug was at the core of the operation."

"You should have told me, Scotty."

"Perhaps, but I was trying to protect you and keep the drug a deep secret. It's enormously powerful and could easily be manipulated for terrible purposes."

"Well, it seems your secret is out. How did Luke learn about it, and how'd he get his hands on it?"

"There was a security breach at CIA—someone was stealing the drug. I have reason to believe that the vice president may have been involved."

"The vice president?" repeated the president, his body stiffening. "So the vice president knew about the drug, but nobody bothered to tell the president." His red face looked ready to explode.

Olds decided to get straight to the point. "I have to ask you, sir—did you ever have tea with Congressman Luke—alone or with the vice president present?"

"What are you implying?"

"It's only a question, sir."

"The answer is no, but the vice president has been urging me to meet privately with Luke at Camp David. They set up a meeting last month, but I called it off at the last minute. I can't stand the bastard…He's been fanning the opposition to my foreign policies—calling my administration too passive. Me, passive? That's a bucket of shit." The president charged out from behind his desk and plunked himself down on a couch. He paused for a long time, as if struggling to control his fury.

Olds waited patiently.

"The vice president is quite enamored with Congressman Luke. Says he has a unique perspective on foreign policy matters…says that I should hear him out." The president stood up again and began pacing back and forth. "You don't really think they were planning to use that drug on me, do you?"

"I believe it's a possibility. Look at the facts…Luke was slowly taking over Congress with the drug. I think the next step was to give it to you—to turn you into their puppet—engineer a quiet coup."

The president's posture dropped, and he narrowed his eyes in amazement. "The drug is that powerful?"

"Yes."

"What evidence do you have?"

Olds handed the president the transcript from Luke's chief of staff. The president put on his reading glasses and quickly perused it, focusing on the written comment on the last page.

"You got anything else?"

"A voice recording of CIA director Goodwin ordering the assassination of two US citizens with knowledge of the drug. I also have the testimony from a high-ranking CIA official stating that Goodwin ordered Wilhelm Kronig killed."

"Wilhelm? I heard he was missing. Why in the world would the CIA kill him?"

"To keep the drug and their plot secret. When the CIA official balked, Goodwin implied that the assassination order came from high up. That would only be you or the vice president."

"It sure wasn't me. Where is Wilhelm now?"

"Do you really want to know?"

"Yes."

"In a swamp in North Carolina with a couple of bullets in him. Nobody knows yet."

"Geez," said the president, resuming his pacing, rubbing his palm against his forehead. He reached over to the phone on his desk. "I'm going to call the vice president."

"I would advise against that, sir. Time is of the essence. I would respectfully recommend that you immediately fire Goodwin. Put someone in charge to clean up this mess before it's too late. Everything is in turmoil over there. The CIA has been cooking the intelligence to support Luke and the vice president."

"Like what?"

"Claiming that the aluminum tubes in Iraq are nuclear centrifuges despite ample evidence to the contrary. They've also been ratcheting up production of the drug, and who knows what they're scheming to do with it. You need to move quickly, without the vice president's knowledge—before he can try to intervene."

"I've heard there's been a lot of turnover at the CIA since the appointment."

"That's an understatement. All the experienced hands are bailing. Give Goodwin and his cronies more time and they'll destroy the agency. They'll pack it with yes-men, glad to manufacture whatever intelligence the vice president and Luke's followers want—painting you into a corner."

"I can't fire Goodwin...I just appointed him. The Senate just confirmed him. How would that look to the American people? How would that play out politically?" The president threw his hands in the air, not waiting for an answer. "I'll tell you how it would look," he shouted, "like I don't know what the hell I'm doing." He jabbed a finger at Olds. "Isn't that what my critics have been charging all along? I'd just be giving them more ammunition."

"With all due respect, sir, it's too late to worry about that. You need to make a quick surgical strike. Make up any excuse; just get rid of him...otherwise the situation will worsen by the minute."

"What if Goodwin resists? He has a lot of allies on the Hill."

"You're the president. Threaten to charge him with treason if he balks; tell them you know about the drug. Tell him you know about the vice president's possible involvement. That will scare the hell out of him. If you want, I'll be the messenger."

The president collapsed hard on the sofa. "This is all happening too quickly. I need some time to sort through it." He paused. "Who would I put in charge at CIA? Not you—politically that would never fly."

"How about James Lamont? He has the credibility and experience."

"Jimmy?"

"It's your call, sir, but I think he's the best man for the job in this situation."

"Would he take it?"

"I don't think he wants to be the permanent director, but if you ask, I'm sure he's willing to take over in the interim, until things settle down."

CHAPTER FIFTY-NINE

"HANK, COME HERE quick," screamed Ellie Smith, co-owner of the Hidden Pines Motor Court, sitting in the motel office watching the five o'clock local news.

"What's wrong?" he asked, rushing into the room. She pointed to a perky young blonde reporter standing against a backdrop of police cars and yellow caution tape.

"I'm here on Route 17 beside the Great Dismal Swamp, about seventeen miles north of Elizabeth City. As you can see, there is a lot of law enforcement activity behind me. Helicopters have been flying back and forth all day. The police have cordoned off the area and have closed one lane of Route 17, so if you're heading to Norfolk or other points north you should take an alternative route or expect long delays."

Hank looked at Ellie. "So what? This has been on the news all day."

"Wait," said Ellie. "Just watch."

"We've been following the breaking news since early this morning when a passing motorist discovered a car in the swamp."

"Oh yeah," said Hank. "I saw that motorist interviewed earlier. He claimed he pulled over to check out a rattle in his car. Bullshit, he probably pulled over to take a piss."

"Shush," scolded Ellie.

"Police investigators earlier reported that the driver of the car had been shot multiple times. The police have confirmed a second body at the site, shot in the head. The second victim was reportedly wearing a motorcycle jacket and motorcycle boots. No motorcycle has been located at the scene, although there are unconfirmed reports that a helmet has been recovered."

Hank gave Ellie a worried glance. "You don't think this has anything to do with those two suspicious characters from Hawaii?"

Ellie said nothing and focused her eyes back on the television. The network interrupted the reporter's feed, switching to a hastily called news conference in Raleigh. A heavyset bald man with a dark suit and a solemn face moved in front of a row of microphones. Behind him stood several uniformed officers, flanked by the American and North Carolina flags. The caption at the bottom of the screen indicated that the speaker was the director of the North Carolina State Bureau of Investigation.

"I have a statement to read. I will not be taking questions. This morning at 10:11 a motorist reported a vehicle partly submerged in a swamp near Route 17 in Pasquotank County. The highway patrol investigated and discovered the body of the driver, still in the vehicle, shot several times through the jaw and the chest. The State Bureau of Investigation was called in. A search of the area turned up another victim, about twenty feet away, shot once in the chest and once in the head. The search for other possible victims continues. The circumstances surrounding the shooting and the motives are unknown and under investigation. Based on initial evidence at the scene, however, we believe that another shooter, or shooters, may have been present and may have fled on a motorcycle."

Ellie touched Hank's hand.

The reporters started launching questions at the speaker, but he raised his hand for them to stop.

"As I previously indicated, I won't be taking questions. Let me finish the statement. This is very important. We have positively identified the driver of the car. His name is Wilhelm Kronig and he is the former deputy director of the Central Intelligence Agency. Mr. Kronig has been missing since last Friday. The identity of the second victim is unknown. Because of the circumstances, the FBI will be taking over the investigation."

The director walked away from the microphones, ignoring a frenzied barrage of questions.

"Oh my God," said Ellie. "Those two muddy people on the motorcycle, and the woman covered in blood—wasn't that last Friday?"

Hank turned on Ellie. "I should never have let you talk me out of calling the police. I knew something was wrong. We shouldn't have given them a room."

"Should we go to the police?" asked Ellie.

Hank shook his head. "We didn't keep a record of them staying here. We took their money but wrote nothing down. That's a violation of regulations. They could shut us down, even charge us with tax evasion."

"They wouldn't do that for something so small—letting someone spend a night without a recorded payment."

"Not normally, but if those two murdered some big-shot CIA official then all bets are off."

"Maybe."

"Look, we saw the blood…We suspected foul play, but we didn't do nothing. We let them stay the night and we took their money—like a hush payment. You know what that makes us, Ellie—it makes us accomplices. Plus, you disposed of the evidence—you threw out that pile of bloody clothes. It's already been taken by the trash collectors."

"It's worse. I gave them fresh clothes, I helped them escape."

"We're in big trouble."

"But we didn't know. I even felt sorry for them. People will understand."

"I don't think so. Prosecutors can twist it around, make us look like monsters…and I got a fucking criminal record."

"But that was long ago and you were innocent."

"Don't matter—I'm still an ex-con. Three fucking years in prison for a burglary I didn't do. Letting that no-good prosecutor scare me into pleading guilty. It was all rigged. It still is. Nobody here knows I'm a jailbird except you. If we go to the police, it'll come out." Hank gritted his teeth and pointed to their operating license, framed on the wall. "I lied on the business application. I didn't check that I had a felony conviction. That's enough to ruin us." He gave Ellie a hard stare. "We need to stay quiet. Pretend it never happened."

She sighed heavily. "You're right…We need to keep our mouths shut."

CHAPTER SIXTY

CONNIE INHALED DEEPLY at the front-page headline in the *Washington Post*: "Former CIA Deputy Director Shot Dead in North Carolina."

It was the second headline in three days to feature the CIA, and both had given her a jolt. Two days earlier she'd read, "President Fires New CIA Director Goodwin."

Connie felt her stomach tighten, thinking back to her last vision of Wilhelm Kronig, leaving the Hyatt hotel with Bill and Cheryl. She was sure they were dead too.

It seemed very curious that the president would summarily fire, without explanation, a man he had just recently appointed. The discovery of Wilhelm Kronig's body intensified the mystery. The news networks and the talk radio stations buzzed with speculation. Connie wondered whether the firing had any ties to Kronig's death and Alana and Ryan's disappearance.

Six days had passed since their meeting at the Hyatt Regency Hotel. She had called Kronig's cell phone numerous times but the calls all went to voice mail. Nor did she have any success reaching Ryan and Alana on their cell phone.

In the interim she'd begun working on an article based on her conversation in the park with Kronig. However, when she listened to the tape, she realized that what he had told her about the drug and its use in the war on terror wasn't part of the recording. All that was on tape was his assertion that the new CIA leaders wanted Ryan and Alana erased. Everything else had been off the record. Furthermore, her interview with Ryan and Alana was not helpful. They recalled nothing about their previous lives and were ignorant about how they'd arrived in

Hawaii. All they'd told her was that two people claiming to be CIA agents had attempted to abduct them.

Connie devoured the news reports surrounding Kronig's death, but found no mention of anybody else in the car or at the scene, other than the second victim. She sensed a cover-up and began revising her article.

. . .

Two days later Connie watched as Aaron Retzler reviewed her first draft, scribbling small markups using a red pen. When finished, he handed it back to her and took off his tortoiseshell glasses. "I'm sorry, Connie, but it's lacking. All the references to the drug are based on your previous unsubstantiated article and on what Mr. Kronig told you *before* he turned on the tape recorder. As I understand it, everything else was strictly off the record. There isn't any corroboration."

Connie curled her lips in frustration. "It's no longer confidential if the source is dead."

"It is by my standards. This isn't the *National Mirror*. We have a reputation to uphold. We can never betray a source, dead or alive. You should know better."

She knew he was right, but it was so exasperating to be sitting on a breakthrough story and unable to move on it. "What if I do a piece just on Alana, without mentioning the drug? The public still remembers her from the trial. I have proof she moved to Molokai afterward. I have her recorded interview from the Hyatt, where she says two CIA agents tried to abduct her. I have Kronig's recorded statement that the CIA wanted her dead. I could title it 'The Strange Disappearance of Alana Shannon.'"

"Where do you think she is now?"

"Dead, along with Ryan Butler. Maybe their bodies will turn up, maybe not."

Retzler pressed his fingers around his chin. "Okay, go ahead with the disappearance angle, but remember the story is fluid, and if their bodies are discovered, or if they reappear, everything will change. I'll also have to send it over to the CIA before we publish."

"Why?"

"Because we're intimating that the CIA assassinated American citizens. That's a big deal. They have a right to comment. So your article better be ironclad."

"I'll get right on it." She started to leave.

"Before you go, what about your piece on Congressman Luke?"

"It's stalled. The two interns don't want any press. They believe that their allegations contributed to the congressman's resignation, so they feel partially vindicated—and the pregnant intern's family has reached a private financial settlement with Luke's lawyers. So there's nowhere to go."

"What about the staffer in Luke's office?"

"Jason?"

"Yes. Will he come forward?"

"I tried that. He'll only go public if the interns need him to back their stories. He wants to move on…He says that any revelation that he leaked to the press will ruin his career. He's just started working for another congressman."

"And Jason never saw the drug or witnessed anybody putting it in the tea."

"No, he only surmised it."

"So we're at a dead end on the drug, the tea sessions, and the rapes."

"Unfortunately, yes."

CHAPTER SIXTY-ONE

TOM CLIFFORD HAD had a difficult week. Never in his twenty-two years as a police officer had he drawn his gun or been assaulted. His kind of duty didn't lend itself to danger. In the summer he directed traffic, recovered missing property, and responded to noise complaints. In the winter he monitored vacant vacation homes.

What had happened at the beach house was a growing enigma. Several hours after the assault, he'd regained consciousness in his police car. The first thing he remembered was the frantic squawking of the police radio imploring him to respond. When help arrived, they searched the beach house, finding nothing incriminating. He had scribbled down the DC license number of the Chevy, and the police department issued an APB, but nothing showed up.

Some of his fellow officers started ribbing him, joking that maybe he had fallen asleep and made up the assault story as a cover. One of the younger officers flippantly called him Rip van Winkle. His vehement and angry denial surprised his colleagues, but it didn't stop the mocking. When he claimed that his assailant resembled George Clooney, someone posted a fake report on the break room bulletin board: "The Duck Police Department is searching for a man who looks like George Clooney; so is every woman in America."

Clifford wasn't sleeping well, replaying the incident in his mind and worrying about the fate of Aida and the man and woman on the motorcycle. He was also disgusted at how easily he had been overtaken at the beach house. He knew he was a poor excuse for a cop, too old, too timid, and too out of shape. His wife was right, he thought, he should retire.

Over the next few days, the story became increasingly bizarre. The police department tried unsuccessfully to reach the owner of the house, Martin Henley. Except for the residence in Duck, there were no phone numbers or addresses for him. Furthermore, Mr. Henley's name didn't appear anywhere in the real estate records for the house. Instead the documents indicated that a financial investment firm in the Cayman Islands, Epstein Global Associates, owned it. Under Cayman law, the names of the firm's officers were secret.

Officer Clifford didn't know Aida's last name and had never recorded the license plate number of her Buick. Nor did he remember Bill and Cheryl's last names.

The next bombshell hit when the District of Columbia Department of Motor Vehicles reported that the license plate number of the missing Chevy wasn't in their database. Although Clifford knew he had recorded it correctly, he suspected the other officers thought he had messed up.

The motorcycle in the garage was the only solid evidence. According to the Maryland State Highway Administration, the cycle's plate linked back to someone named Anthony Haig in Baltimore. When Clifford followed up with the Maryland State Police, he learned that Haig had been killed in a bar fight six years earlier. Furthermore, the address on the registration was of an abandoned house in Baltimore.

Everything was at a standstill until the *Washington Post*, one of several national newspapers to which the department subscribed, arrived at the Duck Police Department. Officer Clifford stared at the headline—the same one that had shocked Connie Blythe: "Former CIA Deputy Director Shot Dead in North Carolina."

However, it was the picture of Wilhelm Kronig that made his hair stand on end. He was sure he was looking at the face of Martin Henley. When he read that the killer could have escaped on a motorcycle, he called the FBI.

CHAPTER SIXTY-TWO

THE MEMORIAL FOR Wilhelm Kronig took place at the historic
Georgetown Lutheran Church. Hundreds of mourners attended,
including two past presidents, four previous CIA directors, members of
the intelligence community, and numerous congressional
representatives. Maddie sat in the front pew, dressed in black, next to
Kronig's two weeping daughters and their families. James Lamont,
whom the president had just appointed as interim director of the CIA,
was a few rows back.

Several speakers, including a former president, spoke eloquently of
Kronig's long and distinguished service to his nation. At the completion
of the memorial service, a smaller contingent followed the funeral
procession to Arlington National Cemetery.

After the twenty-one-gun salute and the playing of taps, Lamont
spotted Maddie away from the others, leaning against a tree, as if
needing it for support. It was a cold, gray, and windy day.

"How are you holding up, Maddie?"

She wiped tears away. "Not well, James, but I'll be all right
eventually. He was a wonderful man…It's going to be very difficult to
go on without him. He never should have died the way he did."

"I know," said Lamont, reaching out and clasping her hands. "What
are you going to do now?"

"I'm not sure. Wilhelm was very generous in his will…I'm financially
set for the rest of my life." Her eyes welled. "It's hard to believe that I
started working for him and his family over thirty years ago…cleaning
their house and scrubbing their floors." She shook her head in
amazement.

"He was a very special human being."

Maddie reached over and hugged him, whispering into his ear. "I can't stop thinking about our last conversation. I'm sorry I hung up on you and Scotty…I was so upset. I thought I could trust Marko. Never for a second did I believe he would harm Ryan or Alana. If something bad has happened to them, I'll never forgive myself." She trembled.

"Don't worry, Maddie, they are safe. We had doubts about Marko, but he came through in the end."

She breathed a huge sigh of relief. "You don't know how much that means to me—I've been so worried about them."

Lamont patted her on her back.

She looked at him through wet eyes. "And the operation you were planning with Wilhelm? I know you can't tell me…but it would be wonderful to know that he didn't die for nothing—that it was for a cause."

"His death was not in vain…It made a big difference. I can't tell you how—you will just have to take my word for it."

…

Several hours later Lamont returned to Langley. He called Marko into his office. "Why weren't you at the funeral?"

"I didn't want to see Maddie. I didn't know what to say if she asked about Ryan and Alana."

"She did ask. I told them they're fine."

"Are they?"

Lamont changed the subject. "Your actions in North Carolina were absolutely inappropriate. Please tell me why it was necessary to drug them. To bind them and put them in the trunk of your car. Why didn't you just tell them that you were taking them to the Justice Department?"

"I was under orders to kill them—I was debating what to do."

"You were contemplating carrying out an illegal order?"

"I'll be straight, I was conflicted. When Luke resigned, I saw the bigger picture. I decided to bring them in and to turn over the cell phone."

Lamont studied Marko's deadpan face. "I find it difficult to understand you, Marko. Do you feel anything?"

"Not much...occasionally anger."

"I'm disciplining you for violating agency protocols. I am suspending you without pay for thirty days and demoting you one grade. The demotion is effective immediately, but I'm delaying the suspension. I need you with me during the transition to handle Dr. Cameron and to retake control of the drug manufacture."

"I understand," said Marko flatly.

"I'm not sure when the suspension will start. I'll have to play it by ear. Now, you said you had something to tell me?"

"Some disturbing news. We received a draft article from that reporter with the *Beltway Insider*, Connie Blythe. Her boss, Aaron Retzler, sent it over for comment. It's about the disappearance of Alana and Ryan and it mentions Kronig. It's extremely damaging."

"Shit," said Lamont. "Let me see it."

CHAPTER SIXTY-THREE

BILL AND CHERYL'S room at the Federal Correctional Complex, Butner, was nothing like a prison cell. It reminded them of an efficiency apartment, fitted with a queen-size bed, television, separate bathroom, and minikitchen. A single window looked out to a thick stand of pine trees.

Their quarters were in a special, highly secure building, separated from the others at Butner by an immense concrete wall. The security personnel wore tan uniforms without insignia. James Lamont told them that the CIA used the facility for the interrogation of state enemies and for the temporary housing of high-level security risks. They had no idea what that meant. Other than the guards, they never saw or heard anyone.

The authorities strictly regimented their lives. Meals arrived three times a day—typical nondescript institutional fare. At ten in the morning, a guard escorted them to the small gym for forty-five minutes of exercise. At two in the afternoon, they were let outside for forty-five minutes to walk back and forth in a walled concrete courtyard. At four they visited a small library to borrow books and DVDs. There they could surf the Internet but couldn't use e-mail. On the return to their room, they could stop by a small store to purchase snacks, frozen meals, and sundries.

Their greatest challenge was the isolation and boredom. Although it had been only seven days, it seemed like a lifetime. They spent most of their hours watching television, viewing movies, or reading. Their only other diversion was occasional bird and squirrel activity outside their window.

Their conversations centered on whether they wanted their memories restored. Cheryl was hesitant, disliking what she had learned about the woman she used to be. Bill was curious, wanting to know who he was and what his connections were to Cheryl and the CIA. Ultimately the CIA made the decision. Shortly after news broke that the president had appointed James Lamont as the interim CIA director, they received a terse communication advising them that their memories would be restored on Saturday.

The night before, Cheryl couldn't sleep. Her tossing and turning kept Bill awake until he finally switched on the lamp. She was sitting up in bed, staring at the wall and rubbing her hands together on her lap. He gently touched her shoulder. "I know you're worried, so am I. But we have to find out who we really are. We can't go on not knowing."

She grabbed his arm. "It's not just that. I keep thinking back to what Mr. Kronig said about my hair in Washington. I told him I liked it brown and he said of course I did—I was told to like it that way."

"I remember, so?"

"Well, what if I was told to love you and you were told to love me? What if it none of it is real...What if it's just the effect of the drug?"

"It can't be. I know that I love you, Cheryl. Nothing can change that."

"How can you be so sure? Maybe it's all been a drug-induced spell."

"But Mr. Kronig said we had been lovers in the past."

"But I was married to another man and you were a lawyer in Arizona. How could we have been lovers?"

"I don't think Mr. Kronig would lie...What would be the purpose?"

She took a very deep breath. "You've heard the expression *lover's quarrel?*"

"Of course."

"Have we ever had one?"

Bill's face lost expression. "Nothing major."

"And we've never had a real fight, have we?"

"No."

"Does that seem normal? We've shut ourselves away from the rest of the world…living in our own cocoon. Maybe it's all an illusion. I'm just so afraid that we won't feel the same way about each other after tomorrow."

Bill stroked his fingers through Cheryl's hair, saying nothing, reluctant to tell her that he shared the same fear.

…

The next afternoon a guard led them to a small sterile room at Butner. A few moments later James Lamont entered carrying a silver case. He closed the door. "Are you ready?"

"Yes," they answered in unison, surprised to be alone in a room with the newly appointed CIA interim director.

Lamont pulled two syringes out of the case. "You were initially given a very large dose of the drug, and it will take an equally large one to snap you back. After that we can discuss your options."

"Why can't we discuss them now…before we're given the drug?" asked Cheryl.

"Because in your current states you can't fully comprehend your situation or the ramifications of your choices. You need to understand the full context to make a reasoned decision. I owe you that."

Bill went first: Lamont inserted the syringe into his arm. He had expected his memories would come rushing back in a flood of revelations and overpowering emotions, but it was not like that at all. Instead it was as if he were slowly awakening from a deep sleep and recalling an incredible dream.

Across from him Lamont was holding Alana's arm, preparing to inject the drug. He realized that she had been right—he did feel different about her. On Molokai he had been in love with a mirage—not a real woman.

CHAPTER SIXTY-FOUR

As THE NEEDLE penetrated Alana's skin, her eyes widened slowly. She looked at Ryan, and her mouth curled into a tender smile of recognition. She spread out her arms to embrace him. "Oh my God," she cried. "We're back together—for real!"

He rushed in and passionately kissed her lips, feeling his heart thumping against hers. He melted in her warmth. Despite their living together on Molokai for the past two years, it seemed as though they had been apart for a very long time. She was no longer Cheryl, a phantom, but Alana—the very real, radiant, smart, vivacious, and beautiful woman he had fallen in love with so long ago.

They continued kissing and embracing until Lamont interrupted. "There will be plenty of time for that later. So has everything come back?"

"Yes," they both said, still staring moonstruck at each other.

"How could we have believed we were Bill and Cheryl Parker from Colorado?" asked Alana, shaking her head.

"It seems impossible."

Ryan looked around at the four empty pale-green walls. It was the same room where they had initially received the drug. Wilhelm Kronig and James Lamont had been there, outlining the plan, briefing them on the setup on Molokai, and reviewing the backstory of their fictional lives in Colorado. Ryan had reviewed and signed the contract, just below Alana's signature. Then Lamont had injected the drug. After that there was only Molokai.

Suddenly the full realization of Kronig's murder hit Ryan hard. Kronig had been their friend and protector, pushing back when Marko advocated killing them and convincing Lamont to hide them on Molokai. He recalled how much he hated Marko and how they had fought in the past.

Ryan's own story was clear. He had grown up in Allentown, Pennsylvania, the son of a steelworker. After earning all-American honors at Temple University, he signed with the Chicago White Sox as their top pitching prospect and played two years in the minors before a car crash ended his career. After earning a law degree, he spent the next twenty years trapped in a cold marriage, plodding toward a partnership in a prestigious and stuffy Philadelphia law firm. His life took a radical turn when he met Alana.

He recalled the first time he'd seen her, at the hospital. She greeted him with such a dazzling smile and such luminescent green eyes that he could hardly speak. She was stunningly beautiful, with a model-perfect face…bright-blonde hair, soft cheeks, full lips, a sculptured nose, and a lovely lissome figure. When she reached out to shake his hand, the warmth of her touch stole his breath away. It was love at first sight, but there were complications. She was the young wife of an old baseball buddy, Steve Shannon, whom Ryan was visiting at the hospital. Steve was in a bizarre and unexplained coma.

The mystery surrounding Steve's medical condition pulled Ryan and Alana deeper and deeper into the world of espionage and unlocked the secret of the drug. His recurring nightmare of shooting a man on a boat in the Caribbean was not a dream at all, but a real and desperate act he had taken to rescue Alana from a rogue CIA agent. That incident and the subsequent cover-up snared both of them in the CIA's web. Their brief fling ended when the CIA forbade further contact. Alana returned to her husband, who had strangely recovered from his coma. Ryan became a lawyer for the EPA in Arizona, carrying with him the very deep secret of the drug. Although they were separated for years, he never stopped yearning for her.

Ryan's work with the EPA required him to travel extensively, studying the environmental and legal impact of water desalination plants throughout Europe and the Middle East. Although he believed he had severed all CIA ties, he later learned that the agency had manipulated him into smuggling coded documents during his travels, putting his life at risk, but gaining crucial intelligence for the nation.

On the personal side, Ryan's wife divorced him and he never remarried. Despite a string of girlfriends, he couldn't forget Alana. Years later, when he learned that she was on trial for shooting her husband, he rushed to her defense, knowing that his secret was the key to her exoneration. Thrown together again, they quickly rekindled their lost love.

...

"Here are your options," said Lamont, drawing Ryan back to the present. He handed them three folders, each showing the imprint of Epstein Global Associates on the cover. Inside were photographs of houses and detailed climate and demographic data for towns in California, Alaska, and Arkansas. "These are your relocation choices. As you can see by the photos, all the houses are upscale but located on the outskirts of small towns in remote areas. It is imperative that we continue to minimize Alana's chances of recognition. I'm willing to amend the contract to allow you to retain your memories, providing you agree to fully cooperate."

"What about Molokai?" asked Alana. "Can't we go back to our house?"

"That's not an option. You were compromised there. Connie Blythe could track you down again."

"But that's where we want to go," said Alana, desperately looking to Ryan for confirmation and support.

Ryan took her hand. "I agree, we want to go back to Molokai."

Lamont took a deep breath. "That's only possible if two conditions are met. You'd have to resubmit to the drug and resume your lives as Bill and Cheryl Parker. I'd also need an assurance that Connie Blythe will not track you down or disclose anything that has happened over the past few weeks."

They balked at the conditions. They had no desire to lose their memories again and they were outraged that Connie Blythe could dictate their future.

Ryan now remembered that Alana detested Connie. Writing for the *National Mirror*, Connie had first labeled her the Porn Star Murderess, a name that stuck in the popular press.

CHAPTER SIXTY-FIVE

THE LINCOLN CONTINENTAL idled in a no-parking zone in the curved driveway outside the entrance to Connie's office building. The driver, an air force staff sergeant, opened the back door for Connie and Aaron Retzler. The sergeant took his position behind the wheel.

"Where are you taking us?" asked Retzler.

"To Andrews Air Force Base; there you will join Director Lamont. A jet's waiting."

"Nobody said anything about a jet on the phone," said Retzler.

"Those are my orders, sir. That's all I know."

It all had occurred fast. Fewer than forty-eight hours after he had sent Connie's article to the CIA, Retzler received a call from the agency's public information office with an urgent request that he delay publication. The call included an invitation to meet with interim CIA director James Lamont. If they agreed, a car would pick them up at their office at 9:00 a.m. on Friday, and they should plan to be away for at least six hours.

It took them an hour to snake through the midmorning Washington traffic to Andrews Air Force Base just outside the Beltway in Maryland. The driver parked at a small building at the end of a runway far from the hub of military activity. He escorted them to the entrance, through a metal detector, and inside to a lounge where James Lamont waited.

When Lamont saw them, he put away his cell phone and quickly strode over, extending his hand. "Good to see you again, Connie, and it's a pleasure to meet you, Mr. Retzler. Thank you for accepting my invitation. I can explain more when we are airborne. First, we need to reach an understanding. What I am going to tell you and show you is strictly off the record. You can't disclose anything I say or anything you see today. Is that acceptable?"

Connie didn't like it. "What if it confirms things we already know?"

"I'm talking about new revelations—that doesn't impact what you may have already substantiated."

"Then what's the point?" asked Retzler.

"To show you the bigger picture."

Connie started to balk, but Retzler interrupted her. "We will agree to that."

They walked out the other side of the building, onto the tarmac, and up the steps into a small white unmarked private jet, settling into facing leather seats. The only others on board were the pilot and the copilot.

"I know this trip may seem unusual," said Lamont as the jet taxied, "but I want to explain to you why publication of the article would be so damaging. I also want to show you something—that's why I'm flying you to North Carolina."

"Where in North Carolina?" asked Connie.

"We'll be landing at the Raleigh-Durham Airport in about forty-five minutes. There's a car waiting for us, and from there it's another forty-minute drive to our destination. It will all become clear when we get there." He abruptly changed the subject. "Should be a beautiful day for flying—we'll talk more when we're in the air."

. . .

Five minutes after takeoff, the pilot came on the intercom. "As you requested, Director Lamont, we just crossed five thousand feet."

Lamont's expression turned solemn. "For security reasons, it's best not to talk on the ground. What I'm going to tell you is extremely sensitive. Your article alleges that the CIA ordered the assassination of two US citizens, in direct violation of the law. Furthermore, your article indicates that you have a taped statement from the late Wilhelm Kronig confirming the allegation." He stared straight at Connie. "From our previous conversation, and from reading your draft article from two years ago, I know you suspect that the CIA has been employing a secret drug that influences human actions and memory. You probably suspect that we gave the drug to Alana Shannon and Ryan Butler. Am I correct so far?"

"Yes," said Connie.

"Granted, the article you sent over doesn't mention the drug and only focuses on the whereabouts of Alana Shannon. Even given that limited scope, you are sitting on a powder keg. Alana Shannon is a public figure, and your article implies that the CIA killed her. It will stir up questions and suspicions that will lead to further speculation and accusations until there's a media firestorm. After all, she was once the darling of the tabloids. You realize that, don't you?"

"It's a possibility," said Retzler.

"So let me tell you what's at stake. Simply put, the lives of thousands of people. The drug is amazingly powerful, and we have been using it to interrogate al-Qaeda prisoners at Guantánamo and elsewhere. The media believes that enhanced interrogation means torture. That's partly true. However, our greatest breakthroughs have come from the drug. We have foiled three major terrorist attacks in the United States, France, and Belgium. Without the drug, the death toll would have dwarfed that of 9/11."

Lamont stopped for effect, waiting for his words to sink in. "We are also using the drug offensively. We've released detainees under its influence with orders to disrupt the terrorist networks. We came very close to finding and killing Osama bin Laden. If the existence of the drug becomes public, all our progress against the terrorists will be reversed. I'm telling you flat out that publication of your article could lead to the deaths of many innocent people at home and abroad."

"The job of the press is to uncover the truth. Now you want to censor us?" asked Connie.

"No, I want you to censor yourselves. To put your country first."

"A free press is central to our democracy," said Connie.

"So you're willing to have blood on your hands?" asked Lamont.

"That's not fair," said Retzler.

"It's fair, all right. There is a precedent for the press to hold back when lives are at stake and the United States is directly threatened. During the Cuban missile crisis in 1962, the Kennedy administration approached reporters from the *Times* and the *Post* and asked them to hold their stories about the planned blockade of Soviet ships to Cuba. The papers complied. That crisis brought us to the brink of nuclear war—one misstep and it would have been all over. What if the papers had rejected the request? Maybe today we'd still be digging out from a nuclear holocaust, assuming any of us survived."

"Those are just scare tactics," countered Connie.

"I know you want a Pulitzer, but let me ask you—how proud would you be if that medal was stained with the lifeblood of thousands, maybe millions of innocent people?"

Retzler broke in. "Let's say we decide to go ahead and run the story...I assume you will take legal action to block publication."

"No. That would give the story credibility. However, we will vigorously deny everything. Again, I'm requesting that you voluntarily withhold the article, for the good of your nation."

"If I remember correctly, during the Cuban missile crisis the *Times* and *Post* agreed to delay publication, not to bury it," said Retzler.

Lamont sighed. "This is no different. If the information comes out from some other source, you are free to run your article and any others. It wouldn't matter at that point."

"But someone else would get credit for the scoop," said Connie.

"Is that all you care about? Who gets the credit?"

Retzler interrupted. "I promise you I will give it serious thought. That's all."

The pilot came back on the intercom, "We're beginning our initial descent."

They looked out the window as the jet glided over ribbons of blue lakes interspersed by thick evergreen forests.

CHAPTER SIXTY-SIX

FORTY-FIVE MINUTES after landing at Raleigh Durham Airport, Connie, Retzler, and Lamont sat in a small room at the Federal Correctional Complex, Butner. The door opened and in walked Ryan Butler wearing a navy-blue shirt and pants resembling medical scrubs. Alana followed him wearing similar clothes.

"Hello, Connie," Ryan said, looking into her eyes.

Connie was stunned to see them alive. She also realized that something had changed since Washington. Their fear and confusion were gone, replaced by recognition.

"So you remember me now?"

"We remember everything," answered Ryan.

"Let me remind you that you can't use anything discussed or revealed here," said Lamont.

"We understand," said Retzler, realizing that they had walked into a trap.

"What happened to you?" asked Connie. "Last time I saw you, you were leaving with Mr. Kronig. Now he's dead."

"We were there when he was killed, but we're not allowed to talk about that," said Ryan, looking to Lamont.

"How come you're still alive? How did you get away? You were the real targets, weren't you?" asked Connie.

"As I said, I can't discuss what happened. The important thing is that we are safe and the forces that wanted us dead are no longer a threat. That's all I can tell you."

"Then what's the purpose of our meeting?" asked Retzler, suspecting that he already knew the answer.

Ryan spoke again. "We want you to see that we are alive and safe. We also want you to know how we ended up in Molokai. After the murder trial, with the help of Mr. Kronig, we voluntarily signed a contract with the CIA. We agreed to submit to the drug and to relocate to Molokai. Because of Alana's celebrity, she consented to cosmetic surgery. We did it for our own safety but also for the country—to protect the secret of the drug. We know that Mr. Lamont has briefed you on its importance in the war on terror."

Connie glared at Lamont, her eyes on fire. "You've brought us all the way here so they can try to talk us out of running our story?"

"We want our lives back," said Ryan. "We want to go back to Molokai, to our home. If you publish your article, that will be impossible. The media will track us down and hound us for the rest of our lives. We will never be free. So we are asking you to forget about us…not to write about us."

"I'm sorry, I can't do that."

Alana exploded. "If it hadn't been for you, none of this would have happened. Mr. Kronig would still be alive today and we'd still be on Molokai. I don't understand why you couldn't leave us alone. Why you had to come searching for us, tracking us down, wrecking our lives. Now you want to ruin them again just to sell newspapers."

"The public has a right to know what happened," argued Connie, her voice rising.

"That's enough!" shouted Retzler, abruptly standing. "I've seen and heard all I need—we won't be running the article. We'll leave now."

Connie stared in disbelief, aghast that her boss would suddenly end the meeting and squash the story. Her hands gripped the arms of her chair tightly.

…

Lamont remained behind, so it was only Connie and Retzler returning to Washington. Connie quietly seethed during the car ride from Butner to the airport, not wanting to argue in front of the driver, knowing the topic was top secret. However, as soon as they were in the air, she lit into him. "Why the hell did you stop the interview?" she shouted.

"Continuing would have been pointless."

"Why? You're allowing the CIA to intimidate us. We're talking about freedom of the press and the public's right to know."

Retzler sighed. "It's not that easy, Connie. Think about it…We've just been played. The story's dead—I recognized it was a trap when Alana and Ryan walked into the room."

Connie pulled back her head in confusion. "What do you mean?"

"What was the title of your article?"

"'The Strange Disappearance of Alana Shannon.'"

"And has she disappeared?"

Connie slumped back in her seat. "Well, no. We now know where she is—so all we have to do is change the title."

"Change it to what? We promised not to reveal anything we learned today. Well, today we saw her and she's alive, so there is no disappearance and consequently no story."

"But we know from Kronig's tape that the CIA ordered her murder."

"He never used the word *murder*, he said *erased*—and she hasn't been erased, has she?"

"We can still run the story without mentioning anything about that happened today."

Retzler took off his glasses and riveted his eyes on Connie. She stared back defiantly. "Let's dissect your article, shall we? The CIA allegedly orders Alana and Ryan killed. Alana and Ryan leave Washington with Wilhelm Kronig, who offers them protection. Somebody kills Kronig, and Alana and Ryan disappear. End of story. The strong implication is that somebody killed them too. Now we know that's not the case…They're both alive and safe. However, we can't reveal that, because we promised Mr. Lamont confidentiality. If we print the original story, we're misleading the public, implying that the CIA killed her. If we print the truth, not only are we potentially harming national security, but we are reneging on a promise of nondisclosure—an action that could damage our reputation and poison our credibility."

Connie glowered.

"Even if we were to run the story as we now understand it, there is no real news. All we have is the now-dead deputy director saying the CIA wanted to kill Alana and Ryan. However, we have nothing to back up his statement. And the CIA didn't kill them—they're fine. So again, where's the story?

Connie sulked.

"Add to that the national security concerns and the direct appeal from Alana and Ryan."

Connie rose in her seat. "Ryan and Alana are not our sources—they're the story. We have no obligation to protect them."

"No, we don't, but Alana is right. Your visit to Hawaii set this off. Your story may be true, but it's weak journalism. If we release it, we will be stirring up a hornet's nest and, ultimately, we will be the ones getting stung."

Connie clasped her arms over her chest in frustration. What made her especially livid was the realization that Retzler was right—they had been played.

CHAPTER SIXTY-SEVEN

AFTER CONNIE AND Retzler departed, Lamont stayed behind with Ryan and Alana.

"Do you really think they'll drop the article?" asked Alana.

"Yes. Retzler will rein her in. He sees the bigger picture. He told us that he would shut it down and I trust him—he's a man of his word." Lamont glanced at his watch. "A few days ago I laid out your options. You've had time to talk it over. What have you decided?"

Ryan spoke. "We want to go back to Molokai, but not under the influence of the drug. Now that we know who we are, we want to keep our memories—it's who we are."

"But I thought you liked being Bill and Cheryl Parker? You said you were in a state of bliss on the island."

"We were—but it wasn't real," said Alana. "It all seems like a fog. Without our past, only a part of us existed. We don't want to go back to that. We don't want to lose each other again."

"As I told you before, the only way you can return to Hawaii is under the drug. Otherwise it's too risky. I don't have to remind you that you signed a contract agreeing to relinquish your memories."

Alana's eyes flashed. "The contract didn't say anything about a hit man trying to kill us in a swamp. It didn't say one of your agents would bind and gag us in the trunk of a car. I think that's enough to void the contract."

Ryan piled on. "Even if we agreed to go back under the drug, what's to stop it all from happening again? Maybe something new will trigger a memory, or someone will recognize us like before, and we'll start searching again for our real identities. It could be a continuous cycle."

Lamont recognized that he was probably right.

"Alana and I have talked it over—we refuse to resubmit to the drug. We're not signing any new contracts with the CIA, period."

Lamont smoothed his fingers along the sides of his mustache. "You realize that we don't need a contract. We did that to protect you. We could force the drug on you."

"You wouldn't do that, would you?" pleaded Alana.

"Don't test me."

CHAPTER SIXTY-EIGHT

THREE DAYS LATER Lamont sat in a briefing room at the FBI's J. Edgar Hoover Building in Washington, watching a slide presentation on the investigation into Wilhelm Kronig's murder. FBI field agent Maria Sanchez was the presenter. Although she was very professional and businesslike, Lamont took note of her attractiveness—black hair pulled straight back, highlighting large walnut eyes and arching eyebrows. Her trim figure fit smartly into a dark, tailored business suit.

Bruce Marko and Jack Carter, associate director of the FBI, were the only others present. Lamont and Carter had a long history, although it had not always been a cordial one. Most of the time they worked well together, but the CIA had occasionally tried to put the brakes on FBI investigations, claiming national security interests. This had led to several shouting matches, but ultimately the CIA always won out.

Agent Sanchez clicked for the next slide, and an aerial shot of the murder scene appeared on the screen. Circled in red were Kronig's Cadillac and the body of the motorcycle man. "From the damage to the trees, we estimate that Mr. Kronig's car left the highway at a speed of between fifty-five and sixty-five miles per hour," said Sanchez. A laser pointer traced the trajectory. "We assume that the driver either swerved to avoid an object, was forced off the road, or became incapacitated."

The next slide was an artist's sketch of Kronig's body in the car. "Mr. Kronig was shot three times. We believe this was the first bullet." A dotted line appeared on the screen. "From Kronig's forward position, the bullet entered at a 270-degree angle, passed through his jaw, and lodged in the passenger side door below the window. The second and third bullets were fired at close range and entered into his upper rib cage and his heart at an angle of approximately three hundred and thirty degrees." Two more dotted lines materialized. "The first bullet likely incapacitated Mr. Kronig, and the last two killed him."

Lamont was relieved that she was showing artist's sketches—he didn't want his last memory of Kronig to be of some gruesome photograph.

Next appeared a sketch of the motorcycle man prone on the ground. "The second victim was found nineteen feet away on his back—shot once in the shoulder and once through the brain, above his left eye. We also recovered three bullets that missed. The entry angle of the injuries indicates that the bullets were fired from the vicinity of Kronig's car, probably from within." More dotted lines appeared.

"Have you found the weapons?" asked Lamont, although he already knew the answer.

"We recovered a Colt M1911 next to the second victim…Ballistic tests confirm that the bullets that hit Mr. Kronig were fired from that gun."

"How about the other weapon?" asked Marko.

"Kronig's shoulder holster was empty. He usually carried a Glock 23 with a nine-millimeter clip…the same caliber that killed the second victim. We've searched for the gun using metal detectors and high-tech scanning techniques—but nothing's turned up."

"Have you identified the second victim?" asked Marko.

"No. We have checked his fingerprints and dental records, but there are no matches in any of our databases. Furthermore, we have no reports of a missing person with his description. All we know is that he was wearing a motorcycle jacket and boots."

"Is that's why the initial investigators thought a motorcycle was present?" asked Lamont.

"Yes…and we found a motorcycle helmet nearby. Tests confirmed that the hair particles in the helmet matched those of the second victim."

"Where did you find the helmet?" asked Marko, wondering how he had missed it.

"It was near the road in a thicket of brush, completely covered in mud."

"So what do you think happened?" asked Lamont.

"As reported in the papers, we believe a third person, or persons, may have been present and fled on the motorcycle. However, we've found no evidence of anybody else at the scene."

"What's your best theory?" asked Marko.

Agent Sanchez shrugged. "We don't have one. There are a number of alternative theories, all with gaping holes. The entire scene is a forensic nightmare. The swamp swallows up everything. The rain and the shifting tides have erased all footprints and may have swept away some of the physical evidence. Furthermore, if there was a third person who fled by motorcycle, that person might be anywhere by now. We don't know where to begin looking. We don't have a description of the motorcycle, we don't have a description of the person, we don't have fingerprints, and we don't even know what time the shooting took place. All we know is that the third shooter's clothes would have been muddy, but that's not much to go on."

Carter interjected. "And we still don't have a motive…nor do we know what Mr. Kronig was doing in the swamp or where he was headed." He raised an eyebrow at Lamont. "So that's the current status of our investigation—unless there's something else you would like to offer?"

To Lamont, it was the first indication that Carter suspected the CIA knew more than it was letting on. "I have nothing to add." Carter thanked Agent Sanchez for the presentation and indicated he needed to have a private discussion with Lamont.

CHAPTER SIXTY-NINE

As SANCHEZ AND Marko departed the FBI briefing room, Lamont and Carter positioned their chairs to face each other. Both men were in their early fifties. Carter, a former college football player, was tall and athletic, with broad shoulders and a tapered waist. He wore his salt-and-pepper hair cropped tight on the sides and short on top.

"There's a new development, James, which I need to share with you. A police officer in the town of Duck, North Carolina, has come forward. He believes that Mr. Kronig kept a beach house on the Outer Banks under the name of Martin Henley. Could that be true?"

Lamont flinched at the mention of Duck and hoped that Carter hadn't noticed. "I know he liked to vacation at the beach, but he never indicated where. Have you tried locating Mr. Henley?"

"Mr. Henley doesn't exist, and the beach house in question is owned by Epstein Global Associates in the Cayman Islands." Carter paused, giving Lamont a knowing look. "I seem to recall that the CIA has had arrangements with that firm in the past." He folded his hands in a tent in front of his face, waiting for Lamont's response.

"It is possible that Kronig may have kept a house at the beach under an assumed name—so what?"

"Because according to this police officer, some unusual events recently occurred there."

"Really?"

"It started when the officer intercepted a man and woman on a motorcycle searching for Mr. Henley's house. Neither wore a helmet as required by North Carolina law, and both were peculiarly dressed—ill-fitting sweat clothes and muddy shoes." Carter emphasized the word *muddy.* "They claimed they had bought the clothes at a thrift store in Elizabeth City after their motorcycle spun out. The man carried a Hawaiian driver's license but had no registration card for the cycle." Carter paused again.

Lamont gave no response and Carter continued. "Elizabeth City is only seventeen miles from the scene of the shooting, and all of this occurred around the time that Kronig disappeared." He paused again, watching Lamont. "I think you can see where this is leading?"

"Perhaps," answered Lamont, his eyes steady and unblinking.

"It gets stranger. The man on the motorcycle claimed to be Henley's nephew. Since the officer knew Henley, he led them to his house where Henley's housekeeper, Aida, vouched for them. And by the way, the officer's description of Aida bears a striking resemblance to Kronig's housekeeper—Maddie—whom I believe you know."

"Of course I know Maddie."

"The officer suspected that something was off-kilter. The next day he noticed a new car parked in front of the Henley house, a Chevy Malibu. He rang the doorbell and a man he said resembled George Clooney greeted him. The man indicated that he was an old friend of Mr. Henley and that Aida and the two people on the motorcycle had left earlier that morning."

Lamont's body immediately stiffened. Marko had never mentioned anything about talking to a police officer at the beach house.

Carter cocked his head. "You know, earlier this morning Agent Sanchez remarked to me that Bruce Marko reminded her a little of George Clooney. Strange coincidence, don't you think?"

"I don't put much stock in coincidences."

"Here's the thing. The officer questioned the man and it soon became apparent that he didn't really know Mr. Henley. The officer pulled his gun and a confrontation commenced. The next thing the officer remembers is waking up in his police car several hours later."

Lamont tried hard to hide his fury at Marko—he was hearing of this encounter for the first time. Beneath a calm exterior, his blood boiled. *I'm going to kill him,* he thought.

"It turns out that the license plate on the Chevy was counterfeit and the plate for the motorcycle was registered to a dead man. Nothing adds up, does it?"

Lamont stayed silent, avoiding Carter's gaze, imagining that he was strangling Marko.

"The officer remembers the first names of the man and the woman on the motorcycle, Bill and Cheryl, but can't recall their last name. They told him they were married. We're about to make a request to the Hawaii Department of Motor Vehicles. We'll be asking them to query their database for the last names of all persons named Cheryl and Bill, or Cheryl and William, who live at the same address. That should narrow it down."

"You're going to have to pull that request," Lamont stated loudly and forcefully.

Carter raised his arms in a gesture of surrender. "I knew it from the start. This had the stench of a CIA fiasco all over it. So how are we going to handle this? The usual? You demand that we halt the investigation citing national secrets. I resist, until I'm ordered to do so by someone higher up."

"We could play it that way, assuming you want to go through the all the hassle and the waste of time. Or I could just have the president call your boss."

Carter shrugged his shoulders. "I hate fighting with you, James...I never win. I'll put an end to that angle of the investigation."

"I'll need more than that," commanded Lamont.

"What?"

"Has the police officer talked to anybody else about this incident?"

"We've instructed him to stay quiet and to only deal with our agents, but he's already shared his account with his police chief and some of the other officers."

Lamont clenched his jaw. "Then he's going to have to retract his story."

"How the hell are you going to get him to do that?" asked Carter, shaking his head.

"Just work with me on this."

"You bastards get away with murder, don't you?"

"I trust you mean that figuratively."

"Only you would know for sure."

CHAPTER SEVENTY

RETURNING TO LANGLEY from the FBI briefing, Lamont burst into Marko's office. Marko glanced up from his computer with a vacant stare.

"You're fired," shouted Lamont. "Pack your things and get out of here."

"Now?"

"Yes, now."

"What did I do?"

"You neglected to mention that you assaulted a police officer in North Carolina."

"I had to—he was about to blow everything. He wanted me to open my car trunk. Ryan and Alana were in there—I had no choice."

"And tell me again, what were Ryan and Alana doing in the trunk of your car?"

"Look, James, I made a mistake. But if the officer had seen them, it would have been all over. I couldn't have talked my way out of that."

"And is there a reason that you haven't told me about this before?"

"You didn't ask," answered Marko in a deadpan voice.

Lamont's face turned crimson. "I instructed you to tell me everything that happened when you were together with Alana and Ryan."

"Technically, we weren't together—I was in the house and they were in the trunk. Besides, I didn't think it was relevant. I figured the policeman would wake up later, wouldn't know what happened, and that would be the end of it."

"You really thought that?" asked Lamont, dumbfounded.

"I know, I messed up. I didn't know what the hell I was doing—it was very confusing. I was under orders to kill Ryan and Alana and I almost did. When I came to my senses, I was ashamed—I didn't want you to know about the cop. I was hoping it would never come out."

"You felt ashamed? I thought you didn't have emotions."

"Sometimes I do, but it takes a lot for them to surface. When I was a kid, my dad would beat me if I cried—he said he wasn't going to raise a sissy. Then he beat me if I laughed—he said life wasn't a joke. I watched him knock my mother around...She just took it. She never fought back, she never cried; she never showed any reaction at all. She told me that he could hurt us physically but never mentally...that we should never give him that satisfaction. So I learned from her. I hid my feelings until I was numb. After he killed my mother, I saw a lot of shrinks. I recall one saying that I was damaged goods."

Lamont stared at Marko, unsure what to think. He had never talked about his past before and had never indicated that his father had killed his mother. For a brief instant he felt sorry for him. Yet Marko had related this horrific story without showing even the slightest hint of hurt or sorrow—as if it were someone else's life. "Go get some boxes to clear out your desk and files," snapped Lamont, determined not to give in. "I'll have you escorted out of the building and your credentials rescinded. Anything you take will need to be cleared through security."

"Can't you give me some more time? What about the drug manufacture? Who will handle that? And what about the interrogations? Nobody else knows the full story of the drug except you, Scotty Olds, and me. And there's also the Black Box operation."

Lamont realized that Marko made sense. In his anger he hadn't thought through what he would do without Marko.

"Who will replace me?" Marko asked.

"That's not your concern."

"Not any of Crowder's people, I hope. They can't be trusted."

"Just go get the boxes."

...

Marko left the office and Lamont sat behind the desk. Except for a few scattered papers, the desk was clear. The white office walls were completely blank. There were no personal effects anywhere, nothing to suggest that the office belonged to anyone. Lamont's anger slowly subsided. Marko was right, he thought, nobody else could step in without extensive preparation. It would mean sharing dark secrets with a new and untested individual. "God damn you," he whispered under his breath. He had a million things to do now that he was interim director. He didn't have time to groom a replacement, and there were no obvious candidates. He knew he still needed Marko with him.

Marko returned with boxes. "Are you going to sit there and watch me pack?"

"It shouldn't take long—there's hardly anything here." The edge faded from Lamont's voice. "What will you do now?"

"I don't know…This has been my whole life. I'll have to weigh my options—if I have any."

"Put the boxes down. Sometimes you drive me up a wall, but you're right, I need you here to help me. It looks like I'm stuck with you for a while."

Marko dropped the boxes. "So you're not firing me?"

"Not yet. But one more screwup and I'll kill you with my bare hands."

CHAPTER SEVENTY-ONE

IT HAD BEEN a crazy whirlwind since Officer Clifford relayed his story to the FBI. The FBI agent instructed him not to talk to anybody about the matter until he got back to him. The next day the agent called and asked if he could meet with him and another official at the FBI regional office in Norfolk, Virginia, the next morning at ten. Officer Clifford agreed, and the agent again reminded him not to discuss the matter with anyone, not even his wife.

Clifford called his chief and told him he was taking a personal day. He told his wife that he had confidential business to take care of and couldn't tell her what it was. She reacted with worry and suspicion—he had never done anything like that in the past.

He didn't sleep well that night, mulling over everything that had happened and apprehensive about the upcoming meeting. He left before sunrise, wanting to give himself plenty of time, and arrived in Norfolk two hours before the scheduled meeting.

He bided his time at a diner, gulping pancakes and drinking too much coffee. When he arrived for the meeting, he cleared security and ended up alone in a small room with two chairs. A gray glass panel covered one wall, and the others were empty. He recognized it as a room for interrogating suspects.

A few minutes later the FBI agent entered along with a distinguished mature man in a silver suit and blue tie. They all shook hands, and the FBI agent immediately excused himself.

"My name is Skip Baxter. I work for the National Security Council at the White House, handling matters related to domestic terrorism."

Clifford could hardly believe that somebody from the White House would want to interview him.

"The FBI has shared with me your story about the two people on the motorcycle and the assault by the man at Mr. Henley's beach house who reminded you of George Clooney. He also briefed me on your suspicion that Mr. Henley and Mr. Kronig are one and the same."

"That's correct," answered Clifford, his voice cracking slightly. The room felt very warm.

"Our meeting today must remain absolutely confidential, as it concerns a grave national security matter. You can never reveal anything that we discuss. If you do, we will prosecute you. Understood?"

"Yes," Clifford replied, caught off guard by the gravity of the man's words.

"Good, so let's get down to business. You are correct. Wilhelm Kronig used the name Martin Henley as an alias. The beach house in Duck is a CIA safe house—that's why its ownership is fuzzy. I assume you are familiar with safe houses?"

"Only from what I've read in books and seen in the movies."

"When not being used for official purposes, it served as Mr. Kronig's vacation home...a perk for someone in his position." Baxter leaned forward and lowered his voice. "What we have here is a very delicate international situation. An agent of the Russian government murdered Mr. Kronig."

"Russians?" Clifford shot back, feeling his armpits sweat.

"Yes, but Mr. Kronig wasn't the target. We are confident that the Russian government had no idea that he was the driver of the vehicle—they would never assassinate a former deputy director of the CIA."

"An assassination?" repeated Clifford. It seemed like something out of the movies. "Then who was the target?"

"This man," said Baxter, handing a photograph to Clifford.

Clifford's jaw dropped as he stared at the picture. "I don't understand. That's the man I stopped on the motorcycle who claimed he was Mr. Henley's nephew. His name was Bill. He wasn't a Russian."

"His real name is Anatoly Popovich and he speaks fluent English. Mr. Kronig and another CIA agent were transporting him to the safe house when the assassin struck on a motorcycle, forcing Mr. Kronig's car off the road and into the swamp. A shoot-out took place, resulting in Mr. Kronig's death. Fortunately, the CIA agent in the car was able to take out the assassin." Baxter stopped for a second, waiting for Officer Clifford to absorb what he was telling him. "You also met the CIA agent—she was the woman on the motorcycle who told you she was Bill's wife, Cheryl."

Clifford's jaw dropped.

"I know this is a lot to grasp all at once. After the shoot-out, the Russian and the CIA agent escaped on the assassin's motorcycle. You intercepted them on the way to the safe house, where they had previously planned to rendezvous with Kronig's assistant, Aida, whom you know."

"You mean she works for the CIA too?"

Baxter didn't answer. He sat back in his chair, looked hard at Clifford, and slowly shook his head. "You have a knack for being at the wrong place at the wrong time, Officer Clifford. The fourth person you met at the house, the George Clooney look-alike, is a CIA fixer. I'm sure you are familiar with that term?"

Clifford nodded.

"His job was to clean up after everyone left—to remove any evidence that the Russian had been there. You came close to botching the operation. I know you were only doing your job, but he needed to get you out of the way—he had no choice but to disarm you."

Clifford swallowed hard. His world was turned upside down. "So who is the Russian—what's his name again?"

"Popovich. At one time he was a close adviser to the Russian president and was purported to be his personal banker. He recently fell out of favor at the Kremlin and feared he would be imprisoned. He escaped to the United States several weeks ago with damaging information concerning shady financial dealings involving high-ranking Soviet leaders, including the president. He carried papers documenting secret foreign bank accounts, shell companies, kickback schemes, and payoffs to prominent politicians in eastern Europe. Popovich wanted to go to the press, but the CIA took him into protective custody to debrief him. Popovich was convinced that the Russian authorities would try to kill him, so the CIA decided to move him to the safe house. Obviously we had a security breach."

"What does this have to do with me?" asked Clifford. The room felt stifling.

"We need your help. We have two requests. The first is a simple one. We want you to keep quiet about the two people on the motorcycle and the events at the beach house. I'll get to the second request in a moment. First, let me tell you why we need to keep this secret.

"We are currently immersed in important negotiations with the Russian government regarding the war on terror. As you know, they hold veto power in the United Nations Security Council, where we are pushing a resolution to authorize sanctions against nations doing business or otherwise providing assistance to Iraq, Iran, and North Korea…the axis of evil, as the president calls them. The Russians have been playing hardball, demanding ridiculous concessions in exchange for their acquiescence. Are you following all this, Officer Clifford?"

"I think so."

"Now, can you imagine the fallout if word leaked that the Russians had assassinated the former deputy director of the CIA on American soil? It would poison the well. Of course, they would deny any involvement. In response, Congress and the American people would demand aggressive retaliatory actions. The Russians would counter by refusing to assist us in any way, and would veto the UN resolution."

"So they're just going to get away with it?"

"Not exactly. Popovich is cooperating, and we know what he knows. We can use that information as clout over the Russians. If they don't cooperate, we will threaten to leak Popovich's documents. We can do it in dribs and drabs—a kind of Chinese water torture. We will be positioned to exert undreamed influence over the Russian leaders."

"This is all way above me."

Baxter leaned forward again in his chair. He lowered his voice. "Earlier I told you we had two requests. In addition to keeping quiet, we want you to lie."

"Lie? How?" Sweat dripped from Clifford's forehead.

"I know that lying goes against your principles, but this is the big leagues. We're talking geopolitical realities and raw power. Like it or not, that is the world we live in."

"What do you want me to lie about?"

"First, let me play a message for you. I will play it only once, so listen carefully." Baxter took a small device out of his pocket and pushed a button.

Clifford reeled when he recognized the voice.

"Officer Clifford, this is the president of the United States. I know that Mr. Baxter has briefed you concerning the gravity of the situation surrounding Wilhelm Kronig's murder. I have just read your profile. You have been a steadfast law enforcement officer for over twenty years, and I thank you for your dedicated service. In a few moments Mr. Baxter will ask you to do something that may seem wrong. However, it's crucial to the security of our country that you cooperate. Through the long history of our nation, many patriots have been called upon to make great sacrifices, sometimes with their lives. Today we are at war against a new enemy, terrorism, and we need your cooperation to keep America safe and free. I know I can count on you. God bless you, Officer Clifford."

Baxter again pushed a button on the device. "I just deleted the message." He put the device back in his suit pocket and traced a finger along the cleft of his chin as he waited for Clifford's reaction.

Clifford stayed quiet for a long time, amazed and humbled that the president of the United States had sent him a personal message. "What do you want me to lie about?"

Baxter stood up and placed his hand reassuringly on Clifford's shoulder. "This will be hard. We want you to tell your chief of police and your fellow officers that no confrontation took place at the beach house. We want you to tell them that you fell asleep in the car and you were too ashamed to admit it, so you made up the entire story."

"They'll fire me."

"Possibly, but I doubt that. They will discipline you for sure, and you'll probably lose some pay. I also know that this will be excruciatingly embarrassing for you and your family. You can take solace in knowing that you are making an important sacrifice for your country—the kind of selfless act that the president mentioned."

"I have my twenty years in. I can retire at any time. My wife has been nagging me to."

"That may be your best option. We are also prepared to offer you financial compensation."

"What?" Clifford asked, looking perplexed.

"Think of it as a token of appreciation from a grateful nation."

"That won't be necessary. I will tell the chief and everybody else that I fell asleep. I could never let the president down."

END OF PART 2

PART 3

CHAPTER SEVENTY-TWO

ANYONE WATCHING THE couple descending the stairs from the prop plane at the Molokai Airport would have thought they were tourists, dressed in Hawaiian floral-print shirts and shorts—until they both knelt and simultaneously kissed the ground.

They retrieved their luggage and took a taxi to their house, just off the Kamehameha Highway, on the ocean. As the taxi sped away, they held each other closely and kissed in a long embrace. They could hardly believe it had been less than a month since their abduction. Yet before them stood the house they'd thought they would never see again. The newly planted grass needed cutting and the tropical plants needed pruning, but beyond that nothing had changed.

Entering the front door, they both let out a tremendous sigh of relief. Everything looked the same as they had left it. The breakfast dishes were still on the table, the cooking pans on the stove. Clothes were scattered across their beds, reminders of their frantic dressing when the CIA agents arrived. They walked outside to the veranda, looking out at the beautiful expanse of blue ocean and the green-walled cliffs of Maui and Lanai in the distance. The flowers in the vases had wilted, but everything else seemed perfect. Holding hands, they walked across the back yard to the small sandy beach. They removed their shoes and waded in. The soft water felt wonderful caressing their ankles.

They spent the afternoon straightening the house, washing dishes, disposing of spoiled food in the refrigerator, and sorting through the mountain of mail that had piled up. It felt as if they were in a dream.

As the sun lowered, they opened an expensive bottle of a cabernet sauvignon they had been saving for a special occasion. They poured two glasses and curled up on the veranda sofa. As the sun dipped, the water turned from blue to silver to gold. A diamond-studded sky slowly materialized.

The sudden sound of the doorbell shattered their peace. They reacted with alarm. Cheryl's face flushed hot as the panic struck, and she feared another horrible surprise. She wished they had a gun in the house.

"You stay here, let me get it," said Bill. He went back through the house to the front door, stopping by the kitchen to grab a butcher knife.

From the veranda Cheryl circled around the side yard to the driveway and observed a Molokai police car parked in front. She ran back to the veranda and into the house. Bill stood at the doorway talking to someone. "Who is it?" she asked.

"It's Sergeant Keahi."

"Hello, Mrs. Parker," said Keahi when he saw her. His voice was formal and his expression cold. "I heard you arrived back on the island. I wanted to make sure you were all right after the way you ditched me."

"We're fine," said Bill. "Please come in, Sergeant."

"I'd prefer to stay here…and I'm no longer a sergeant, thanks to you. I'm just Officer Keahi now. You pulled a horrible stunt on me. When you weren't here when I came to pick you up, I was beside myself with worry. I thought something terrible had happened, and I blamed myself for releasing you. I called out your names and searched all over. I even checked your sailboat at the harbor. I got a warrant to search the house. It looked like you left in a hurry. I was worried sick that the kidnappers had come back for you. Then we got word from the feds that you were fugitives—that you had bought plane tickets to the mainland. So tell me, what happened?"

"We're sorry," said Bill, "We didn't mean any harm. After the events at the airport, we feared for our safety—so we ran away."

"Where did you go?"

Cheryl spoke. "After you dropped us off in town, we took the ferry to Maui and caught a flight to Chicago. From there we went back to visit our family in Colorado. We stayed with relatives in Denver trying to figure out what was happening and what we should do. We had no idea why anyone would want to kidnap us."

"Well, I guess you figured it out, 'cause you're back."

"The CIA caught up with us in Colorado. It turns out it was a case of mistaken identity. The CIA was searching for a man and a woman who had stolen classified documents. They were acting on a tip. Someone familiar with the case was vacationing on the island and spotted us. He thought we resembled the missing couple and notified the CIA."

Bill took over the conversation. "They were very apologetic. They showed us pictures of the two people they were seeking—there were some similarities. They convinced the feds to drop the charges."

"I wondered why they suddenly dismissed the case. If not for that, I would have lost my job. When the feds found out that I had let you go, I was in big trouble. The department suspended me without pay pending an investigation. They wanted to charge me with a crime—aiding and abetting fugitives. It was a very tough time for my family and me. The department reinstated me when the feds dropped the charges, but they gave me a letter of reprimand and a demotion...a pay cut too."

"We didn't mean for anything bad to happen," said Cheryl. "We feared for our lives and thought that our only chance was to escape. Looking back, we know that running away was a silly overreaction, but at the time it seemed like the only thing to do. We weren't thinking rationally."

Keahi's face softened slightly. "You know the Hawaiian way, we don't take things too seriously and we don't hold grudges—life is too short for that. But I wanted you to know that you let me down. Uncle Eddie would have been very disappointed. I thought we were friends."

"We still are," said Bill. "Is there anything we can do to make it up to you?"

"No. Just stay out of trouble and don't ask me for any more favors."

...

Bill and Cheryl watched at the doorway as Officer Keahi drove away.

"I feel so bad for him," said Cheryl.

"We only did what we had to do," answered Bill, putting his arm around her and pulling her close.

CHAPTER SEVENTY-THREE

CONNIE BLYTHE FEVERISHLY typed on her computer and didn't look up when Aaron Retzler peered into her office.

Retzler wasn't sure whether she was ignoring him or hadn't seen him. "Connie—do you have a minute?"

She jumped at the sound of his voice. "How long have you been there?"

"Not long. I didn't want to interrupt you…You seemed off in another world. I heard you were looking for me."

"I need to brief you on a new story I'm working on. It could be big."

"It doesn't involve the CIA, does it?" asked Retzler, frowning.

"No, it involves the army—based on a website tip. Do you remember all the publicity a few months ago about the rescue of an aid worker in Afghanistan?"

"Sure…our first skirmish against the Taliban."

"The official version goes like this—as our troops entered the city of Herat, a seven-man squad got separated from their platoon and wound up south of the city in a small village. One of the villagers spoke some English and told them that a female American aid worker was being held hostage at a medical clinic there. The squad leader decided to investigate. As they approached the clinic, armed Taliban fighters emerged and opened fire. During the gun battle, three Taliban fighters were killed. One of our soldiers was shot in the leg, and the aid worker was rescued unharmed."

"I recall they handed out medals."

"A Silver Star to the squad leader and a Purple Heart to the injured soldier."

"So who contacted you?"

"One of the soldiers…Corporal First Class Wayne Jackson. He told me the official story was a sham. They had been ordered to keep quiet about what really happened. Jackson and two others in the squad made a pact that they would tell the truth when they were released from the army. Jackson is the first, honorably discharged last week."

"So what's the real story?"

"The villager never said the aid worker was being held hostage…He just wanted the soldiers to know that an American was there. She had been providing medical care and the villagers were trying to keep her presence hidden from the Taliban. The tribal leader for the area had deployed a couple of his fighters to protect the clinic. They weren't Taliban."

"Shit," whispered Retzler.

"The soldiers didn't know what to expect, so they split up. Four approached from the front and three from the back. When they drew near, two men came running out of the hospital waving rifles and yelling. None of the soldiers understood what they were saying, so they raised their weapons in defense. The squad leader, a young lieutenant, shouted for them to release the aid worker. They responded in Pashto. This went back and forth for several minutes—neither understanding the other. Finally a man dressed in green scrubs came out of the clinic and shouted in English for the soldiers to lower their weapons.

"The lieutenant wasn't sure what to do and ordered his men to hold steady. In response the fighters pointed their rifles back at the soldiers. One of our men in the back panicked and opened fire. All hell broke loose, and the three Afghans were killed in a hail of bullets."

"But I thought one of our men got hit in the leg."

"He did, but it was friendly fire. It was a terrible setup, soldiers in the front and back firing into the middle."

"Do you have other sources?"

"I spoke to the two other soldiers, still in the army. They confirmed everything."

"Wow."

"Not exactly. They're still in uniform and they're under orders not to contradict the official version. I can use their stories for backup, but not their names—at least not until they're discharged. So I'm referring to them as Soldier A and Soldier B."

"We'll need more than that. What about the others in the squad?"

"Two of them were later killed in combat. Jackson said the others wouldn't challenge the official story. One is the injured private—he has to wear a leg prosthesis and doesn't want his Purple Heart discredited. The other is the lieutenant."

"Did you follow up?"

"The private wouldn't take my call, and the lieutenant said he wasn't allowed to comment, but I sensed discomfort in his voice. I think he may come around. I also tracked down the aid worker. She confirmed that she was never a hostage. I have a telephone interview scheduled with her for tomorrow."

"You're right, this could be very big." He smiled. "Nice to see you excited again. Are we still friends?"

Connie extended her hand. "Friends."

"And you're willing to forget about the CIA?"

She gave him a pained nod. "For now."

CHAPTER SEVENTY-FOUR

DEBBIE CLIFFORD PUT down her book and studied her husband, Tom, as he stood knee-deep in the surf, his fishing rod bent toward the ocean. When he turned to wave, the morning sun shone off his white hair and caught his face in a wide smile. It was a beautiful winter day on the Outer Banks, sunny, with highs in the low seventies. In the distance pelicans glided effortlessly over breaking waves. In front of her chair, skinny-legged sandpipers darted back and forth at the water's edge. The beach was mostly deserted, and the only sounds were the roar of the ocean and the cries of seagulls.

Two weeks had passed since Tom Clifford retired from the Duck Police Department, and she hadn't seen him so relaxed and contented in years. There were other changes too. His stride was more purposeful and his posture more erect. He projected a newfound self-assurance that reminded her of the cocky young man she had married so long ago. He was also more attentive and affectionate. All this despite having left the police force in disgrace.

She was still trying to make sense of what had happened. After the assault at the beach house, she noticed that his mood darkened and he had trouble sleeping. He was unusually quiet and withdrawn, but snapped at the smallest provocation. She didn't press him, but he finally opened up. He told her that he was ashamed at how easily he had been disarmed and subdued. He told her that he was a joke as a police officer. He told her that the younger officers made fun of him. Then he confessed the real reason for his gloom. He said that right before he lost consciousness in the assailant's chokehold, two terrifying thoughts flashed across his mind—that he was going to die and that he had wasted his life.

She did her best to console him, to convince him otherwise, but he remained downhearted. She suggested he speak to the police psychologist, but he resisted, saying it would be too embarrassing. Therefore, when he later took the day off and refused to tell her where he was going, she suspected it was to see a psychologist in another town. From that day on, things changed rapidly.

When he arrived home that evening, he seemed different, as if a tremendous weight was gone from his shoulders. He smiled for the first time since the incident and seemed remarkably serene.

"I've made a decision. I'm going to retire," he announced.

She rushed to him, wrapping her arms around him in a tight hug. This is what she'd wanted all along. It meant that she could leave her nursing job at the hospital. They had talked about this for years—they would buy an RV and drive around the country.

"Have you picked a date yet?" she asked excitedly.

"Tomorrow. I've already spoken to the chief."

She was stunned. "Tomorrow? Don't you need to give more notice than that?"

"Not under the circumstances."

"What circumstances?"

"If I don't retire, they're going to suspend me and begin disciplinary proceedings."

Her face became ashen. "Discipline you for what?"

"I lied about the incident at the beach house. It never took place. I fell asleep in the car. It's happened before. I didn't want anybody to know, so I fabricated the whole story."

She studied his face as he averted his eyes. She didn't believe him for a second. After three decades together, she had become a very good lie detector, and he was a pitiful liar. However, she couldn't fathom why he would claim that the assault had never occurred.

The following day he signed the retirement papers. A few of the senior officers held an impromptu retirement party at a local pizzeria. It all felt very uncomfortable.

She hoped the incident would stay quiet, but the next day the news hit the *Outer Banks Sentinel*:

"The Duck Police Department confirmed today that a reported assault on one of their officers never actually occurred. In a sworn statement, Officer Thomas Clifford, a twenty-two-year veteran of the force, admitted that he fabricated the story to cover up that he had fallen asleep in his police car. He further indicated that it was not the first time he had slept on duty. Police Chief Phillip Anderson indicated that Clifford suffers from narcolepsy, an affliction that triggers uncontrollable sleep episodes. Clifford has retired from the force."

Debbie knew that the narcolepsy claim was bullshit, offered by the chief to save face. However, Tom's reaction puzzled her the most. He didn't seem bothered at all by the public disclosure and the accompanying ridicule. In fact, he basked in the notoriety. He carried himself with a smug swagger and a confident demeanor, suggesting he had done nothing wrong or shameful.

Their retirement plans quickly fell by the wayside. Tom announced that he wanted to visit Washington and tour the White House, the FBI, and the State Department. Debbie was astonished; he had never expressed any interest in going to DC before. Furthermore, he displayed a sudden fascination with current events, especially those involving the United Nations and relations with Russia. He scoured the Internet for news, took books out of the library, and even purchased subscriptions to *Time* magazine and the *Washington Post*. When she questioned him about his new interests, he just gave her a Cheshire cat smile. She knew that he was hiding something, and she suspected it all had to do with the day he'd disappeared.

. . .

Breaking her thoughts, a wet golden retriever came ambling down the beach, its owner straggling far behind. The dog made a beeline for her and stopped in front to shake, spraying her with smelly seawater. Afterward the dog ran off toward Tom.

After petting the gleeful animal, Tom placed his rod in its holder and walked back to her, sitting down in his beach chair. "Dog got you wet?"

"Yeah, but who can resist a golden?"

He placed his hand over hers. "Such a beautiful day. Last month who would have thought we'd be here? I'd be driving around in the patrol car, bored to death, and you'd be at the hospital. I know I let a lot of people down, but I'm glad I lied. It got us here."

She turned to face him. "Which lie are you talking about?"

"What do you mean?"

"You never fell asleep, did you?"

He stared at his feet, moving his toes back and forth in the sand. "No."

"Then why did you say you did? It makes no sense."

"I wish I could tell you, but I can't."

"It has something to do with the day you disappeared, doesn't it?"

He nodded, still staring at his feet.

"You know you can trust me, Tom. Talk to me."

"I made a promise. I can never tell anybody what happened—not even you."

She studied him for a long time. "Okay," she finally said.

His face rounded in a contented smile. "But I can tell you this—you would be very proud of me if you knew the truth."

"I've always been proud of you," she said softly, wrapping her hands around his arm and leaning her head into his shoulder. They sat together quietly, watching the waves crash against the shore. She liked the new Tom.

CHAPTER SEVENTY-FIVE

LAMONT HAD BEEN interim CIA director for several weeks when Scotty Olds came visiting. He welcomed Olds into his office at Langley, and they sat next to each other on a couch under a portrait of the president.

"How's it going?" asked Olds.

"Busy as hell, but we're undoing the damage. Most of the senior staff are back, and we've managed to pull in the doctored intelligence."

"It's scary how close they came to pulling it off—using the drug on Congress and scheming to use it on the president."

"Do you really think they would have gone through with it?" asked Lamont.

"It seems so. At the vice president's insistence, they had set up a private meeting at one of the cabins at Camp David. They wanted it packaged as a one-on-one get-together—an opportunity for the president and Luke to exchange ideas and sip tea. They even had the press corps lined up to come in for a few minutes and take pictures of them holding up teacups."

"Bastards," mouthed Lamont.

"The president didn't want to do it—he hated Luke, but the vice president kept pressuring him and the public relations people thought it would look good. Fortunately, the president found a last-minute excuse to bow out."

"And they were planning to ratchet up production of the drug. Do you know what they intended to do with it?"

"No, but it's easy to guess. As I told the president, this was a quiet coup attempt."

"Has the president talked to the vice president?" asked Lamont.

"No. He's cut the vice president off. He's refused all requests for meetings and has taken him out of the intelligence loop. The vice president is totally isolated and he's furious."

"I know. He's been calling me, demanding a meeting. I've been putting him off until I heard from you."

"Don't talk to him; that comes directly from the president."

Lamont smiled. "There's something satisfying about refusing to take his calls. I bet he's going crazy. Do you think he knows that we know?"

"Probably," said Olds.

"What about Goodwin and Crowder?"

"I had a long sit-down with them. I played them the message that Marko had recorded on his cell phone. I made it clear that if they refused to go quietly, the Justice Department would launch a criminal investigation."

"Good riddance," said Lamont.

"And now Dr. Cameron's dead."

"Yes, a freak tragedy—killed by a hit-and-run driver only a block from his apartment building." He gave Olds a knowing smile.

"He had it coming."

"You know, Wilhelm warned us of the drug's danger. The smartest thing would be to destroy it all," said Lamont.

"Maybe someday…although I'm afraid it's too late to get the genie back in the bottle." Olds changed the subject. "I read O'Brien's report on that police officer in North Carolina. Are you convinced he will stay quiet?"

"O'Brien believes so, and that's good enough for me. He did a fantastic job posing as a representative from the White House and the National Security Council."

"Did the police officer take the money?"

"No. The message from the president was all he needed—he didn't want money. He's an honorable man."

Olds raised his eyebrows. "What message from the president?"

"O'Brien came up with the idea. He made the tape himself. I listened to it—he sounded just like the president. He's a master at imitation."

Olds frowned.

"I know you don't approve of our methods. We've had this conversation before. We do what needs to be done."

"I don't want to know," said Olds.

Lamont got up from the sofa and walked over to his wall safe. He opened it and removed a document. "Ryan Butler and Alana Shannon are back in Hawaii. They've resumed their previous lives as Bill and Cheryl Parker. They signed a new contract."

Olds smiled. "I'm glad to hear that. If it hadn't been for them, we wouldn't have made the connection between the drug and the tea sessions. We wouldn't have had Marko come forward with the cell phone evidence. Without them, it's likely the coup would have succeeded."

"We owe them big—although they have no idea about any of this or the role they played."

"So did you finally give them what they wanted? What they were holding out for?"

Lamont handed him the document. "I'll let you decide—here's the new contract."

CHAPTER SEVENTY-SIX

THE MAN SNORKELED in the clear waters of the Pacific Ocean, off the west coast of Molokai. Below the surface was an amazing world of coral reefs and tropical fish, their colors iridescent in the streaming sunlight.

He pulled his head above the water, took off his mask, and surveyed his surroundings. The sky was deep blue with scattered puffs of white clouds. The lush verdant cliffs of Molokai loomed in front.

He swam over to the white sailboat and climbed up the ladder. He grabbed a towel and dried himself. The fresh ocean breeze felt invigorating against his wet skin. He looked back toward Molokai and saw her in the distance, still snorkeling, her legs making small splashes as she glided across the water.

He went to the galley, opened the refrigerator, and pulled out a bottle of champagne and two chilled glasses. He placed them on the table at the back of the boat and returned for the platter of cheese, mangoes, strawberries, and chocolates. He had just finished setting the table when he noticed her swimming back to the sailboat. He watched as she climbed aboard wearing a skimpy black bikini and smiling radiantly.

"It's so beautiful out there, even more glorious than I remember. So many tropical fish today, and the water is so clear. I even saw a leopard ray and more green sea turtles."

"I saw them too."

She smiled. "It's wonderful to be home, Ryan." She walked over and kissed him.

"We're not supposed to use our real names."

"I know, but it's hard not to; and nobody can hear us here."

"It's just we need to get into the practice of calling ourselves Bill and Cheryl, so we don't slip up. Your aunt Janet is going to be randomly checking in on us, so we have to be careful not to make mistakes."

"Yeah, my aunt," she said sarcastically. "I hate these stupid made-up names. And I hate what they did to my nose and my eyes. Someday I'm going to have surgery to put my nose back the way it was…and restore my eye color too. I've been thinking of letting my hair grow out, go back to blonde. Get rid of this hideous brown."

"You can't. We made an agreement. You know what happens if we renege."

She sighed. "I know—it's just a dream. I just want to be the woman you fell in love with."

"You are."

"But I don't look the same. You fell in love with a green-eyed blonde with a straight nose."

"And now I'm in love with a beautiful brown-eyed brunette with a cute little bump on her nose. Call me fickle."

She smiled. "Okay, you're fickle."

Ryan wrapped the champagne bottle in a white cloth and popped the cork. He poured two glasses and handed one to her. "A toast…to paradise lost…to paradise found."

They chinked their glasses and sipped the bubbly.

He continued. "Let's forget all about Cheryl and Bill Parker and celebrate that we're home, together, in this wonderful place—and we know who we are."

"I'll drink to that."

They took more sips, looking out to the water and the island as the boat gently rocked with the waves.

"I felt like such a phony the other day," said Alana. "Giving Officer Keahi that ridiculous story they made up for us about visiting our nonexistent family in Colorado."

"Me too, but that's how it must be." He gazed into her eyes. "We have nothing to complain about. We're back where we want to be, and we're finally free to be ourselves."

"It's wonderful, isn't it? To know who we are. To really be together."

They drank more champagne.

Alana's face flushed as the glow of the alcohol started to work its magic. She smiled seductively at Ryan. "Remember, before everything went crazy, we talked about taking the boat out and engaging in a little extracurricular activity."

"I like the way you say *extracurricular*…You almost make it sound dirty." He wrapped his arms around her, kissing her with a hint of tongue. She brought her hand behind his neck, gently caressing it, and playfully bit his earlobe.

Ryan immediately responded. He knew that she felt his rise through the fabric of his bathing shorts. He reached around behind her and pulled the string of her bikini top.

"Hey, what are you up to?" She giggled as it fell to the deck.

"I want to check out a certain crescent birthmark that I'm especially fond of."

"You think I'm that easy?"

"I know you are."

She gave him a sudden shove, pushing him backward. She ran over to the side of the boat. "You'll have to catch me first," she said, laughing, and dove into the water.

Ryan moved to the boat rail, watching as she disappeared beneath the water. When she surfaced, she waved her bikini bottom in her hand. "I'm not going to need this." She threw it back over the side of the boat. Then she splashed water at him. "What's the matter, afraid you might get it wet?"

Ryan pulled off his bathing suit and jumped in. He swam to her and they held each other in a tight embrace, mouth on mouth, their legs entwined, drifting together in the blue, blue waves of the Pacific Ocean.

THE END

AFTERWORD

This completes my trilogy of thrillers featuring Ryan Butler and Alana Shannon. If you would like to learn how Ryan's and Alana's lives first intersected, how the CIA ensnared them, and what really happened in the Caribbean, read my first novel, *Breaking Free*. If you would like to know more about Alana's story, her murder trial in North Carolina, the secret of the hypnosis drug, and the CIA's ultraclassified Black Box operation, read my award-winning second novel, *Beyond Top Secret*.

To some readers, a powerful hypnosis-enhancing drug may seem a bit of a stretch. However, the concept is premised on Project MKUltra—a secret and illegal CIA program that used drugs and hypnosis to manipulate mental states and brain functions. The project began in the 1950s and continued until its public exposure in 1975. Congress convened hearings, but by then most of the documents had been destroyed. Information about the project is readily available on the Internet.

On a personal note, every few years I have the good fortune to stay at a condominium in Maui that offers a stunning view of Molokai. With binoculars I can make out houses along the island's shoreline, and I like to believe that one of them belongs to Ryan and Alana. Often I see a white sailboat in the waters just off Molokai, and I imagine that Ryan and Alana are there, snorkeling, sharing lunch, or making love on the deck. Someday I may take the ferry over to Molokai and try to look them up. I'm sure we would have much to discuss.

ABOUT THE AUTHOR

Rob Lubitz has held numerous high-level government positions. He has served as a senior United States Department of Justice official, state courts administrator (Florida), Governor's Crime Commission director (North Carolina), sentencing commission director (North Carolina), and juvenile justice director (Arizona). A criminal justice expert, he has been quoted in the *New York Times,* the *Wall Street Journal,* the *Washington Post, U.S. News & World Report,* and *ABC World News Tonight.* He was formerly a US Air Force officer with a top-secret security clearance.

He has published two previous thrillers, *Breaking Free* and *Beyond Top Secret.* The latter received a Gold Medal in the 2015 Readers' Favorite International Book Contest. He lives in Arizona with his wife, Joanne, and one obnoxious cat.

www.ingramcontent.com/pod-product-compliance
Lightning Source LLC
Chambersburg PA
CBHW071124170626
46809CB00002B/491